GW00400241

Two Lost

Years

A novel set in 1960s London

Edmond Morris

© 2018 Edmond Morris

All rights reserved. No part of this publication may be reproduced, stored in a retrieval system or transmitted in any form or by any means, electronic, mechanical, photocopy, recording or otherwise without prior consent of the copyright owner. Nor can it be circulated in any form of binding or cover other than that in which it is published without similar condition including the condition being imposed on a subsequent purchaser.

All the characters in this book are fictitious and any resemblance to actual persons, living or dead, is entirely coincidental.

First published worldwide in 2018.
Cover design by Rob Noble 2018.

*

Other books by the author writing as Steve Morris.
Fiction:-
'In Kinabalu's Shadow' – a war novel set in Borneo before and during the Japanese occupation in WW2.
'Mario's' – a novel set in India covering the disturbing subject of child sex abuse.
Memoir:-
'Borneo Bound' – an account of the author's time as a VSO volunteer in the 1960s.
Musical Dramas for primary schools – writing as Steve Ringwood.
'War and Piece' – a tale of WW2 evacuees.
'Jason' - the Greek myth brought to life.
'Adam Goes West' - settlers encounter the Lakota Indian tribe in America.

Chapter 1

Liverpool, June 2017

The end of The Beatles' 1964 ballad 'And I Love Her' slowly faded away as the coffin slid soundlessly and efficiently on its final journey. The song had been chosen by the deceased when his bowel cancer had been judged terminal and he'd said it marked an important time in his life. He'd planned his own funeral down to the last detail but didn't explain his choice of music so none of those present had any idea why he had asked for that particular track to be played or what it actually meant to him. As far as it was known he was not a Beatles' fan despite spending his childhood and youth in the city they'd made famous around the world.

The chief mourners, his daughters Louise and Ellen, turned from their front pew and slowly walked to the back of the chapel in Liverpool's Springwood crematorium. Louise, the elder of the two and the shorter, self-consciously brushed away an escaped tendril of dark hair from her forehead and kept her head down. Ellen, tall and willowy with her blond hair tied back in a ponytail stared straight ahead and held her head high as if defying people to dare look at her. They stopped at the exit door for the living and stood one on each side facing each other. Neither of them had wept openly during the brief service that had marked the passing of their father but each had shed a silent tear as they were sad to lose the man who had raised them. Louise looked up with concern at her younger sister who was looking very pale and received a wan smile in return. Both of them knew that they would have a lot to face over the next few hours and wanted the whole day to end as soon as possible. They would, of course, make an effort just as their father would have expected. He was always a stickler for doing things correctly.

Their own husbands and children, the two teenage boys of Ellen's and Louise's daughter, were the first to pass them. Both men smiled at the women and Ellen's partner touched her gently on the cheek. Louise's husband muttered something inappropriate about how his father-in-law had hated the cold but wouldn't be complaining now. Louise gave him a warning glance and he quickly ushered their daughter outside to view the many floral tributes.

The next to leave were their father's many friends, acquaintances and ex-colleagues who had filled the chapel. He had been a much respected headteacher for many years in a local primary school and, although it was over ten years since he retired, there were a great number of people who had turned up as they loved and admired him for his dedication to the school he had worked in for over thirty years. A good number of ex-pupils of all ages were also in attendance, spanning the years that he had spent at Edale Primary School since he had started teaching there in 1966. Some were already retired themselves.

Most mourners shook hands with the sisters and others nodded respectfully. All mouthed similar platitudes as they filed past.

'Such a nice, fine man'

'A pleasure to know'

'My favourite teacher'

'A wonderful Head'

'Everyone respected him'

'Such a nice man'

' I owe him so much'

'We'll all miss him'

And so it went on until the chapel was empty and the council workers could move in and prepare for the next cremation.

After the assembled throng had admired the flowers and read the dedications, all similar to the comments made earlier, they chatted in small groups with people of their own generation who had known or worked with Jack James before his retirement. Soon they started to drift away to their cars to resume their own lives. They felt they had done their duty by attending and were satisfied in the knowledge that so many others had noticed them there.

A few close friends had been invited by the sisters back to the family home for drinks and nibbles. Their husbands took the children to their own homes as their wives thought they would find the funeral tea far too tedious. There was no other family other than Louise's and Ellen's own as Jack's wife Susan, their mother, had died of breast cancer five years earlier and neither Jack nor his wife had any siblings or even cousins that the sisters knew about. The funeral limousines moved off slowly and were followed by a couple of cars as they made their way down Springwood Road and along Mather Avenue until they turned left into Rose Lane and came to a halt at the three bedroomed terraced house where Jack had been born and died. The house had been bought new in the 1930s by his grandfather and when their son, Jack's father, had married in 1938 he had brought his wife to live with them in the house. Jack was born in 1942 but never knew his father as he was killed in Burma a few months before the war against the Japanese ended. His mother, who had been in her mid-thirties when she married had brought him up with her in-laws and was delighted with her clever boy who won a place in the local grammar school and then went to college to train to be a teacher. None of her friends or indeed her had ever stayed at school over the age of fourteen. She was sorry that his grandparents had died before he went to college as she knew they would have been very proud of his achievements. Her own parents, who had lived in Cumberland, died shortly after the end of the war so she was totally dependent on her husband's parents for a place to live. When Jack had started school she had gained a small measure of independence by taking a part time job as a telephonist. She never remarried and later in life lived frugally and relied on her small widow's pension to pay her way. They had left her the house so she didn't have to find any money for rent.

With the help of the next door neighbours, elderly spinsters Peggy and Dorothy, the sandwiches and cakes were taken out of their tins and the kettle turned on. Peggy insisted that Louise and Ellen should be free to greet and mingle with their guests as they arrived so she said that, with her sister, they would cope with the catering.

More kind remarks were whispered ever so sincerely at the door as the guests assembled in the front room. This room was always kept ready for any visitors and was never played in by Louise and Ellen when they were children nor by their father when he was a boy. It was decorated and furnished in the post-war style unchanged from when their father had brought his wife to live there. He'd made few changes after his mother had passed away so It hadn't altered much over the decades and still had the wooden framed Ercol chairs and low coffee table so typical of the era. In pride of place was a large radiogram with a collection of 78s still stored in the side compartment. There was a carpet on the floor but not a fitted one so the sides of the floor from the carpet to the skirting boards were dark stained wood. The girls had spent a happy childhood in Rose Lane and had many fond memories of their parents and the neighbours who always had time to chat to them.

Peggy wheeled in the wooden tea trolley laden down with comestibles and her sister followed taking orders for tea or coffee. There was whisky or beer for the men but most refused as they were driving. The bottle of sweet sherry for the women remained unopened. Away from the crematorium the mood was somewhat lighter and the guests soon started swapping tales about Jack and his somewhat strange foibles. His long-time deputy, Marcia, mentioned how he always shunned publicity and hated having his photo taken. Another colleague commented that Jack was happy to allow the press to report on the many achievements of the school but always refused to be included in the articles. Louise added that he even hated being in family photos and they had very few snaps to remember him by. The general opinion was that he was a very private and modest man who didn't like any fuss. One of his friends from the Mossley Hill Bridge Club he had regularly attended said that he always insisted on everything being done in a particular manner and that he became quite upset if the regular routine was changed for any reason. All agreed that Jack hated surprises. Louise and Ellen exchanged knowing glances as they were well aware of their father's fear of change. He had refused to join the technological age and never owned any communication device other than a land-line telephone. All his correspondence was by traditional letter post.

After about an hour of chat the small gathering started to break up and, with more condolences, drifted away. The ever helpful neighbours were the last to leave as they had taken on the chore of washing up the used crockery and cutlery in the kitchen. Before they left Louise asked them if there was anything they would like to take from the house for themselves before the contents were sold at auction.

They thought for a while and then Peggy said, 'If you don't mind I would love to have the tea trolley as I've always admired it and think it adds a certain style to any occasion.'

Dorothy agreed so the trolley was dutifully wheeled through the front door, down the steps to the pavement and then into the house next door. The elderly ladies were obviously overjoyed with their acquisition and couldn't stop smiling at each other despite it being a sombre occasion.

Now that Ellen and Louise were alone they sat down and jointly sighed.

'Well, that's cheered them up,' said Louise.

'Good,' replied Ellen. 'They deserve it as they were always such good neighbours. Now we have to get down to dealing with all the official stuff.'

'Too true,' answered Louise, 'but hopefully it will be quite straightforward as we're the only beneficiaries and are also executors. The solicitor will deal with all the legal bits and we can split the rest of the work between us. I don't mind sorting out the house and the car if you'd go through all the banking and pension details. We can work together to contact any of Dad's friends who are in his address book and couldn't make the funeral.'

Ellen smiled, 'That's fine by me. I thought the cremation went very smoothly. Dad would have been most impressed as he'd planned it so carefully. I hope the undertakers have taken the flowers to the hospice he'd been in as requested. He'd have liked that as he was well looked after there and, in any case, he always hated waste.'

Louise suddenly looked very tired and felt quite emotional. She had held herself in check for the day and now it was over suddenly realised what had happened. Before the funeral she had kept busy and hadn't really thought about the now overwhelming fact that she would never see her father again. Leaning forward she rested her elbows on her knees and put her head in her hands. She began to cry quietly. Ellen moved beside her on the sofa and put her arm round her. They sat motionless for an age before Ellen withdrew her arm and stood up. 'I know it's very sad,' she said,' but we just have to get on with it as best we can. Once everything is sorted out and the house is sold we'll soon get back to our own lives and families.'

'You're right,' agreed Louise. 'But not yet. We'll make a start next week. Is Monday okay for you?'

'Fine. However, one thing. If another person had used the words 'nice' or 'lovely man' to describe Dad I would have screamed. They made him sound so ordinary and staid.'

'They were only being kind,' said Louise, 'and they were probably right. He was a rather boring man. He never did anything adventurous. He went to school, then college and then back to school again. Then he retired. Not a particularly stellar life but one that suited him. Do you think he ever hankered for something more?'

'No way!' exclaimed Ellen. 'It was impossible to make him do anything exciting. If you remember he wouldn't even take us to London for a holiday. Mum so much wanted to go and see where he had lived before they met. When she died he just continued on as before although he did spend more time with our kids – he seemed more relaxed with them than he'd ever been with us.'

'And, although I'm sure he loved Mum, he was never demonstrative. It was almost as if he thought that if he became too close to us everything would fall apart.' Louise stopped talking and looked pensive for a moment before adding, 'do you think he really enjoyed life?'

'I hope so,' replied Ellen. 'It'd have been a terrible waste if he'd spent his whole life wanting something that he couldn't have.'

'Oh well, I suppose we'll never know. Let's go home now and make a start on sorting everything out on Monday.'

*

The next week was filled with activity for the sisters. Some of it seemed pointless and a total waste of their time and most of it unnecessarily complicated and confusing. They wanted to sell their dad's car straight away but found it had to be in one of their names. It appeared that dead people can own a car but can't sell it as they are unable to sign the forms. Their solicitor said that when probate had been granted then they would be able to sell the house, car and everything else they wanted to be rid of. He'd said it would only take about five weeks as the estate was small and the value below the figure that would have triggered inheritance tax. He had added that that was one benefit of having a terraced house in Liverpool as they weren't worth very much compared to houses in London. In the meantime Louise had the car and the house valued. She knew the furniture was virtually worthless and her father hadn't owned any valuable jewellery except for a couple of rings they guessed had belonged to his mother. Louise took the gold band and Ellen the ruby engagement ring. She tried it on and it fitted perfectly. There were no other saleable items and nothing they wanted to keep. Certainly nothing electronic.

Ellen busied herself going through a mountain of old bank statements, bills, insurance and pension documents. Most of it was so out of date that it could just be shredded but she knew that she had to notify a number of companies and government departments about Jack's death. Some of them required a copy of the death certificate. Eventually she reached the pile dealing with his State and Teachers' pensions. The State pension was easy to sort out but his pension from his long teaching career was a little more difficult so she went right back to the earliest documents in the file to work her way through to the present. When she read the details of his original pension settlement she was puzzled and called Louise to the sitting room where she was working.

'Look at this,' she said.

'What,' asked Louise.

'These dates don't add up,' replied Ellen. 'We know that Dad went from Liverpool to Avery Hill College in 1960 and then started teaching in London in 1963.'

'That's right. And then he came back to Liverpool to look after his mother in 1966. She died soon after his return so sadly we never met her. He then got a job teaching at Edale Primary and married Mum in 1974. He carried on working at that school until he retired.'

'Yes,' said Ellen, 'but this document says that he only worked for the ILEA in London until 1964. There's no mention of any other teaching job between then and his return to Liverpool. There must be some mistake. I'll phone the Teachers' Pensions Agency and ask for clarification. Can you remember the name of the school he taught in when he was in London?'

'I know it was in a place called Plumstead and the school was Vicarage something or other. Probably Vicarage Road School as lots of schools are named after the road they're in. After all we both went to Booker Avenue Juniors, imaginatively named after Booker Avenue itself.'

'Okay, when I phone I'll ask them.'

After phoning the Agency Ellen called to her sister again. 'I've just spoken to a helpful woman at the Agency and she says the details must be correct. She pointed out that Dad would have queried it if his details were wrong as he would have lost some of his pension. She couldn't help with the name of the school as they only kept a record of which local authority paid his salary. There were only two in his whole career; the Inner London Education Authority and Liverpool City Corporation.'

Louise shook her head. 'Does it really matter after all this time? We've got enough to do without worrying about Dad's past.'

14

Ellen disagreed. 'I want to know what he did for the two years he wasn't teaching. He never said anything to us or, as far as I know, to Mum when she was alive. I hope he wasn't in prison.'

'Don't be silly,' exclaimed Louise. 'He wouldn't have been allowed to carry on teaching if he'd been inside. Anyway, how can you find out what he did all those years ago?'

'I probably can't but I'm going to have a try anyway. I'm going to check back as far as I can using the internet.'

'Well, the best of luck. I thought we'd enough to do without wasting time researching   father's early life.'

Chapter 2

London, August 1963

The postman had just called at the door of the run-down terraced house in Pattison Road, Plumstead, south-east London and handed over a long cardboard tube. The young man who received it took it through into the kitchen where he opened it carefully and held up the document rolled inside.

It asserted:-

JACK ARTHUR JAMES

CERTIFICATE IN EDUCATION

AVERY HILL COLLEGE

1963

Art read it over and over again. All his hard work had paid off at last. He already knew he had passed his exams as a letter had arrived a few weeks earlier listing all the results of that year's cohort at the teacher training college he had attended for three years. But to see his name on the official certificate made the whole thing seem more real and somehow he felt that he was now a proper adult. He carefully re-rolled the certificate and pushed it gently back into its tube. He wanted to show it off to everyone in the nearby pub but knew that it wouldn't be a good idea among people who had left school at fourteen or fifteen. At best they would look at it with little interest and some might be hostile to the neighbour they had befriended when he was just an impoverished student. Many of them had helped him out over the last three years with odd meals, free drinks and even with finding local holiday jobs for him in the long holidays. The extra money had been very useful and enabled him to pay the £4 per week rent on the house for the whole year rather than having to go home between terms and have to search for new accommodation again when he returned from Liverpool. His grant of £260 a year wouldn't have been sufficient to allow him the luxury of his own house however decrepit that might be. He could pay for his food with around a pound a week and with beer at less than a pound for ten pints then, with his holiday jobs, he could afford to survive so long as he kept an eye on his spending. He'd bought no new clothes for the three years he'd been at college.

He rented the house from an elderly couple in Woolwich who had been left it by their friend, an old lady who had lived there since her marriage at the turn of the century. It was fully furnished in an old lady style with worn chintzy furniture and a lot of plastic flowers. There was one open fire in the living room and a one bar electric fire in the kitchen. London at that time, as with many other cities, was smokeless which meant that only special fuel could be used. Most people complied with the law but some still burned wood when it was dark as the smokeless fuel was expensive and difficult to light. They thought no one would know but actually everyone did as they could smell the smoke from the wood burning as they walked down the road. The bedroom had no heating as there were no power points upstairs. On really cold nights Art put newspaper between the blankets for extra warmth and it wasn't unusual to find frost on the insides of the windows come the morning. The previous owner had thoughtfully had the kitchen wall knocked through to the outside toilet so that it could be accessed from inside the house. Not very hygienic but it saved him going outside on cold wet mornings. There was no bathroom but a small Sadia water heater above the kitchen sink fitfully provided the hot water he used for washing plates, clothes and most of himself. Once a week he would make his way into Woolwich to visit the Public Baths where he could have a luxurious wallow in deep piping hot water for one shilling which included a sliver of soap and a rough council towel. The water was controlled from outside the bathroom by the male attendant and Art had to shout if he wanted more hot or more cold water to be added to the mix. During term time at college he had been able to sneak into the PE department at the end of the day and use the showers next to the gymnasium but now he had to make do with the slipper baths a mile away.

Art was the name he had affected when he started college as he thought it sounded more interesting than Jack and was part of his middle name anyway. He was fairly tall at about six foot and of an athletic build as he had always been active as a footballer and cyclist. His hair was curly and was a mixture of colours. From being platinum blond as a baby his hair was now made up of various shades of colour. In some light it took on a red tinge but it was predominantly light brown. His hazel eyes were alive and twinkling and his ready smile made him a favourite with men and women alike. He had made few close friends in the college because he hadn't stayed in the Halls of Residence as most students did. They spent their time in the 'Dive', a bar on the Avery Hill Campus and rarely ventured off the college site. Art thought this wasn't a good idea as he wanted to mix with people of all ages from different walks of life. He reasoned that he would be a better teacher if he knew a little about how the families of his pupils lived. His teaching practices had all been local and he had been allocated a place in a junior school that was near his house by the Inner London Education Authority Division 6 Office. The school was Vicarage Road Junior School and was typical of the many London schools built in the last few decades of the nineteenth century. It was quite small with only a two form entry and was surrounded by houses built originally for workers in the Woolwich Arsenal in the 1840s. They stretched in neat rows up the hill from the River Thames until they reached Plumstead Common. At the end of each terrace was a slightly larger house with a bay window. These were originally for the foremen to live in but many had since been converted to small shops or public houses.

The pub nearest to his house was called the Star and Garter and was run by a permanently sour looking landlord called Ted and his downtrodden wife Nell who rarely made an appearance behind either bar. Ted ran the pub on his own despite having to serve in both the public and the saloon bars.

He was suspicious of everyone and everything and hated leaving a customer alone in one bar while he served in the other. No-one knew why but it was joked that he worried about the furniture being stolen while his back was turned. However, he looked after the Courage beer very well and kept his prices low. He even did a small trade in selling cheese and onion rolls. Most customers only bought them once as the wedge of cheese quickly tapered off to nothing at the back of the roll and the onion, instead of a slice, was a single ring. They looked well-filled from the front so he sold quite a few to the passing trade.

The only entertainment was a dartboard called a fives board as it only had the numbers five, ten, fifteen and twenty round the edge and the doubles and trebles were half the width of a normal dartboard. It made the arithmetic much easier. On a Saturday night a family from across the road brought in a Dansette record player and a few of the wives and girlfriends would dance. The evening often ended up in a fight as the owner of the player seemed to like accusing any man he didn't know of looking at his wife in a lecherous manner. As she was a very large and dowdy lady who didn't speak to anyone other than her own family it was really stretching a point that anyone would be interested in making advances to her. But a challenge was a challenge and the scrap took place on the pavement outside until the protagonists were separated by the other men. No serious harm was ever done as few blows were landed and the fights were mainly pushing and wrestling.

Art liked the pub and enjoyed the company of the various families who frequented it on a regular basis. Sunday lunchtime was a men only affair as the women were expected to stay at home and cook the Sunday roast. The men wore their best suits as if they had just come from church although few actually attended a service. The pub was only open for two hours so drinking was swift and hard. Ted sometimes put out bowls of roast potatoes on the bar which were heavily salted to encourage more drinking though thirst. As usual, he also kept the key to the inside toilet in his pocket. It was normally only for ladies to use as the men were expected to use the outside urinal which had no roof and was only cleaned when it rained. Ted would begrudgingly hand over the key to the inside facility to a man if he pleaded with Ted that he needed a 'number two'.

*

It was quite a warm August and Art, thanks to Tony a friend from the pub who'd found him a job for the holidays, was sweltering in a plastics factory on a new industrial estate near Plumstead Station. It was boring work operating an injection moulding machine and trimming the pieces of plastic as they were spewed out into cardboard boxes. Most of the pieces were recognisable as joints used in plumbing. Sometimes he would be asked to leave the machine and take empty boxes to other machine operators and take away the filled ones. This was more interesting and cooler and he could stop for a short chat with his fellow workers and keep his distance from the hot machines. At least, Art considered, he could see an end to the drudgery and was excited about the prospect of starting out in his career as a qualified teacher. The thought of having to spend the rest of his life in a factory doing the same repetitive job every day was something he couldn't imagine and he was very thankful for his good education and the opportunities it presented to him. He knew he would still have to complete a successful probationary year but that didn't worry him as he had been praised by lecturers and teachers in all his teaching practises for his good discipline and well thought out lessons. His experience at grammar school, where he had been Head Boy and had taken a number of lessons for absent teachers had stood him in good stead and given him confidence. Meanwhile he would save some money to see him through to his first pay day at the end of September. A proper salary. He loved the idea of being regarded as a professional and having a salary instead of a weekly wage or a government grant.

Art had been told to report to the headteacher of Vicarage Road Juniors on the Friday before school started properly on the following Monday. He was a little scared about this as he was well aware that he would now be expected to be in charge of a class all on his own and needed to make a good impression on the man who would oversee his first possibly shaky steps as a teacher. They had met before and Art had quite liked the tweedy man who smelt of pipe tobacco and wet raincoats. His name was Mr Dixon and he had told Art that he enjoyed music and sometimes played his violin in assemblies. He also told Art that the class he would be taking was a year four class which meant they were in their last year before going on to secondary school. It was unusual for a novice teacher to take the 'top' class but one of the staff had taken early retirement and the other permanent teachers preferred younger children to teach. There was a parallel class so he would hopefully be able to have some help and advice from the experienced teacher taking those children. There was also the niggle at the back of his mind as to how to treat the other teachers in the school. There was so much staffroom etiquette he knew he had to assimilate to avoid falling out with his much more experienced and older colleagues. He'd been told that one heinous crime he could commit was to sit in the chair of one of the established teachers or, even worse, use their personal mug for his tea.

*

September came soon enough and it was time for Art to put on his only suit and tie to meet Mr Dixon in his office at the school. Walking in the main door it appeared strange as the school was so silent. Art had never been in a school when there were no children around and it seemed a lonely and dull place without the joyful chatter and constant clatter of the pupils. He made his way up the boys' stone staircase flanked to shoulder height by sage green tiles to the first floor where the junior school was housed. As with all such schools the infants were on the ground floor. The eight junior classrooms were arranged with six at one end of the large hall and two at the other. At the end by the two classrooms were the head's study and the school office as well as a spare room which served as a library and general purpose room for group and remedial work. The staffroom and staff toilets were at the other end of the hall by the group of six classrooms. There were no indoor toilets for the children. They had to go outside to the open-topped facilities in the junior playground.

He knocked softly on Mr Dixon's door and waited for a moment until he was called in. Mr Dixon was sitting behind his large desk and was casually dressed with a pullover over a checked shirt. Art couldn't see his trousers but guessed they were probably something like cords but almost certainly not jeans. Mr Dixon smiled warmly. 'Welcome to Vicarage Road,' he said. 'I hope you'll be very happy here. We're quite a friendly bunch when you get to know us and everybody is willing to help if you just ask.'

'Thank you,' replied Art. 'I have rather mixed feelings. I'm excited about teaching a class of my own but at the same time worried I might not get it right.'

Mr Dixon laughed. 'You won't get it all right. Everyone makes mistakes. Just make sure you learn from them and nobody is injured or dies. I'm still trying to get it right as you put it after thirty years.'

'I'll certainly try my best,' said Art, 'and I hope you and the rest of the staff will be willing to put up with me.'

'We will. Even the older teachers remember their first year in the job even though I'm sure many of them would prefer not to. Be confident but don't overdo it. Now sit down and I'll explain the timetable to you and give you your register with the class two list of names. You can then go and look around your classroom and have a chat to my deputy Miss Powell. She is the teacher of class one, the other fourth year class, so you can discuss with her the books and stock you'll require for Monday.'

After half an hour Art left the office with a thousand questions still unanswered. He had his class list and noticed there were forty-two names on it. The register had to be completed from the list and, Mr Dixon had stressed, was a legal document that must be kept up-to-date twice a day in case of fire or other unspecified disasters. His children and all the others in the juniors were also in teams called houses and it was apparently his job to organise the collection of team points for the week so a cup could be awarded in assembly to the winning team. This was supposed to engender a healthy competitive spirit that would help with good discipline and motivate the children to work hard and pull together. He was also worrying about other work he had to do, such as dinner and playground duties, take the boys in the fourth year to football, help out with swimming coaching, teach something called boys' craft and prepare his class to take an assembly every half term. None of these 'extras' had been included in the training at Avery Hill College so they were now additional items to add to his main concern about actually teaching all day every day. He decided to go to his classroom and see what was there before searching out the woman who would be teaching the other top class.

He found his classroom as it had a large white number two painted on the blue door. It had four panes of glass in the door, three frosted and one plain glass. Inside, it was a reasonable sized room with a high ceiling from which hung eight lights with grubby cellulose shades that had possibly once been white. There was a large clock on the wall with a wooden cased speaker hanging next to it facing the windows. The windows were tall and he noticed that it would be impossible for children to look out of them as the sills were a good five feet from the floor. A window pole with a curly metal top was in the corner behind his desk and a large dark brown cupboard like a wardrobe stood in the corner near the door. Art's desk was fairly large with two drawers; one with a key in the lock. He presumed that was where he should keep the register. There was another table situated at the back of the room and two large blackboards on the front wall. The boards slid on runners to reveal another blackboard behind them which would enable him to keep anything he had written for another occasion if required. A bookcase stood to one side with a rather tatty looking collection of paperbacks and what appeared to be a complete set of Ladybird books. The children's desks, with inkwells containing white ceramic pots and desk lids that lifted up, were in pairs and with seats attached and placed in neat rows facing the blackboards. There were twenty-one such units, just enough for the forty-two on roll and Art immediately wondered how to arrange who sat where as he didn't know anything about the children. The Head hadn't passed on any information at all about the class, not even their reading ages or any notes about children with special needs, so it was difficult to decide on the best seating plan. He was well aware that if he left it to the children then chaos would ensue and all the likely troublemakers would gravitate to the back of the room with the quiet boys and girls at the front.

He opened the cupboard and found the shelves fairly well stocked with pencils, boxes of white and coloured chalk, notebooks, art materials and paper. There were also some textbooks for mathematics and English. The maths books were for a fourth year class and there were two types named Alpha and Beta so that after he had taught the particular topic or skill for the week the more able pupils could work on the more challenging sums in the Alpha book and the other children use the easier Beta. The English books were a grammar book called 'First Aid in English' and a book of comprehension exercises with questions which appeared to be at the same level of difficulty for every child. His desk drawers yielded up an interesting collection of objects including a box of drawing pins, a metal ruler, bottles of ink, blotting paper, drawing pins and scissors. Art was now ready to go and meet his new colleague in the room next door.

He could see through the glass panel in the door that she was sitting at her desk. Appearing to be of an indeterminate age he guessed she was probably in her late forties. A large woman with her too black hair pulled back severely in a style reminiscent of an earlier era. Art wasn't sure which one but Edwardian sprang to mind. A governess. That's what she reminded him of. A governess in an Edwardian novel. He knocked gently.

'Come,' she called and Art entered the classroom. He was immediately struck by the number of signs and notices taped to the walls. They were everywhere and in large letters exhorted the reader to improve in all aspects of their life.

'No daydreaming'

'No talking'

'No fidgeting'.

'No calling out'

'Always work in silence'

'Be tidy'

'Keep your hands to yourself'

And so on to cover every possible misdemeanour and eventuality that could possibly occur to or be considered by a ten year old child and quite a few which might encourage new and exciting possibilities to lighten the day.

She looked up at Art and smiled a thin smile. 'I suppose you're the new teacher for class two. I'm Joan Powell the deputy head. I'm surprised you've been given the responsibility of one of the top classes when you're only a probationer but I suppose it's inevitable as most of the other teachers prefer taking the younger children and It's useful to have a man in the fourth year.'

'I'm Art James. I've seen Mr Dixon and he said I should come to you to find out more about what I'm expected to teach and what I'll need from the stockroom for Monday.'

'The usual subjects,' she replied. 'Mr Dixon gives us a great deal of freedom so it's really up to you. Some of the parents will want their offspring to go to one of the local grammar schools so you'll have to concentrate on them. There's no official eleven plus exam in London but all the children will be tested in maths, English and verbal reasoning in the Spring and the results of those tests will decide which attainment band they are put in. If they are in the top band then they can apply for a place in one of the selective schools and go for an interview. The others, virtually all the children from this school, will go to one of the local comprehensive schools. Most mornings are taken up with maths and English and the afternoons spent in doing other subjects such as games, art, craft, history and geography. You've no need to bother with scripture or music as the local vicar takes our classes once a week for religious education and I'll take your class for singing. You will have your only free time during the scripture lessons. For music we'll swap classes and you can teach mine a little geography if that suits you.'

'Thanks, I'm happy with that,' Art said. 'Do we have to show all our lesson plans to Mr Dixon?'

Joan laughed,'you can forget all that now you've left college. No aims or methods or outcomes to record. All he wants is a brief note in your record book each week about what you intend to cover in the various subjects. Something along the lines of, "Multiplication of fractions and prime numbers" for maths. You will have to fill in a timetable so I'll tell you when your class will have PE, games, swimming and craft lessons. I'll take you to the stockroom now and we can sort out the exercise books you'll need.'

He met the remainder of the staff at lunchtime when they went to the Rose Inn for a pie and a drink. Art had a soft drink as he didn't want to make a bad impression then noticed that all the others had plumped for the alcoholic variety. He was now worried they might think him a bit of a weed. There was general chitchat about the holidays and very little was said about the upcoming new school year. Art listened politely and only spoke when asked a direct question. These turned out to be thankfully few in number and, when they had found out where he was from, where he lived and his marital status they appeared to lose interest in him. All were older than him but a couple of the women looked to be a bit nearer his age. One named Carol was from Belfast and told him she was in her third year of teaching. She was pleased that he was from Liverpool as she had some family there and they discussed the pros and cons of living in London compared to their own quite similar cities. Art was pleased to find someone he felt that he could befriend as the other young woman appeared rather keen on trying to impress the older teachers with her upcoming wedding and the elaborate plans her parents were making for the big day scheduled for the following year.

In the afternoon Art carefully wrote the names in the register, boys first followed by the girls and drafted out his timetable to show Mr Dixon. After talking to Joan about the children in his class, he worked out a seating plan which he hoped would keep apart the pupils who she had earmarked as possible troublemakers. He made little folded pieces of paper with the names on and placed them on the desks. Then he put a pencil and a rough workbook on each desk followed by a lined paper and a squared paper exercise book. That, he thought, should be enough for now. Joan had also told him that most of the children would bring their own cartridge fountain pens so the stick pens and the ink bottles would only be needed for a very few of the class. He next looked at the bare walls and display boards and wondered what he could do to make them a little more attractive. In the stockroom he had seen a pile of coloured sugar paper so he went and fetched a mixed assortment and used the drawing pins to cover each display board a different colour. He then cut out some black paper in different shapes and pinned these on top. Standing back he admired his artistic efforts and thought that at last the room was beginning to look more welcoming.

There was a knock on his door and Carol came in. 'Wow,' she said. 'You've been busy. I just popped in to see if you wanted any help but I see I'm wasting my time.'

'No,' Art replied quickly, 'I'll need all the help and advice I can get. Were you scared the first time you had a class of your own?'

'Petrified. And I didn't sleep for two nights before the first day of term. Actually it all went reasonably smoothly. You think the children will somehow know you are new to the job but that isn't the case. They want you to like them so you'll have a short honeymoon period before they start to form an opinion. Just make sure you set the boundaries straight away and don't fall into the trap of being king of the kids as that's a sure recipe for disaster. Be firm and fair but let them know that you are in charge all the time.'

'Thanks. I'll do that. But there seems to be so much I don't know about the school routine.'

'You'll soon pick it up. The children will help as they're rather full of their own importance as it's their last year in the juniors. As you will have to choose some of them to be monitors then they'll be falling over themselves to be helpful and make a good impression.'

Art groaned. 'You see. That's the first I've heard about monitors. How many should I pick and what are their duties?'

'I think you should work that out with Joan. She's taught the fourth year kids here for about a hundred years so she'll be able to guide you. I've been stuck with the first years since I started. They're okay but I'm a little bored with Janet and John books. I'm off now so I'll see you on Monday. Try to relax this weekend.'

'I'll try. I'm going to watch Charlton play tomorrow so that might take my mind off school for a few hours. See you.'

At home Art thought about his day. All in all it had been reasonably successful although he was still anxious about the many unanswered questions concerning the daily school routine. He checked that he had two clean shirts for the following week and didn't have to pay a visit to the laundrette in the parade of shops on Plumstead Common. He was looking forward to the football match tomorrow and hoped for an improvement on the previous season when the team had only just avoided relegation to the third division. So long as

32

Eddie Firmani, the South African centre forward, was knocking in the goals there was a faint hope of being promoted to the first division for 1964. There was still a long way to go and Art knew the team needed a good start to the season as they never performed very well when the pitches became bogged down with mud. He had bought a standing season ticket with the money he earned in the holiday. It would mean he could stand on the vast east terrace which it was said could hold fifty thousand supporters but gates rarely topped fifteen thousand since they had languished in the second division for the past six seasons. As well as watching the game Art enjoyed meeting up with some supporters he knew and joining in the witty repartee for which football supporters were universally renowned. One of these, Bill, he also saw in the Star and Garter and they often met up to travel on the 177 bus or sometimes the train to go to the match.

Now that he had done as much as he could to prepare for school he grilled a pork chop, boiled a few potatoes and heated up a small tin of peas for his dinner. He ate these in the kitchen listening to his small transistor radio and after washing up decided that it would be a good idea to go for a couple of pints in the pub and see if any of the regulars were there to play a game of of darts or just chat. Sunday would be the worst day as he knew he wouldn't be able to put Class Two out of his mind. He'd just have to deal with that.

*

Monday went by in a blur. Art sat down that evening on the sagging sofa at home and sighed out loud. It had been a day of mixed feelings. It had started well enough when his class had quietly filed in and taken their seats. They had looked at him with a mixture of curiosity and trepidation. He had written the date and his name on one of the boards and welcomed them with a brief speech about how he was looking forward to the year ahead and how he hoped they would all make excellent progress by working hard and concentrating in lessons. There had been no visible reaction so he called out the names in the register. They answered 'yes sir' to their names and he made a short blue line in the morning square opposite each name to record those present and a red circle for the few who were absent. An electric bell rang and he knew this was the signal to go to morning assembly. They lined up at the door in two rows, boys and girls and filed out to the hall. Their classroom and that of class one were the furthest from the hall and when they arrived class one were already lined up at the back. Art's class lined up in front of them and the children then sat cross-legged on the parquet floor waiting for the other classes to arrive. A chair was strategically placed at the end of each class which the teacher sat on to keep an eye on the children. When all had sat down, Mr Dixon, who had been sitting on a chair at the front, stood up and announced the first hymn. Art's career had truly started.

The rest of the day went very quickly as Art struggled to put names to faces. His seating plan seemed to work as there were no incidents of bad behaviour. But, he reflected, as Carol had predicted it was still early days and he would have to remember not to relax too much. He was looking forward to tomorrow and the new events and experiences it might bring. It would also be the first time he had taken a PE lesson on his own as student teachers had never been allowed to take PE unless accompanied by a qualified teacher. Something, he'd been told, to do with insurance rather than the safety of the children. Tuesday was also the day he was timetabled for playground duty; another new adventure and hurdle to overcome.

Chapter 3

Liverpool, July 2017

Louise and Ellen were in the house in Rose Lane finalising the clearing out of their father's possessions. They had sorted out his clothes and bagged up any reasonably decent jackets and trousers for the charity shop down the road. The rest of the clothes together with any bedding and towels had been put out for the dustmen to take away. They weren't interested in his fairly large collection of books and intended to phone a local second hand bookshop to see if they could make a few pounds selling them. The furniture, paintings, crockery and collectibles would go to auction and be collected later that week. Louise had arranged for the white and electrical goods to go to a charity that helped people with little money to set up home. Then it was only the house and car to be sold and the whole time-consuming and rather sad business would be over. At least, that was how Louise saw it. Ellen was still keen on digging into their father's past and solving the mystery of the two year gap in his teaching record.

'I'll be so glad when this is over,' said Louise to her sister with a tired smile. 'It's taken longer than I thought. At least we won't have to do it all again as Dad was our only remaining older relative.'

'That's true,' replied Ellen thoughtfully, 'but I'm still going to carry on trying to find out more about 1965.'

'You're worse than a dog with a bone,' Louise laughed. 'Have you found out anything yet?'

'No, I've been too busy with all the banking and insurance documents to do anything about Dad's past. I'm also a little worried about what might crop up. Don't want any nasty surprises. A friend said a good place to start could be social media websites. There's Facebook where you can look up groups set up by schools and ex-pupils. There might be some information about Vicarage Road School. Someone could have mentioned Dad as one of the teachers.'

'He was only there a couple of years. Probably not remembered by anyone. But I suppose it's worth a try.'

'Come home with me and have a cuppa and I'll give it a go.'

They left Rose Lane and went to Ellen's house where she switched on her laptop and waited for the annoying Window's jingle to tell her it was ready. She opened the Facebook site. It was fairly easy to negotiate so she put in a search for Vicarage Road School. Of the results that popped up only one was for a school in London and she noticed there was a public group she could access so she clicked on it. The page came up with a number of class photographs and comments by ex-pupils. Many of the photos seemed quite old but she couldn't find one from her dad's time there. But, scrolling down the comments from pupils she found at least one pupil had written about him. However, what she read stunned her so much that she had to read it again and then she called her sister. 'Louise, come and look at this. Please tell me what's been written about Dad is some sort of joke.'

Louise read the item on the screen. 'I hope it is,' she breathed softly. 'Otherwise we've a lot more sorting out to do. How can we check if what it says is true?'

'More research?' suggested Ellen. 'At least we have the name of the pupil who wrote the item and those who replied to the original post. I'll read all the other contributions about the school first to see if there are any more mentions of Dad. I'll do that when I get home and call you if I find out more.'

'Do we really want to?'

Chapter 4

London, December 1963

The end of term. All the Christmas carols had been more or less tunefully sung and the parties had ended. Art looked round his classroom and prepared to tidy up a little before going home. He'd had an interview with the headmaster and the Division 6 inspector Mr Lewis earlier in the week and they had expressed satisfaction with his work so far. Mr Dixon went so far as to say he thought Art would make an excellent teacher but the inspector was more circumspect and said that there were still another two terms to go before Art's probationary period was ended. Art was pleased that the term had gone well and that his relationships with the staff had blossomed despite a small altercation with the school caretaker about tennis balls going on the school roof from the playground.

His class had responded well to his teaching and they now had a good relationship based on mutual trust. He had introduced some more interesting work by teaching some basic science and taking small groups in his own time to the Science Museum in Kensington. These were on Saturdays when Charlton Athletic were playing away. The children enjoyed going on the train and the tube as much as the museum itself as it was the first time many of them had ventured outside Plumstead or been on a train. At the parents' meeting earlier in the month a number of the mums and dads had thanked him for the extra time he put in with their children. In the New Year he thought he might take some of the children to watch a Charlton match if he could persuade the football club to help out with some free tickets. The parents of Paul Hayes, one of the cleverer boys in his class, had been very complimentary about his efforts and had expressed a willingness to help out if Art ever needed another adult for any visits. Art had been very pleased to receive the offer and thanked him for his interest. Their son Paul was probably the best dressed of all the boys and was always willing to help Art in break times to put things out or clear up. They got along very well and Paul was one of the few children that Art chatted to almost as an equal. However, Paul was not very popular with the other children and many of them seemed wary of him and kept out of his way. Art wondered if that was because the boy was clever and came from a relatively well-to-do family.

It was the first Christmas for three years that Art was able to go home to Liverpool and see his mother. All his other Christmases had been spent working in the local Post Office in Woolwich sorting and sometimes delivering the mail. It had been quite well paid but meant he couldn't be home for the festivities. He had always felt guilty about this as his mother was on her own apart from a few close friends and neighbours who popped in to see her over the Christmas period. But, as they had their own families, she had spent Christmas Day alone although Art always telephoned to wish her all the best. 1963 would be different and he was catching the train from Euston with a load of presents for her that he could now afford. He'd asked his friend Tony from up the road to keep an eye on the house while he was away and set off happily down Spray Street to Woolwich Arsenal Station. Tony was almost twice Art's age, well built with slicked back black hair and although he was clearly a tough character they had got on well from the start. They first met playing darts and Art had thrown a treble twenty which was a difficult feat as the doubles and trebles were very narrow. Tony, looking very serious, had said that he'd break his arm if he did it again. Art was obviously worried that he might actually fulfil his threat until Tony grinned and slapped him on the shoulder. 'Only joking, I'm really quite gentle with people I like. And you're one of them.'

Art was visibly relieved but made sure that he didn't throw any more high scoring darts that evening. Tony was a foreman in a plastics factory near Abbey Wood which was how he had managed to find a holiday job for Art. He was a bit of a mystery. Local rumours said he had a long criminal record for various serious assaults and most men in the pub kept well clear of him. The women however found him fascinating and always tried to be near him. He was originally from Hull and lived further up Art's road with his common law wife June and their baby daughter.

Art left the train at Mossley Hill Station which was very convenient for his mother's house as the station was actually in Rose Lane. He walked up the road passed the Rose of Mossley pub and a parade of local shops until he reached the terrace which he had known intimately since he was a toddler. He stood and looked at the house where he had been born. It looked exactly as it had in the 1950s. Same paint, same net curtains, same broken gate, same untidy hedge and, no doubt, just the same inside. He put his key in the Yale lock and pushed open the door, dragging his bags behind him. 'Hello,' he called. 'I'm home.' There was no reply so he dropped his case and parcels in the hall and went to the kitchen. It was empty and he could see through the glass panel in the back door that the garden was also deserted. Had he given his mother the wrong details? He didn't think so. He went into the back room and found his mother asleep in one of the armchairs. She looked so peaceful he was reluctant to disturb her. He shook her shoulder gently and her eyes opened. She took a second to focus and then realised who it was.

'I was well away,' she admitted. 'I've been busy cooking and getting everything ready for you. I'm so looking forward to Christmas with you home. It'll be like old times again.'

She pushed herself up from the chair and Art noticed her grimace and exhale as she straightened up. 'Are you okay?' he asked.

'Yes, I'm fine. Just a touch of rheumatics in my old age. Nothing to worry about.'

Art thought she looked a lot older than her sixty years and more frail than he remembered. At least he could now afford to come home each holiday and possibly in the half terms. He might buy a car and then they could go out for picnics to her favourite spots on the Wirral and in North Wales. Possibly even a trip to the farm in Cumberland where she had been born. It brought to his mind one of her stories about when she was a naive teenager and had asked her father why they kept a bull if it was so dangerous. But any trips would be for the future and now he just wanted to have a rest and catch up with a few of his old school friends who hadn't left the city to live their lives elsewhere. There weren't very many of them still in Liverpool but he thought some might have returned home for Christmas. A couple of drinks in the Rose of Mossley or the Athletics Club would be a great idea. He went up to his bedroom at the front of the house and unpacked his clothes and a few books. The room was just as he had left it with the same old furniture that had been his mother's before her in-laws died and she had moved into the back bedroom. That was when Art, or Jack as was known then, had moved from the box-room to the larger bedroom with the cast iron fireplace which now housed a small electric fire. He suddenly thought that his house in London wasn't anywhere near as comfortable as his family home and was a little ashamed. As a qualified teacher he should have moved up in the world and what had been tolerable or even amusing as a poor student would no longer be acceptable. If his mother saw his cold and poorly furnished house she would be very surprised and probably upset that he hadn't bettered himself after leaving home. She'd no idea how difficult it had been for him making ends meet on a small grant and holiday work. Sometimes, towards the end of terms, he had lived on toast and tea for days.

Christmas was quiet. Art had met a couple of old friends but had found the going tough. They no longer had similar interests and weren't really interested in each other's new lives away from their grammar school. To begin with it had been a bit of a competition to show who had made the most progress in the world but they all soon realised that none of them had very much to show for themselves since leaving school and the conversation drifted to reminiscing about teachers they had tormented and boys they disliked for spurious reasons. He decided that he wouldn't bother contacting them next time he was home and thought they almost certainly felt the same.

He would soon be back in his classroom with the children whose company he enjoyed despite the few, usually boys, who occasionally challenged his authority. There were some other pupils in the school who caused him a little trouble but he was getting better at spotting areas of possible conflict and defusing a situation before it escalated. The Spring term was to be a busy one and to add to his other duties Mr Dixon had given him the dubious honour of organising the annual school swimming gala in Plumstead Baths which was situated along the High Street down the hill from the school. He wondered why he had been chosen and Carol had told him that no one else ever wanted to do it as it was a nightmare to put together. Half the children had no idea of their ability at swimming and their teachers were little help so every year the event bordered on disaster. She recounted how the previous gala had seen two boys enter the diving competition even though they couldn't swim a stroke and had to be fished out by the lifeguards. This information had depressed Art even more.

Chapter 5

London, February 1964

The Spring term had started well and Art soon slipped into a comfortable routine with his class in school and his life outside. The only part of teaching he didn't enjoy much was the weekly football lesson. The Council bus took him and the fourth year boys to a windswept park where there was an unheated hut. Here the boys changed and, as the school only possessed two footballs, it meant that there was no opportunity for Art to do any skills coaching. The only activity possible was a twenty-a-side game in which most of the boys kicked the ball once if they were lucky and many spent the whole hour standing around with their hands down their shorts for a little warmth as it was freezing in the vicious wind. Art started the lesson with a run round the field but any warmth generated by that soon dissipated with the following inactivity. He tried to encourage the more interested boys to pass the ball and spread out but the game always degenerated into a mass of forty small boys chasing after the football in the vain hope that they might actually make contact with the heavy, muddy object. As they wore their own kit it was impossible for them to remember who was on their side so no team ever knew if they had won or not. It was a relief to

Art and his charges when he blew the final whistle and they could all return to the hut, change and then jump back on the bus to return to the warmth of the classrooms. Art made mental plans to try and improve the football lessons for the following year by persuading the Mr. Dixon to buy some more balls, a few traffic cones and coloured bibs to enable him to actually improve skill levels and organise small sided games so each boy could have more time on the ball. The bibs would help identify the players in each team.

The dreaded swimming gala date loomed ever nearer and Art began to panic as he had to rely on the class teachers to put forward children's names for the various races. Each teacher took their own class swimming but the lessons were taken by a qualified swimming instructor at the baths. Because of this most of the class teachers had no idea of the level of competency of each child or which strokes they could perform adequately so they relied on the children putting their names forward for the events in which they thought they could do well. The lists of names and events were dutifully handed to Art so he could compile a programme for the afternoon. Parents were going to be invited to watch and sit in the balconies which were above the poolside changing cubicles on both sides of the pool. Art was starter and Joan, the deputy head, was to record the results at a table in the corner. As the pupils were in teams they scored points for first, second or third places and these were added to the ongoing total on a small blackboard. Two responsible and numerate non-swimmers were given the job of keeping the scoreboard up-to-date. Three teachers were to decide on which children had come first, second or third and then give those successful a card to take to the results table for recording. All the other teachers and assistants were either looking after the non-swimmers or supervising those changing in the cubicles. Boys were down one side of the pool and girls down the other. These teachers, known as whips, had to marshal the swimmers for the races and line them up ready for Art to start each race. At the end there would be a relay race with double points for the winning team. The diving competition had been dropped. Nothing could go wrong.

The big day arrived all too quickly and the blue local authority buses ferried the children class by class to the baths. Art was the first to leave as he was in charge of setting everything up with the able assistance of Paul Hayes from his class who, although a good swimmer, had a verruca which made him ineligible to enter any races. He told Art that his family would come to watch anyway as they always supported school events. When they arrived at the baths Art sent his non-swimmers to sit in the balcony at the end designated for them and told the others to get changed ready for the races. He then set up the table and chair for Joan, the results blackboard and had a word with the two lifeguards on duty giving them a rough idea of how the gala would proceed. They were to stand one on each side of the pool with long poles to rescue any child in difficulty. Each pole had a wire loop at the end for any drowning child to cling on to and be pulled to the side. The swimming teacher was nowhere to be seen so Art assumed she wasn't very interested in seeing how well or otherwise she had taught the children.

Soon the baths was full of excited children, parents and frazzled teachers trying to keep order and prevent children falling into the water before their race. It was time to start. Mr Dixon clapped his hands and called for silence which was observed by the children if not their parents. He made a short speech welcoming the visitors, encouraged sporting behaviour and declared the gala open. Art lined up the six children for the first race, blew his whistle and watched them struggle their way down the pool to the shallow end. Great cheers greeted the winner and the twenty-five races for the afternoon were under way. His young assistant, Paul, was doing a sterling job lining up the swimmers and proved very useful as he knew all the children and could make sure they were swimming in the correct age group. He even had some idea which children were weaker swimmers and put them in the outside lanes near to the lifeguards. Art was very impressed and wondered what he could give the boy as a small thank you for his efforts. He decided that a card would be about right as Paul's family were obviously quite well off and a present wouldn't really be appropriate. He looked up to where Paul's parents were sitting and Mr Hayes gave him a wave. Art noticed that a young lady was sitting between him and his wife and wondered who she was. He liked what he saw; she was slim with long blond hair and dressed casually in a black sweater and slacks. He guessed that she must be a relation, possibly Paul's older sister or an aunt.

The gala came to its conclusion without too many mishaps and no drownings. The only embarrassment Art had suffered was when he started a backstroke race without telling the competitors to start in the water. The resultant attempted backward jumps and dives had caused some amusement in the gallery. The gala had been a close contest with the green team coming out victors by winning the final race which was the relay. The children changed back into their school clothes and the buses returned them to school class by class. Art made a point of thanking everybody who had helped and Mr Dixon shook his hand and congratulated him on a successful event. Art was very pleased and decided an extra pint in the Star and Garter that evening would be well deserved.

The next week was half term but Art had made no plans to go to see his mother in Liverpool. He just wanted a week to himself to reflect on how his career was progressing now that he was half way through his first year and to try and work out how his life in general was going. He knew that he should, and would, have to move out from the hovel that had been his home for over three years. It was too close to the school and many of the children knew where he lived and he saw them regularly when he went shopping. They didn't really intrude on his life and were unfailingly polite but he found it difficult to relax and the constant calling of his name or the ubiquitous 'sir' ensured that everyone was aware he was a teacher. At least children weren't allowed in pubs so that was one place he could escape work. There was also a small problem with the family who lived next door to him. Their son had just moved up to the juniors from the infants and wasn't well behaved. It wasn't really surprising as his family life was pretty dire. There were constant shouting matches between the parents who roundly abused each other in strong Scottish accents. Art was fairly sure the father used his belt to try and control the boy.

Art's pay wasn't exactly great but he thought he might be able to afford a small place in nearby Welling which was more upmarket and only a short bus ride from the school. A car was also still in his thoughts as he'd passed his test during his last year in the sixth form before going to college. He didn't think he could manage to finance both ideas at the same time so he decided to do nothing until the summer holidays when, hopefully, he would have completed his probationary year to the satisfaction of the divisional inspector and his headmaster. He would also have more time in the long summer holiday to look at the various possibilities in the housing market and go round a few used car salerooms. Meanwhile he would continue with his teaching and enjoy the warmer weather and the cricket season. The novelty of being paid to enjoy all that free time was never far from his thoughts.

After half term was over and he was back at work he sat at his desk at the end of another day marking some English compositions when he sensed someone was watching him. He looked up and Paul was standing in the doorway. 'Come in,' said Art. 'What do you want? School's been over for ages.'

Paul was obviously embarrassed and stared at the floor. Eventually he spoke. 'Not sure how to put this. Remember the gala before half term?'

'Yes, you were very helpful. What about it?'

'Well, my sister was watching the races and she said she liked the look of you and told me that she wanted to meet.' Paul was, by now, bright red to the roots of his tousled blond hair and unable to look directly at Art.

'That's very nice,' replied Art as calmly as he could manage. 'Was she the young lady sitting with your parents?'

'That's her. She insisted I tell you. Sorry. Was it the wrong thing to do?'

Art was delighted but tried to hide how he really felt. 'Please tell her I'm very flattered. I'd love to meet her. What's her name?'

'Judith, but everyone calls her Jude.'

'When can I meet her?'

'Now would be a good time,' came a voice from outside the doorway. 'I came with Paul to find out what you'd say without you knowing I was here.' She appeared in the classroom grinning and Paul turned and rushed out past her leaving the two of them together. 'Sorry to be so devious but I didn't know how you'd react. I know you're not married because everyone round here gossips all the time. But you could have a secret girlfriend.'

'No,' replied Art. 'I've not had much time for girlfriends or any other friends for that matter since starting here. I'd really like to take you out sometime. What do you like to do?'

'How about a film? There's a new one on at the ABC starting on Wednesday. It's called Zulu.'

'I've heard of it,' said Art. 'It's had good write-ups in the Evening News. Would Saturday be a good time?'

'Great. I'll meet you outside at seven ready for the last house. What can I call you? I don't want to spend the evening calling you sir.'

Art laughed. 'No, that might raise a few eyebrows. 'Mr James would be far too formal so you'd better call me Art. It's part of my middle name which is Arthur. I thought it sounded less ordinary than Jack which is my first name and the few friends I have in London call me by it. May I call you Jude?'

'Jude and Art it is then. I'll see you on Saturday.'

Jude looked at him intently, smiled and then turned to go. As she left the classroom she called out over her shoulder. 'Can't wait.'

Art sat for a few minutes and wondered if he had done the right thing. He didn't know if it would be frowned upon if other parents and his colleagues knew he had a date with the sister of one of the boys in his class. He decided not to mention it to anyone until they'd got to know each other better. That's if it lasted that long. He hoped it would as she was certainly the best looking girl he'd seen in Plumstead. However, it wasn't a secret he could keep for long. He'd forgotten about Paul who almost certainly wouldn't be able to resist telling his friends so the story would soon be common knowledge throughout the school and beyond.

*

The week flew by and Art spent much of the time at home worrying about his upcoming date on Saturday. What to wear? what to talk about? Should he take Jude for a drink afterwards? How would she get home? His limited experience of taking a girl out anywhere made him even more concerned that he might get it all wrong and she wouldn't want to see him again. He realised she probably knew a lot more about him than he knew about her. From their brief meeting in his classroom he realised she had a sense of humour and wasn't at all shy and retiring but that was purely speculation and he had no idea what she liked or disliked. By Saturday morning he still hadn't found answers to any of his questions. After a school football match on Winn's Common he went down to the slipper baths in Woolwich to make sure he was clean and presentable for the evening. He decided not to wear his school clothes but be a little more casual with a pair of dark green trousers, an open necked check shirt and his favourite Charlton red pullover. As it was still cold out he would wear his only coat which was a fashionable dark blue Crombie.

Art set out for the ABC picture house in plenty of time and considered popping in to the local shop for some chocolates for Jude but he decided it would be better to let her choose what she wanted from the booth in the cinema foyer. He hoped that she wouldn't be waiting for him and was relieved to see that the pavement outside the cinema was only inhabited by young men who were probably also waiting for their dates to turn up. Art joined them and spent some time looking at the advertising posters for future showings. He turned to look up and down Wellington Street but couldn't see Jude coming. Suddenly a black Jaguar car purred up next to him and Jude climbed out of the passenger seat. Her father was driving and gave Art a smile and a wave before speeding off. Art looked at Jude and was mesmerised. She really was the loveliest girl he'd ever seen and he couldn't believe she was actually going to be with him for the evening. She was wearing a green coat with a fur collar and her blond hair shone brilliantly in the bright light of the cinema entrance. Art didn't know what to think or say so he just stood there.

She hooked her arm through his and looked up at him with a smile. 'Well,' she said, 'are we going in or what?'

Art breathed in her perfume and returned to reality. 'Yes. Of course. Now.' He ushered her up the steps towards the ticket booth. 'Where would you like to sit?'

'I'm not going to say the back of the stalls!' laughed Jude, 'As it's our first date. But we'll have a better view from the circle if that's okay by you.'

Art bought the tickets and took her to the small kiosk between the doors to the stalls and asked if she would like some sweets or chocolates but she said she would prefer to wait and have an ice cream in the interval. They went up the stairs to the circle and made their way to the front to have an uninterrupted view of the film. Taking off their coats they folded them and stashed them away under the seats. As soon as they sat down Jude again linked her arm through his and they settled down to wait for lights to dim and the show to start. After about ten minutes of Pearl and Dean adverts and trailers for future shows the main feature started.

*

John Hayes, Jude's father, put down the evening paper he'd been reading and glanced across the large living room to his wife Marion. She was sitting on a sofa and was reading a novel with her feet tucked up beneath her. John always liked to catch his wife when she was unaware he was watching. He smiled at the sight. She really was still very beautiful he thought and she had kept the figure that had entranced him over twenty years earlier. She looked up, smiled, and said,' I wonder how the evening's going for Jude? Should we have invited Mr James to come here before their date or would that have been too formal?'

'Too formal,' replied John, 'these days youngsters are more relaxed about social niceties than we were. I'll never forget the worry I had when I was invited to Sunday tea by your parents. They gave me the third degree.'

'That's because they didn't know you or your family. With Mr James it's different. We've known him for ages through school and especially from the stories about him that Paul tells constantly.'

'You're right,' said John, 'Paul worships him and will miss him when he moves up to secondary school. D'you think it's a good thing for Jude to be going out with Paul's teacher. Could it cause problems?'

'I don't think so,' considered Marion. 'Paul's a sensible boy. He won't try to take advantage. Anyway this might turn out to be the one and only time they go out. Perhaps Mr James was only being polite when he asked Jude to the flicks. He might have thought Paul would be upset if he turned her down.'

'You might be right but she's really grown into a very attractive young lady. But I'm not sure that a poorly paid primary school teacher is what we want for her however nice he is. She should be able to make a better match than that.'

'You snob,' laughed Marion. 'When we met you were a barrow boy on the market and my parents didn't mind too much. Look how well you've done since then. We've got our own house and aren't short of a bob or two. Let's wait and see if anything develops.'

*

In the intermission Art went and bought two ice cream tubs which they ate using the little wooden spoons hidden under the lids. When they'd finished Jude put the empty tubs on the floor, carefully avoiding their coats. She looked at Art. 'Are you enjoying it? I'm finding it a bit bloodthirsty with all those Africans getting shot. It seems a bit unfair that our lot have guns and all the natives have are spears and little shields.'

'I think it's great,' replied Art. 'It's not that one-sided as there seem to be thousands of Zulus against a handful of soldiers. You're right though, there are a lot of people dying.'

The light started to dim and the second half of the film began. Jude settled down in her seat and leaned towards Art. When he felt her shoulder nestling against him he put his arm around her. He was terrified that she might push him away but she just snuggled closer, took hold of his hand and gave it a light squeeze of encouragement. Art wanted the moment to last forever.

It didn't. The film soon ended and the lights came on. Art and Jude put on their coats and made their way to the exit. Jude took his hand again and whispered, 'what now?'

Art looked at his watch. 'It's only just after ten. How about a quick drink and then I'll take you home.'

'Good idea. But you don't have to take me home. I told Dad I'd phone him so he could come and pick me up. I'm sure he'll give you a lift as well. Do you know any of the local Woolwich pubs? I only know the ones around Plumstead Common.'

Art grinned. 'Most of the town pubs are dives and I wouldn't dream of taking you in those. The Director General over the road is reasonably respectable as is the Union Tavern off Powis Street. You choose.'

'The one opposite seems okay and it'll be easier for Dad to find although I'm sure he knows every pub in Woolwich as his business seems to involve most of them.'

They crossed the road and Art held the door for Jude. Inside it was a typical late Victorian pub with various rooms to choose from. They went to the bar at the back and found a table. Jude had asked for a gin and orange so Art bought that and a pint for himself. He took the drinks to the table and sat down, 'What did you mean about your dad having links to the pubs?'

Jude sipped her drink. 'He doesn't talk much about work but occasionally I overhear him on the phone talking to one of

58

his employees and sometimes he mentions pubs in Woolwich and Greenwich. It must be something to do with the security firm he runs. He has a number of business interests locally but I don't know much about them. Mum's the same. She never asks him about what he's doing and just looks after us all.'

'What about you?', asked Art. 'Are you a student?'

Jude laughed. 'No, I'm not the brainy type. I left school a couple of years ago and I work in a dental surgery as a nurse. It sounds good but I've no real nursing qualifications. The dentist taught me all I need to know. It's not very well paid but Dad gives me an allowance for clothes and pays for my car.'

'You've got a car?'

'Yes. It's only a mini and I'm still having lessons. I hope to pass my test this year. Do you drive?'

'Not much as I can't afford a car yet. I passed my test before going off to college. One day I'll get one but I'd like to move to a better house first. Pattison Road is fine for a student but now I'm teaching I should look out for somewhere better. Preferably a bit further from the school.'

'Pattison Road?' Jude looked a little shocked. 'That's a bit of a dump. Sorry, I didn't mean to be rude but I had a friend who lived there and she said they didn't even have hot water or a bathroom. Is yours like that?'

'I'm afraid it is,' admitted Art. 'It's all I could afford on a student grant but now I'm on a salary I'll be able to make some changes. This is my first year in teaching so I've been concentrating on the job. I know from Paul that you live on the other side of the Common. It's an area I don't know well at all.'

'You'll have to come round and meet my parents properly. They'll make you very welcome and Mum's a fabulous cook.'

'I'd like that. Does that mean you'd like to see me again?'

Jude reached out and touched his arm. 'Yes. And you?'

'Try and stop me. How about going out to dinner one evening?'

'I'd love that. I've never been taken out to dinner unless you count family ones. It sounds very romantic. Have you a restaurant in mind? When we go out we usually to go to a Chinese Dad knows. I'd like to try somewhere different.'

Art could only think of one restaurant that wasn't of the greasy spoon variety and that was on the waterfront in Greenwich. He knew it was very expensive but... 'How about The Trafalgar?'

'Wow, I've heard of that. It's posh,' replied Jude, 'I'd love to go there. My friends will be very impressed.'

'The Trafalgar it is then. When?'

'Next weekend? That okay? I'll give you my phone number.'

Without a moment's hesitation Art agreed. 'Yes, that's great but there's no need to give me your number now as It's on Paul's record card in school.'

He thought he could sort out the cost later. The most important thing was that he was going to see Jude again.

*

Jude left Art at the table and went to use the payphone that she had noticed by the door when they had entered the pub. She phoned home and her mother answered. Jude explained where they were and asked if her dad could pick them up. It was soon arranged and Jude put the phone back on its cradle. She paused for a moment's thought. Was she being a bit too forward on a first date? Was Art serious about seeing her again or was he just being polite because her father did so much for the school? She knew she really liked him and hoped he felt the same. Another date, she considered, would help her decide if he was right for her. She'd really enjoyed the evening and had been thrilled when he'd put his arm round her during the film. I hope he kisses me goodnight she thought as she returned to the table. Obviously, with her father collecting them, Art wouldn't have an opportunity to kiss her in the car on the way home but she had a plan.

'Dad's coming,' she said to Art. 'We'd better go outside now to wait for him.'

'Okay, here's your coat.'

Jude put her coat on and took Art's hand as they walked down the corridor to the door. Just before they went out Jude stopped, turned to Art and put her hands on his shoulders. She looked him directly in the eye and leaned towards him. 'It's been a lovely evening,' she whispered. 'I wish it could last longer.'

Art couldn't resist the opportunity and, leaning forward, kissed her on the lips. Jude responded instantly and her arms encircled his neck. He pulled her to him and they held the kiss and the embrace until the door swung open and a man pushed his way past them into the pub. That broke the magic and they went outside to wait for Mr Hayes to arrive. A couple of minutes later the Jag swept up and Jude climbed in the back. Art stood on the pavement unsure of what he should do until Mr Hayes called to him to get in and he'd give him a lift home. Art joined Jude and they set off.

'Enjoy the film?' enquired John Hayes as he drove towards Plumstead Common.

'Yes,' replied Jude, 'although it was a bit bloodthirsty.'

'I liked it a lot,' said Art. 'I'd like to go to Africa some day. If I can afford it. Travelling abroad is very expensive.'

'Well, when you're a headmaster you might have the money,' laughed Jude. 'Dad, Art lives in Pattison Road. Can you drop him off there?'

'Pattison Road eh,' said John. 'I lived in a similar road by the station when I was a boy. Nothing wrong with that although I was glad to move out when I married. Have you had a bathroom put in?'

'No, it's rented. Now I'm earning I'll be on the lookout for a better place. I'm fed up of going to Woolwich for a bath and I can no longer use the showers at college as I used to'

John laughed. 'We had to do that when I was a lad. Do you still have to call out for more hot water?'

'Yes.' Art felt more at ease now that John had opened up a little about his past. 'Here we are,' he called out. 'I live at 19, near the pub.'

John stopped the car and Art got out. Jude smiled at Art and mouthed 'call me soon' as he turned to go. He nodded and thanked John for the lift. The car sped away leaving Art to consider how the evening had gone. He was elated and noticed that the pub was still open so he popped in for last orders.

In bed that night Art found sleep difficult to come by. His mind kept going over the events of the evening again and again. The highlight had been the kiss in the pub. He couldn't wait to repeat the experience. He was sure Jude was special and he was determined to try to make a go of their relationship. At long last he slept.

Art woke early the next morning and decided to go for a walk before the usual Sunday lunchtime session in the Star and Garter. He headed up the hill to the common and sat by the bandstand to try and sort out his thoughts again. He hoped to formulate a plan and map out his future but all his thoughts kept returning to the kiss in the pub. What should he do next? Try to improve his living conditions? Concentrate on his career or focus on the embryonic relationship with Jude? Jude won hands down.

The Star and Garter had the usual crowd of men at the bar when Art walked in. His friend Tony was already half way through a pint and Art asked if he'd like another. Tony thanked him and Art ordered two pints of best. They stood in silence for a minute while they supped and savoured the beer. Eventually Tony turned to Art and asked him how work was going.

'It's going well,' said Art. 'I hope to pass my probationary year so I can be permanent in the school. I like it there. The kids and the staff are all great and I think I'm doing okay.'

'I'm sure you are. The grapevine tells me that you're already well respected and parents hope that their children will end up in your class.'

'That's very flattering. I'm not sure it's deserved.'

'Don't put yourself down,' Tony said. 'I know you're a good worker from when you worked at the factory in your holidays from college. You'll do well whatever you choose to do.'

Art thought this a real compliment from Tony as he much admired the older man despite his rather murky reputation. Some of the locals avoided Tony as he lived with a woman in sin as they thought it. And to have a child as well was the last straw for some of them. That and Tony's reputation as a hard man who was not averse to using violence made him both feared and grudgingly respected. He never spoke about his past and Art never asked. Tony had helped Art settle in as he recognised another northerner trying to learn how to convince Londoners that life wasn't all cloth caps and whippets.

Art couldn't contain himself and told Tony about his date the previous night. Tony listened and asked who the lucky girl was.

Her name's Jude, short for Judith and she lives on the other side of the common. Her dad's got a large black Jag and they've obviously got money. I met her through her brother Paul Hayes who's in my class.' Art paused and raised his glass to his lips.

64

Tony spun round and nearly spilt Art's drink. 'Hayes you say? I know that name.'

Art looked puzzled. 'How do you know Paul and his family?'

'I don't know all the family,' replied Tony. 'But I've heard talk about the father. Only gossip but he's not well liked by some. Are you serious about the girl?'

'I think so. I'm sure what you've heard is wrong or just sour grapes because he's a successful businessman. I've met him a number of times and found him very friendly and helpful. He's always available to come on school trips.'

'Well,' Tony said. 'Just be careful. I hope she's worth it.'

'She is. How about a game of arrows?'

*

After his usual one pan Sunday lunch consisting of a tin of mince, a can of peas and one of new potatoes heated up in the same saucepan and eaten from a bowl using a spoon Art sat on the chintz sofa, swivelled round and put his feet up. The beer and the food made him sleepy and he soon dozed off.

He woke an hour later and decided to go down the road to the phone box to book a table at The Trafalgar for the following Saturday. He got through to the restaurant and booked a table for two and asked if they did a set meal. The price quoted was equivalent to at least a week's pay. He'd picked the Trafalgar because of its reputation but hadn't reckoned it would be so expensive. Never mind, he thought, we can always go to the Woolwich Wimpy Bar next time. If there was a next time. He still couldn't believe that Jude would want to see him on a regular basis. He was still a little shy around girls despite Avery Hill College being coeducational. As an only child in an all boys grammar school he'd not had a lot of experience taking girls out when he was in Liverpool. Certainly not girls as stunning as Jude. His few dates at college had been fun but not really spectacular and nothing particularly romantic had occurred. He'd met a girl named Brenda at one of the Saturday 'Satex' dances held in the basement of Woolwich Polytechnic. She'd been pleasant enough and he'd enjoyed taking her to a dance in Chislehurst Caves but nothing came of it and they drifted apart.

*

Saturday soon arrived and Art made his preparations for the visit to the restaurant. The previous evening he'd been down into Woolwich to the slipper baths but he still had a strip wash at the kitchen sink. He'd agonised over what to wear for a formal meal and had ended up in a pair of black trousers and a sports jacket. It was bitterly cold so he wore his overcoat again. A clean handkerchief completed his ensemble and, after checking for money and keys he set off up the hill to the Common where he crossed the main road to where the Hayes family lived.

The house was bigger than he expected. It was a double-fronted detached Victorian house with its own driveway where two cars were parked. One was the black Jaguar and the other a new Morris Mini-Minor. Art guessed that the red Mini

66

belonged to Jude as lots of trendy youngsters, particularly pop stars, had been buying them since they were first produced in 1959. Straightening his tie for the umpteenth time he walked to the door and rang the bell. It opened so quickly it startled him but it was no surprise to see Paul standing there with a broad grin on his face. 'Come in,' he said. 'She's not ready yet so you'll have to wait in the lounge with Mum and Dad.'

Art wiped his feet on the coconut mat, took off his coat and put it on one of the hooks by the door then followed Paul down the spacious hall and into the lounge. It was, he thought, beautifully furnished with large comfortable looking armchairs and a sofa about the size of his poky living room. There was a cocktail cabinet disguised as a globe in one corner and lots of pictures on the walls that he thought might possibly be original works of art. A large coffee table sat in the centre of the room with various magazines strewn tastefully on top together with a large onyx cigarette box and matching ashtray. He saw Paul's parents sitting watching a large television set and they both stood up when they noticed him. Mrs Hayes, immaculately dressed in a lilac sheath dress turned off the television and her husband who was equally well attired in a three piece chalk stripe suit, white shirt and red tie crossed the room with his hand outstretched to welcome Art. With a firm handshake completed Art was asked to sit down and wait for Jude. Art sank into one of the chairs and wondered what exactly Jude's father did for a living. He looked like a businessman but seemed a little too flashy for someone who worked in the city. He had chunky gold rings and a large wristwatch. Art had also noticed that his tie pin and cuff-links sparkled with what might have been diamonds. His wife sported similarly impressive jewellery including an engagement ring with the largest stone Art had ever seen. If it was a diamond it must have cost a fortune.

'Jude's always late,' said her mother.

'She gets that from you,' joked her husband. 'Don't worry Mr James I'll give you a lift to Greenwich so you won't be late. What time have you booked the table for?'

'Seven-thirty. And please call me Art otherwise I'll think it's a parents evening.'

'Fine by me. How did you come by such a name?'

Art blushed a little. 'It comes from my middle name which is Arthur. My mother calls me by my first name which is Jack.'

Mr Hayes replied, 'Well Art, I'm John and this lovely lady is Marion. I think you might know the boy behind you hopping about with excitement.'

'Possibly. His face does seem familiar,' replied Art as Paul ran round him to sit on the sofa. 'I think he might be the naughtiest boy in my school.'

'Just like I was,' said John with a smile. 'Paul, go and chase up your sister. Tell her if she isn't ready in five minutes we'll all go for a meal without her.'

Art, John and Marion chatted for a while. It turned out that John was also a football fan and supported Charlton as did Art. They discussed how the season was going and the merits or otherwise of the various players. Marion said very little but Art could tell she was sizing him up all the time. He noticed her eyes scrutinising him from the top of his head to the soles of his feet and knew she was critically judging his attire, how he sat, how he spoke and how he conducted himself. He hoped she wasn't too disappointed as he'd done the best he could. At least his shoes were polished. It was all a bit disconcerting and he wanted to get to Greenwich as soon as possible. It was good of John to offer to take them as it wasn't an easy bus journey but he surmised that Marion would have to stay behind to look after Paul.

Just as the conversation was turning to Art's background and his family Jude made her entrance. She was dressed in a simple bias cut blue silk dress with a shawl collar and she was wearing matching blue shoes. Her long blond hair shone and shimmered as she walked. She was, Art considered, absolutely incredible. What on earth was she doing going out with a tramp like him when she could have had her pick of eligible bachelors from the whole of London and beyond?

'You look nice,' said her father which Art thought was the understatement of the year. 'Let's get going.'

They traipsed out to the car with Paul hopping about excitedly in their wake. He wanted to go with them but his father pointed to the house and he reluctantly went back inside. Once under way John chatted to Art about the school and asked what it was like working there. Art was fairly non-committal as he wasn't sure how John felt about the small junior school in a quite poor area of London. He wondered why John sent his son to such a school when it looked as if he could have afforded a private education for him. His unasked question was answered when John said that he had attended the school as a boy and thought that if it was good enough for him then it would do for his children. However he added that he wanted Paul to go to a grammar school at the age of eleven instead of the secondary modern school he had attended. He said that the school he went to was Charlton Central and that he had learned very little there that had been any use in his adult life. Jude joined in the conversation by telling Art that she had also gone to Vicarage Road and then on to the girls' grammar school on Plumstead Common.

Soon they were going along Greenwich High Street towards the Royal Naval College and the Cutty Sark. A right turn took them towards the river and the Trafalgar Tavern with its large picture windows looking over the river to the north bank of the Thames. John stopped the car and turned to Art and Jude. 'Give me a call when you want to come home and I'll drive down and pick you up.'

'That's very kind,' said Art. 'I wouldn't want to put you to any trouble. We could catch the bus back.'

'It's no trouble,' replied John. 'You'd have to catch two buses to get home and it could take ages. Jude, make sure you phone me when you're ready.'

'Okay Dad. Thanks. We won't be too late.'

They clambered out of the car and with a wave John drove off. Art and Jude went into the restaurant and were greeted by the head waiter who, when told they had a reservation, checked in his book on a lectern by the door and escorted them to a table near one of the windows. They sat down and he signalled to one of the waiters to bring the menu and the wine list.

As they perused the menu Jude put her hand on Art's and looked intently into his eyes. 'This is so kind of you,' she said. 'And it's the first time I've ever been taken out to dinner. I hope I don't let you down.'

Art confessed, 'It's the same for me. You're the only girl I've ever invited out to eat so we can make any mistakes together. Anyway, what would you like to eat?'

The whole meal was a delight. Their waiter lit the candles and helpfully steered them through the various courses without making them feel patronised. After coffee and a small glass of Tia Maria Jude leaned back and smiled. 'That was wonderful Art and I really enjoyed it.' She looked at her watch. 'And it's only half past nine. What shall we do now?'

'We could go for a drink in one of the local pubs,' suggested Art. 'The Yacht is just round the corner and it has a terrace overlooking the river. Have you been there?'

'No, but I'd like to. I think it might be too chilly to sit outside.'

Art signalled for the bill with the time honoured method of scribbling in the air on an imaginary sheet of paper and the waiter brought it to him. 'Let me pay half,' said Jude.

'Not this time,' replied Art although he had seen the bill and it was as large as he had expected. 'I asked you so it's my treat. If there's a next time then we can share the cost.'

To his delight Jude replied, 'I hope there'll be a next time, I can't remember a lovelier evening.'

The bill paid with a suitable tip for their friendly waiter they left the restaurant and in two minutes were in the pub. On the way Jude slipped her hand into Art's and gave it a small squeeze. Art was a little taken by surprise and felt a wave of pleasure through his body which came to a focus in his groin. He was a little embarrassed at this turn of events and hoped he could control his burgeoning erection once they were in the pub. Inside they made their way to a table made from an old beer barrel in a quiet corner. Jude insisted on buying the drinks and Art asked for a pint of Courage Best. Art now had time to compose himself and found that by sitting down it was easier to control his obvious excitement. Jude soon returned with his beer and a gin and orange for herself and sat opposite to him. She sipped her drink and looked at Art. I feel I know you already thanks to that brother of mine but I'd like to know more.'

'I hope you don't believe everything Paul tells you,' he laughed. 'I'm sure half of it isn't true. There's not a lot to tell really. I was born in Liverpool and brought up by my grandparents and my mother. My father died in the war. After school I was lucky to find a place at Avery Hill College to train for three years to be a teacher. Vicarage Road is my first job and I'm still learning the ropes. The Head and most of the staff are very kind and help me a lot when things don't go as planned but I think I'm getting there.'

Jude laughed, 'Everyone says you're the best teacher in the school and that includes my father who isn't impressed very easily. I know that a lot of the parents of the kids in your class hold you in high regard especially for your work in science and, of course, I saw you in action at the gala so I know how the children react to you. It was obvious that they respect you and most of the girls are already in love with you.'

Art blushed at that remark. 'I'm glad that I seem to be doing something right but that's enough of me. Tell me about yourself and your family. It's obvious your dad has a very good job because of your house and lifestyle.'

'Okay, here goes. I'm nineteen and you already know I'm a dental nurse. I've no formal qualifications as I learned on the job. I had thought of becoming a qualified nurse but I'm not sure if I'm clever enough to manage the course. As to my family; Dad runs his own business doing all sorts of things. He doesn't talk about it much but it's obviously successful as he can afford to buy us almost anything we want. He spoils us rotten. Paul you know and my mother is just a housewife. That's about all.'

Art wanted to know more about her father's business but didn't like to pry so he changed the subject to music and the many new rock groups starting up, many from Liverpool. He'd missed the early days of The Beatles in the Cavern Club as he was at college in London but was always being questioned about them although he knew very little about their private lives. Jude was the same and, as they were her favourite band, asked all about where they lived and what they were really like. Art could only tell her about the area they came from in Liverpool as it was near to his mother's house. As to their personalities he was stumped and soon realised Jude knew more about them than he did. He'd only been to The Cavern a few times in the holidays and had found it smelly, noisy and overcrowded. Not just that but it only sold soft drinks and coffee so he preferred some of the other clubs which were licensed. Otherwise he just went to the many city pubs to meet a few school friends still living in Liverpool. Most of them were more interested in rugby or football than the music scene.

A glance at the large clock behind the bar when Art went to buy two more drinks showed that it was nearly closing time, When he returned to Jude he suggested phoning John for a lift home. 'I've already phoned,' she said. 'I used the one on the wall when you went for the drinks. He said he'll pick us up out side The Trafalgar in about twenty minutes. Just enough time to finish up.'

Fifteen minutes later they made their way along the narrow passage from the pub towards the road. Art put his arm round Jude's waist and was rewarded by her leaning into him as they walked along. He pulled her towards him and they kissed. It was even more passionate than their previous encounter. They continued to the road but when Art saw that John was already waiting there he quickly pulled his arm away only for Jude to smile up at him and put her arm round his waist instead.

'Jump in,' called John. He beckoned Art to sit in the front with him and Jude sat in the back. 'Had a good time?'

'Yes,' answered Jude. 'We had a great time. The food was excellent. You must take Mum there sometime.'

'Out of my league,' John said with obvious understatement. 'I don't know how Art can afford it. Teachers must be paid a lot more than I thought. Unless he has a private fortune hidden away.'

Art was quick to deny the comment. 'No, I just wanted us to have a great time. I doubt if I could afford to go there again for another month or two.'

'Jude's worth it,' John replied. 'But I'm sure she doesn't expect such treatment every day.'

'I am still here,' complained Jude from the back. 'You don't have to discuss money now. It'll spoil the evening Dad. You always have to bring up costs and prices. I'm not an investment.'

'Point taken. Art, where can I drop you off? At your house?.'

'Yes,' Art agreed. He still felt rather ashamed about Jude knowing he lived in a hovel and hoped he would soon be home before any further revelations about the house were uncovered by John's questioning. Art wondered to himself if he had blown it by being so honest about his circumstances. If John knew what he earned he probably wouldn't let Jude out with him again. After all, she wasn't yet twenty-one so she had to do as he ordered.

The car stopped outside the Star and Garter and Art climbed out. He thanked John for the lift and turned to Jude. 'Thank you for a wonderful evening. I hope you had a good time.'

Jude handed him a piece of paper. 'That's my phone number at work. Please call me if you'd like to.' She glanced towards her father. 'It's more private.'

'I will,' Art promised and closed the car door gently.

There were a few minutes left before closing time so when the car had driven up the road and round the corner towards Burrage Road he pushed open the pub door and asked Ted for a pint of Best. He had a few funny looks from the regulars in the bar and his friend Tony commented on how smart he looked. The record player had been dragged out and a few couples were dancing. Art wasn't in the mood for conversation as his brain was still reeling with how the evening had gone so he sat at one of the round tables and sipped his pint. He tried to analyse what had gone well and if he'd made any mistakes that the Hayes' would laugh about when they got home. Hoping that he'd acquitted himself reasonably well he finished his pint before the Saturday night fracas started and walked the thirty yards or so to his front door. He stopped on the step and looked at the yellow peeling paint. Some changes were needed if he was to continue seeing Jude. Her family with their obvious wealth and posh cars would be a lot to try and keep up with. He hadn't reckoned on how tenacious Jude could be and how she had no problems persuading her parents to agree to nearly everything she wanted. She usually got her own way.

Once back indoors Art made himself a coffee from the small tin of coffee powder he usually only used in a morning. 'I'll bet Jude is having some proper coffee,' he said out loud. 'I wonder what they're saying about me?' He went to bed but couldn't sleep as his thoughts were of Jude and how wonderful she looked and how perfect she seemed. He realised he loved everything about her and couldn't wait to ask her out again. He'd never felt like this before.

*

In the big house on the Common they were indeed talking about Art as Jude was being quizzed by her family. Paul was still up as it was Sunday tomorrow and there was no hurry to rise in the morning.

'Well,' her mother started. 'Tell us all about it. What did you eat? Did you enjoy it?'

'Did he kiss you?' asked Paul cheekily.

'None of your business,' Jude glared at him. 'And if you ask any more silly questions I'll give you a Chinese burn.'

'That's enough,' said John. 'I know you must have enjoyed the evening as you gave him your work phone number. Do you really want to see him again?'

'Yes,' answered Jude simply. 'He's a little shy but good company. I'd like to know him better. Maybe I should start watching Charlton play so I can discuss the game with him.'

'No need for that,' her mother retorted. 'Men prefer to talk to other men about football. It's not really a suitable topic for a young lady.'

'That's a bit old fashioned,' John said. 'I think these days women can enjoy watching all sorts of sports. I wouldn't expect them to actually play games such as football or rugby as they wouldn't be strong enough. There are some women who go to watch Charlton and they can make quite a racket when something exciting happens such as a goal.'

'That's not very often,' Paul scoffed. 'Jude should go and see West Ham if she wants to see goals and excitement.'

'I've no plans to to see either team. And now I'm off to bed.' Jude stood up, took her cup to the kitchen and made her way to her room. Like Art she found sleep hard to come by and it took a long time before she could put him to the back of her mind and drift off.

Chapter 6

London, March 1964

Art had taken Jude out a couple of times since the meal but never again to such an expensive place. They'd gone to the pictures and a dance at the Polytechnic. One evening they'd just stayed in at her house and he'd eaten with the family. That was the evening he'd enjoyed the most as he'd been made very welcome and there was the bonus of watching television for the first time in ages. His relationship with Jude was now more relaxed and they were very happy just to be together. There was no need for a lift from her father as they were only going to nearby venues, mainly in the bustling town of Woolwich down the hill from the Common. So far he hadn't invited her to his house. Partly because he was still ashamed of it but also because he thought it might send out the wrong signal to her father who could misconstrue Art's motives. Art was honest with himself when he considered that John was probably right in thinking the worst. He ached to make Jude his own in every way.

*

Despite trying, Art couldn't remove Tony's earlier warning about Jude's father from his mind. Every time he visited their house he couldn't help looking for any clues as to why John should be disliked, even feared. He had noticed before that Jude's brother Paul had few friends in the class and that they treated him with some degree of deference that was unusual among ten and eleven year olds. It had struck him before but he'd put it down to the fact that Paul seemed more mature and was better off than most, if not all, his classmates.

School broke up towards the end of March, just before Easter, so Art had two weeks to himself. Jude only had a couple of days off work over the Easter weekend so they had planned to go for a couple of walks. As Art didn't have a car he planned walks they could easily access by public transport. It only took a short time by train to reach the Kent countryside so a walk in the Otford area was on the cards. Art knew Otford as a beautiful village with old pubs that he had visited during a geography field trip from college. When John heard of his plans he immediately offered to lend Art a car. Not his Jaguar but Jude's Mini that Art had seen on his first visit. Art was reluctant to agree as he hadn't driven since passing his test in Liverpool before he'd gone to college. He worried about damaging it because of his inexperience but Jude had immediately taken up the offer before he could say anything so it was all decided.

They were to go on Easter Saturday so John asked Art if he'd like to join him in his club for a few drinks on Good Friday lunchtime. This was the first Art had heard of John's membership of a club and, as he'd never been in one, he accepted with alacrity. It might also help him to get to know John a little better in the convivial surroundings of what he expected to be some sort of gentlemen's establishment in the city. John arranged to pick him up from his house on the Friday lunchtime.

*

The club wasn't in the city. It was in a large detached house in Eltham only a few miles away. On arriving John and Art went up a short flight of steps where John pressed a bell by the solid black door. It opened a fraction and then swung open completely and a heavily muscled man welcomed John effusively as they entered. 'Nice to see you Boss,' he grunted. 'Not many here today. Must be a holiday.'

'Thanks Bob,' answered John. 'I'm sure you're right. This is Art. A friend of my Jude.'

They went in and through another door to a rather dim room with subdued lighting and lots of maroon velvet hangings. The walls were covered in dark blue flock wallpaper with gold flowers printed on it. There was traditional club furniture. Lots of leather armchairs and occasional tables. A few men were sitting drinking at some of the tables but no sign of any women. There was a small bar at one end with a couple of empty bar stools next to it. Behind the bar was a small blond barmaid wearing an over-tight green blouse and a black pencil skirt. Art reckoned she was at least forty trying desperately to appear ten years younger. She smiled at John as they reached the bar. 'The usual Boss?' she asked with a smile.

'Please,' replied John. 'What would you like Art?'

'Beer's fine for me.'

81

'Okay. A pint of best and a whisky. Thanks Olive.'

The drinks were soon served and Art followed John to a table in the corner where John sat facing the door. John smiled. 'I always sit here so I can see who's coming in. I like to know what's going on.'

'Why would you want to know?' asked Art.

'Because I own the club. It's one of my small business enterprises. It doesn't make much money but it's useful in other ways.'

Art didn't like to enquire more as to what John meant as he couldn't for the life of him see why anyone would want to run a club at a loss. He wondered what the other ways John had referred to were. He had no idea.

The conversation inevitably turned to football and Art felt on safer ground. A few people drifted in and were always scrutinised by John. Some came over and spoke over-politely to John but regarded Art with open suspicion until John explained who he was. Art was a little uncomfortable with these exchanges and rather wished he was back playing darts in his usual haunt the Star and Garter with Tony and the other regulars. He felt out of his depth. John was a generous host and after a couple more pints Art became more relaxed and asked John about his other business ventures. 'This and that,' was the vague reply. 'I have a taxi firm in the area and provide private security for other businesses that need it. Not a lot to tell really.' That ended Art's questioning. John then started quizzing him in return about his background in Liverpool and his prospects in teaching. Art was honest and

82

told him that it would take many years to reach the top of the pay scale unless he could gain promotion. When he gave John a rough idea as to his annual salary John laughed out loud. 'All that studying and hard work for a pittance. Wasn't there something else you could have done?'

'I love the job. I've never really wanted to do anything else. I know the money isn't brilliant but there's a lot of satisfaction in helping kids learn. I hope I'm making a difference to their future lives.'

'Most commendable,' said John. 'But you must also think of yourself and your own future. You know, there are other ways to make a difference to people's lives. Look at how my family live.'

'Yes, I can see that. You treat them like royalty but I don't know what else I could do. Apart from working for the Post Office at Christmas and odd jobs in factories in the summer I've no other work experience.'

'That's because you've always worked for someone else. To make real money you need to be in charge and control what's happening in your life. People will respect you if you show you're the boss.'

John wouldn't let Art buy a round claiming that it wasn't allowed as he was only a guest and not a member. The club showed no signs of closing even though it was after two o'clock and Art knew pubs kept Sunday hours on Good Friday. When another couple of drinks arrived from two of men on another table John waved to them his thanks and said to Art, 'Let's make this the last one. I'm hungry and if we go back to the house Marion or Jude will soon rustle up a meal for us.'

*

Despite the amount he had drunk John drove them back to his house and they camped out in the spacious sitting room. Art was feeling quite drunk and knew if he shut his eyes he would either fall asleep or the room would start spinning round. He tried his best to focus on John's face and understand a little of what he was saying but it was no good and he couldn't make much sense of what he was being told. He hoped it wasn't important. At last Marion came in with a plate of sandwiches and some pork pies for them to eat. She asked if they wanted a drink and, to Art's relief, John said that a cup of tea would hit the spot. They ate in silence and, when the tea arrived, John told Marion about their day. 'I don't like that club,' she said. 'It isn't a very nice place for a lady to go and enjoy an evening. I prefer a good restaurant or even a decent pub.' Art agreed with her but didn't like to admit it to John.

'It pays the bills,' replied John. 'And it serves a useful purpose.'

Marion grimaced. 'I'm not sure what that is but at least it means some of your cronies don't come here. I wouldn't want the neighbours to see the more unsavoury of them on our doorstep.'

John glanced at Art before replying. 'Now Marion, you know they aren't that bad and they've a lot of respect for our family. They're no trouble.'

'Respect or fear?'

John laughed heartily but Art could see from his eyes that he wasn't amused. 'Well', he said eventually, 'in business you sometimes have to be tough or you'll be trampled on. It's what people expect.' He looked at Art again then said to Marion. 'I'm sure Art wouldn't have the respect of the kids in his school unless he had to wave the big stick now and again. Right Art?'

Art wasn't too sure how to reply honestly so he just smiled at them both and returned to nibbling his sandwich. Marion left the room and John took up the theme again. 'Don't take any notice of her Art. Women don't understand these things. She wouldn't have half the things I buy her if I were a pussy-cat. I know you'll agree.' To Art's relief he heard the front door opening and Jude came in. She looked at the food and at the two men and asked if they'd had a good time in the club. Art felt the need to clear his head so he asked her if she'd like a walk across the Common. She agreed and they set off hand in hand towards the bandstand.

They sat down on a bench in the Spring sunshine and Art wondered if he should mention the disagreement between her parents. He decided not to as he considered it wasn't really any of his business and didn't want either of them thinking he was taking sides. Best left alone. Instead he outlined the plans for tomorrow's day out and Jude listened intently as he extolled the virtues of Otford and what they might see on a walk from the village into the surrounding countryside. He also told her about Lullingstone Roman Villa situated further up the Darent Valley near Eynsford and said they could call in there on the way.

*

Jude was pleased that Art was so enthusiastic about the day trip and hoped that the weather would be kind to them. Easter was quite early in the year and she wondered what to wear. Hiking boots? Anorak? Trousers or skirt? Hat, scarf and gloves? As they were going in the car she decided to take a range of clothes to cope with any weather or terrain. She then considered whether or not to suggest a picnic. Art had mentioned that the village had a couple of old pubs but she didn't know if they did food.

'Art,' she asked. 'Where will we have lunch? I could pack a picnic but it might be too cold to sit out. Do any of the pubs do meals?'

'I think so,' Art replied. 'But we could take some sandwiches just in case. What do you think?'

Jude thought sadly that this was exactly what she'd expected his reply to be. He was so willing to please her that she felt he would agree to anything she suggested. She was really fond of him but wanted him to be a little more demonstrative. She felt that she was making all the running in their relationship. Or was it a relationship yet? She wasn't too sure. On reflection she didn't want to end up like her mother. Stuck indoors most of the time with little to do now Paul was becoming older and more independent. Occasionally she was taken out to be the trophy wife on display to her husband's mates. Maybe she wasn't being fair but that was how she felt.

86

Perhaps Art would take more control of events during their day out. She knew that she loved him and was more than willing to sacrifice all the creature comforts her family offered her to be with him.

*

Art was back in his house and busy planning the trip. He desperately wanted it to be a success and for Jude to have a really great time. He was constantly worried that he wouldn't live up to her expectations and would lose her. The problem was that he'd no idea what she looked for in a man. He knew he wasn't like her father who was rather brash and very confident so if she was hoping for someone similar she would be disappointed. He also knew that as a teacher he couldn't offer her the lifestyle she enjoyed at present. The only way to resolve the problem as he saw it was to just be himself and desperately hope that would be enough. By now he was aware that he was deeply in love with Jude and would do anything to hold on to her.

The next day was bright and sunny; even warm for Easter. Art was in good spirits as he made his way up the hill to Jude's house and found she was, for the first time, ready to join him. Art was pleased as it meant he didn't have to meet her parents for another session in their sitting room. He didn't want any further embarrassment and just wanted to get away and spend the day with Jude. He didn't know that Jude had made an effort to be ready for exactly the same reason. As Art expected, Jude looked like a fashion model in her chosen outfit of slacks, boots and a black and white checked poncho.

Her golden hair was tied back in a ponytail with a black velvet ribbon. She had a coat in one hand and a large bag in the other. She put the bag down and took out the car keys from her back pocket. These she handed to Art who picked up the bag, opened the car and put it on the back seat. Jude went round and sat in the passenger seat as Art clambered in and made himself familiar with the controls. That didn't take long as the mini was a very simple car to drive. They set off, rather hesitantly at first, but soon speeded up as Art gained in confidence. He headed over Shooters Hill to the A20 road which went through Swanley to Farningham where he turned right to Eynsford village and the Roman Villa. Crossing the ford through the River Darent he parked the car, opened his door and went round to open the passenger door and held out his hand to help Jude from her seat.

'What a gentleman,' she smiled. 'Do we need the bag now or will we eat later?'

Art looked at his watch. 'It's only half eleven so we can have a look at the Villa before going further down the road to Otford where we can check out the pubs and decide what to do about lunch.'

'I'll leave the bag in the car,' replied Jude as she took Art's hand and climbed out, 'it's only got a few sandwiches and other stuff in it so we won't want it yet.'

They wandered hand in hand up a track following signs to the Villa and there they were able to view the fantastic mosaic floor and look at the collection of artefacts found during the excavations. Art resisted the temptation to put on his schoolmaster's hat and lecture Jude on what they saw. He just enjoyed seeing her obvious interest in the displays. After about an hour at the villa they returned to the car and headed off down the road to Otford where Art parked by the duck pond and they got out to explore the village.

It was prettier than Art remembered but that was probably because Jude was with him this time rather than his aged lecturer and fellow students. They ambled arm in arm through the village down the High Street and admired the old buildings flanking the road on each side. There were a couple of pubs so Art popped into them and enquired about food but neither of them did lunches. A small restaurant was obviously closed so they returned to the car to fetch the bag which Jude had packed with some food and drinks as well as her scarf and hat. They then retraced their steps down the road until they reached a bridge with the river coursing underneath. Art noticed a path off to the right that seemed to be following the river so they wandered down it past some cottages and eventually found themselves in a quiet meadow with the river meandering alongside.

'This looks like a good place for lunch,' Jude said as she settled herself down on her coat which she spread on the grass and leaned against an old oak tree. 'It really is a beautiful spot and the village looks as if it's unchanged since Adam was a lad. Thanks for bringing me here.'

'The pleasure's all mine. Now what have you got hidden in that voluminous bag?'

Jude took it from him and, like a magician, proceeded to take out a tablecloth and napkins, various tins, plates and cutlery, two glasses and a bottle of Blue Nun wine. She opened the tins to reveal an assortment of sandwiches, sausage rolls, a pork pie, tomatoes and slices of cake. Art was suitably impressed and helped set everything out. 'You knew we would be having a picnic,' he said accusingly. 'What would you have done if I'd taken us into a pub for lunch?'

'I'd have made some excuse about the food on offer or pretended I didn't like the look of the place. Anyway, it all turned out for the best.'

Art opened the white wine using the corkscrew that Jude had remembered to pack and poured two glasses out. He handed one to Jude and they clinked them together. Art meant to wish her good health or some other cliché but as he looked into her cornflower blue eyes he blurted out, 'I do love you.'

Jude wasn't phased and replied,' I know and I love you too.' She put down her glass and took his from him and put it next to hers. Moving round to where he sat she put her arms round his neck and pulled him to her. They kissed in an even more intense manner than before and they lay back on the grass holding each other tightly. Art nuzzled her neck and she sighed contentedly. For the first time his hands explored her body and she unhooked her bra so he could hold her firm breasts. The nipples were erect and Art felt himself responding. Jude put her hands under his pullover and pulled out his shirt so she could caress his naked back. They didn't speak but continued to kiss and cuddle for what seemed like ages when Jude suddenly sat up. 'I can hear someone coming.'

Art sat up as well and saw an elderly lady with a small terrier coming along the path. 'We'd better get back to the picnic,' he said reluctantly. 'I'm hungry and that aperitif has given me a good appetite.'

'Good,' Jude replied, 'and after the main course there could be a sweet.'

'Not just the cake?

'No. Something even sweeter.'

They returned to the picnic and both had their fill. The wine was soon finished and Art lay back with a smile. 'We must do this again sometime. It's the best day out I've ever had.'

'It's not over yet,' promised Jude.

After they had packed away the picnic things they retraced their steps to the car. Art put the bag inside and turned to Jude. He held her by her shoulders and looked her straight in her eyes. 'Is it time for dessert?'

'Not yet,' she murmured, 'There's not enough privacy here. Why don't we drive back to your place? You can make me a coffee.'

'I was going to show you round the ruins of the Bishop's Palace,' replied Art pretending to be annoyed. 'We've come all this way and now you want to go back.'

'It's not the end of our day out,' Jude answered. 'There's still a lot we can do.'

Art opened the car door for her and went round to the driver's door. He opened it and slid into the low seat. 'It's a pity this is a mini. There's not enough room to swing a cat.'

'If you've brought me all this way just to play with a cat I'm deeply offended. There must be a bit more room in your house for swinging things.'

'There is, but it's not as nice as your place. I hope you won't be too critical of my hovel.'

'It's not your hovel as you call it I'm interested in. It's you.'

Art started the car and drove out of the village past the station and up to the main road leading back to London. He had some difficulty concentrating on his driving as his thoughts kept wandering as to what the rest of the day might bring. His thoughts were a mixture of anticipation and trepidation as he realised he would probably be treading ground so far unknown to him. He hoped all would be well.

*

Jude sipped her coffee and smiled gently at Art. He was lying on the ancient chintz sofa with his hands behind his head. He looked very contented. She thought about the day. It had been all she had hoped for. They were both inexperienced but somehow they'd managed to make love in a way that pleased them both. She was happy Art hadn't rushed her and had proved to be a thoughtful partner despite the confines of his single bed. Perhaps the mini would have been more roomy she thought with a bigger smile.

'What's so funny?' asked Art a little worried that he hadn't been good enough for her.

'Just thinking about the car,' Jude answered. 'I was wondering if it was bigger than your bed.'

'Sorry about the lack of space. I've never needed a larger bed before.'

'I'm glad about that. I wouldn't like to think you invited all your girlfriends back here.'

'You know you're the first. And I'm glad about that.'

Jude put down her cup, pushed his legs to the floor and sat next to him. She put her arm round his shoulders and kissed him on the cheek. This was all she had wanted for so long. She felt that she would burst with the love that was overwhelming her and felt sure that everyone would know what they'd done just by looking at her. Should she tell her mother about the day? Well, not all of it of course. And certainly tell her father as little as possible. She knew he still thought of her as his little girl. She had few friends so it would be easy to keep their secret even though she wanted the world to know how much she was in love. She would, however, talk to her parents about the summer holiday to Minehead they were planning. She wanted Art to join them. Her brother would have left the junior school by then so that wouldn't cause a problem. Could she manage to fix it? She thought she could. Art might be a bit wary of such a move but she felt her parents would be only too pleased for him to join them as it would be someone for her father to take to the pub to talk about football and cars. She was well aware that they might not have much time to themselves but that could be worked on later.

It was time to go and Art drove back to Jude's house and parked the car in the drive. They took out the bag and went in. Marion came out of the kitchen to welcome them. 'You both look as if you've had a nice day. The weather was kind. Did you go very far?'

Jude was tempted to reply,'all the way' but decided that might be a big mistake as her mother might realise what she meant so she just replied, 'We went to Otford in Kent. You'd love it Mum. It's a little village full of old world charm, a church and a couple of pubs. You must persuade Dad to take you there sometime. Oh, and nearby is a Roman Villa. That's well worth a visit.'

'Not too sure about that, Your father isn't really one for visiting old ruins. Art, did you enjoy yourself?'

'Yes, thank you,' he said. 'It was a wonderful day. I hope Jude will want to go out for the day again sometime.'

'Any day you like,' Jude answered with a small secretive grin. 'I can't wait for a repeat performance.'

'I am glad.' said her mother. 'The two of you do seem to get on so well. Would you like to stay for dinner Art?'

'Yes please. That would be great. My culinary skills are rather limited.'

'Right,' said Marion. 'Go into the lounge and have a drink. John will be home soon and you can tell him all about your trip.'

Jude led Art by the hand into the lounge and they sat on one of the sofas. She was so pleased that the day had been all and more that she had expected and she didn't want it to end. She heard a car sweep up the drive and then the front door open. Her father was home.

John strode into the lounge and fixed himself a drink from the large globe that opened up to reveal an array of glasses and some bottles of spirits. 'Anyone else for a snifter?' he asked.

'Not for me,' said Art.

'Nor me,' Jude added.

'Okay. I hope you both had a good day. I noticed that the car is still in one piece. Did you make Otford?'

Jude answered before Art could speak. 'Yes, it was lovely. All oldy worldy and the weather was great. We had a picnic by the river. Have you ever been there Dad?'

'No. I prefer the seaside to the country. It smells better. By the way, we must start planning for our summer break in Minehead. Jude, have you got your holiday dates yet?'

'The dentist said I can go any time in August as the surgery is quiet then and he prefers to go away in the winter to somewhere warmer.'

'Lucky bugger,' laughed John. 'I've thought of doing that but I'm not sure Marion would like to fly. I must remember to ask her.'

'Ask her what?' said Marion as she entered the room.

'We were talking about holidays,' explained John. 'Jude says the dentist likes to get away to a warmer country in the winter and I said that you might not like to fly.'

'No idea where you got that from. You've never asked me. Actually I would like to go abroad sometime. Maybe Spain or Italy. Art, have you been abroad?'

'Only on a school trip to France. I enjoyed it but it wasn't really a holiday as we had to practise our French on the locals by buying a list of things from various shops. It was certainly different. At least it means I have a passport if I want to go anywhere else on the continent.'

'Useful things passports,' John commented. 'It might be a good idea if we all had one. Art, are they easy to get?'

'Yes. You need a form from the Post Office. A couple of photographs signed on the back by a responsible citizen and just send it or take it to the passport office in London's Petty France. Not forgetting the fee of course.'

'I don't think I know any responsible citizens. Any idea anyone?'

Art blushed. 'I can sign them. I've already signed a couple for a family in my road. It seems that I'm regarded, with doctors and vicars, as a suitably upright person.'

Marion laughed and said, 'John, at last we are moving in more respectable circles. We must keep hold of Art as our own passport to greater things. I hope you heard that Jude.'

'Loud and clear,' answered Jude. 'Don't worry, I intend to hold on to Art for as long as he'll let me. Now, what about our two weeks in the summer?'

'Well, it's our favourite hotel in Minehead as usual,' said John. 'We always enjoy it there and they make us very welcome. Now I know when you can go then I'll book the rooms next week when Easter is over. The same three rooms as before. Marion?'

Marion glanced at Jude before replying. 'Couldn't we make it four rooms this year?'

'Why? Don't you want to sleep with me? This is startling news.'

'Don't be silly John. I thought that Art might like to join us this year as he and Jude are now quite serious about each other and Jude is a little old for wanting to play sandcastles with Paul every day.'

'I think we should ask both of them about that. What do you think you two?'

'It's a great idea.' replied Jude quickly. She was pleased that the idea had come from her mother rather than having to raise it herself. 'I'm sure Art agrees. You do don't you?'

'So long as it's no bother,' Art diplomatically answered. 'I'd love to come with you. I've never visited Somerset before.'

'Is that where Minehead is? All the time we've been going there I thought it was in Devon,' Marion said. 'They do make super cream teas.'

'Thinking of food again,' joked John, 'you'll never fit into your swimsuit.'

Jude chipped in,' You're right Dad. we'll all need to buy some new outfits. Mum, let's start planning what we need.'

'More expense,'groaned John theatrically. 'Let this be a lesson for you Art. Never mention clothes to a woman.'

Art stayed for another half an hour as the family discussed the arrangements and then left to return home. The next day was Easter Sunday and he just wanted to spend some time thinking about what was happening in his life. Everything was moving on at a fast pace and he wasn't sure he was in control of events that kept rolling in one after the other.

Chapter 7

London, June 1964

John was sitting at his usual table in the club with a large whisky in his hand when the door swung open and one of his many employees rushed in looking hot and harassed. He saw John and immediately went over to have a word with him. John gestured to the seat opposite his and the man sat down still sweating profusely. He took a moment to catch his breath and then addressed John.

'Sorry Boss,' he started. 'There's a problem with one of the collections. Charlie went as usual to the off-licence in Charlton Village but the owner said he was now being looked after by a firm from Lewisham. He said it was the Stevens. He refused to pay up and said they'd told him he didn't have to give us anything no more.'

'Fuck them,' replied John, 'I've had enough of them muscling in on my manor. Go back with a few of the boys and make it very clear to the owner that he still has to pay us. If he argues you know what to do. I'll send a message to Stevens and sort it out. Leave it to me.'

'Okay Boss. I'll take Lenny and Big Dave with me. We'll get the payment.'

John took a sip of his drink and ruminated on the news. He knew he had to do something as he would be regarded as weak if he capitulated even if it was only the once. He would have to approach Alan Stevens and make him understand that Charlton was part of his patch and that as he didn't stray into Stevens area he should restrict his activities to Lewisham and Blackheath where he had operated for years. It really was a pain but it had to be sorted as soon as possible. He had a couple of choices. One was to phone Stevens privately and the other was to pay him a visit, go mob handed and hope he backed down. Both were risky but he decided to try the personal approach first. Why, he thought, were some men so greedy? They had shared the area for years without any real problems. Was Alan Stevens trying to take over his manor completely or was it just a mistake? After all, Charlton was on the border of Blackheath and it would be easy for some knuckle-head employee of Stevens to make a simple mistake. That's how he would play it.

He ordered another drink and the barmaid hurried across with it. He thought about the future and his various business ventures. The club was not making any money but that was irrelevant because it was a useful way of banking his cash from the protection side of his interests. Actually he preferred to call it a security business looking after the myriad of small traders with shops and pubs in the area. His minicab firm was doing very well. He'd jumped on the bandwagon when a loophole in the law had been exposed in 1961 so that cars could take passengers for money so long as they didn't ply for hire. By the simple expediency of having a tiny manned office in Woolwich that people could phone and book one of his cabs they were allowed to pick them up. It was all legal and above board. His genuine security section was also thriving. He remembered the days of the old cocky watchmen and how times had changed and now, instead of guarding holes in the road, his security men and dogs were in demand to pay nightly visits by van to factories and other businesses to make sure they were secure. He wondered if his future lay in his legitimate business ventures but worried that these might also be at risk of being taken over by Stevens and other London firms.

His thoughts then strayed to Jude and Art. He wasn't sure how much Jude knew of his affairs but was sure Art was ignorant of the more illegal side to his work. It was a bit of a problem because he'd hoped Jude would marry a businessman who could hopefully bring greater legality to his ventures. A primary school teacher who lived in a run-down house in a road no better than a slum had never been part of his plans for his treasured daughter. Paul, his son, was easier as he could join him in the business when he was older. Could he tempt Art to work for him in some capacity so that Jude would be better provided for? All that was for the future. There was the problem of Alan Stevens to sort out first. John picked up a folder from the table and started looking through the details of the collections made by his men that week. He was certainly making money from that side of the business but he knew it was risky despite having a local chief inspector in the palm of his hand. The man who, in a drunken moment in the club, had admitted to being heavily in debt through gambling had asked for help. John had paid off the illegal bookies for him leaving an unspoken threat of exposure. It meant that John had prior warning of any police activity likely to disrupt his activities and kept him safe from any prosecutions. He had another drink and chatted to Olive the barmaid about the latest film releases.

Suddenly the door burst open again and the three heavies shambled in. They told John that the matter was sorted and that the off licence owner had paid up in full. This probably meant that he was now paying two firms so John knew he still had to try and diplomatically solve the problem before it escalated. He resolved to do that before going home.

The phone call to Alan Stevens proved to be cordial. As John had hoped Stevens agreed the incursion into Charlton was an error and insisted he knew nothing about it. He said it wouldn't happen again. Although John doubted that was the case he remained polite and the call ended with each wishing the other well. At least for a while thought John as he was sure his rival was testing the water to see what reaction he would get. Lewisham was an area in South London similar to Woolwich with poor housing, poverty and numerous young men with nothing to do except cause trouble. It was a part of London often ignored by the stuffed shirts in County Hall and suffered from a lack of decent schools, housing and jobs. Crime was probably its main export to the rest of London.

With the problem sorted out for now John decided to check out the minicab office in Woolwich and warn the men there that they should stay clear of Lewisham for a while and to report to him if they had any problems. Recently, in north London, there had been some serious gang wars over minicab businesses with a petrol bomb thrown into one controller's office late at night. He thought he would then go to his legitimate security firm's office near Plumstead station and warn them as well although the men who worked from there were more than capable of looking after themselves. The dogs were a good deterrent to anyone with trouble in mind. It would, however, do no harm to have them on alert.

Driving past Shooters Hill police station from Eltham to Woolwich John remembered that he hadn't bought a present for Paul's eleventh birthday. When he arrived at the minicab office he left his car and went to the main shopping street. He spotted a camera store and went in to find something suitable for a young boy to use. Paul had dropped not so subtle hints that a camera was what he wanted most of all. In the shop the assistant showed John the latest cameras. John chose an Instamatic as it was easy to use and load with a film cassette. He added a case and some spare cassettes and flash cubes. He smiled to himself as he paid in cash as the shop was one of the ones he looked after. He knew he would soon receive his money back.

At the office he chatted to the cab controller and some of the drivers. He didn't want to frighten them or they might decide to leave and work for someone else so he kept it low key and just told them to take extra care if they had a fare going near Lewisham or Blackheath. As the cars were unmarked the risk was low but some of the drivers were probably known by the opposition so it was good to be on guard. He decided to have the window and door of the office covered by metal grills and told the controller to have it done as soon as possible. It was just a precaution but, he thought, a sensible one.

It only took him a few minutes to drive to the security office. He pulled into the forecourt and admired the new sign he'd had installed the previous week. In red and gold the sign proclaimed, 'J Hayes & Son. Security – 24 hour service'. He'd added 'son' so that Paul would be flattered and have an incentive to eventually join John in running the business. John hoped that when that time came he would have left the more dodgy side behind. He had needed to be fairly brutal in building up his empire but now he was reasonably well established he didn't want Paul to be involved in that part. It would take a few more years before he could back out with his reputation intact but he really was looking forward to the day when he could be accepted as a proper businessman. Amused at his train of thought he wondered if he would really fit in at Eltham Warren Golf Club, The Round Table or even as a Freemason. He pulled himself out of his reverie and went into the office. A large man with his gut spilling over his belt sat on a desk. He jumped to his feet when John entered and went and sat on the chair behind the desk.

'Hello Boss,' he said, 'to what do we owe the pleasure? You usually only come round on a Friday.'

'Just passing, I thought I'd pop in and see how things are with you and the lads.'

'No problems Boss. All the jobs are covered and there's been no reports of break-ins or other incidents. You know I'll contact you if anything important blows up.'

'Yes,' replied John. 'I just thought I'd mention that we've had a small problem with the Stevens mob. Hopefully it's now okay but I thought you'd better know just in case it blows up again. Tell the guards to be extra vigilant especially at night as Stevens and his men might try some funny business to discredit us.'

'How d'you mean Boss?'

'I don't know but I don't trust them an inch. Just take care.'

John left the office and drove back to Eltham. He thought he deserved another drink before going home.

*

Marion put down the book she had been reading. It was the latest James Bond book by Ian Fleming entitled 'On Her Majesty's Secret Service'. She enjoyed a read in the afternoon before Paul came home from school and she had to prepare the evening meal. It was the best time of day as far as she was concerned. All the chores had been completed and it was her own time to spend as she wished. Her husband John rarely came home before six and Jude didn't finish work until six-thirty so the meal was invariably at seven o'clock. Today would probably be no different. Was that all she wanted? She spent a minute or two with the book resting in her lap and tried to formulate an answer to that question. She had met John one Saturday night at a friend's birthday party in a local church hall when she was fifteen and had been immediately struck by his confidence and bearing. He had dominated the room and everyone seemed to hang on his every word. She had never met anyone like him before and desperately hoped he would notice her. And as he was only eighteen there might be a chance. Lots of people, not just her family, had commented on her good looks but she was rather shy and wasn't at all confident that she was as pretty as they said. After all, she thought, her nose was too long and she was taller than most girls of her age. She was proud of her figure and her breasts had grown exactly as she had hoped when they started developing at the age of twelve. What she didn't realise was that John had spotted her as soon as he'd entered the room and liked what he saw.

He had approached her near the end of the party and asked her for a dance. It turned out to be the last dance of the evening so, of course, it was a slow waltz. He held her tight to him as they shuffled round the floor. He wasn't a particularly good dancer but she hadn't cared as just being in his arms was sufficient ecstasy for that moment. When the music ended he continued to hold her and whispered in her ear. It was the standard request to walk her home but she'd had to refuse as her father was collecting her. He'd then asked if he could see her again and she'd told him they didn't have a

106

phone at home but she could be contacted where she worked in Dolcis shoe shop in Powis Street. Sure enough he popped into the shop on the following Monday and they arranged to meet on the Saturday to go to the pictures. Just like Jude and Art mused Marion.

She knew that at first her parents hadn't approved of John as he was older than her and, they thought, rather too flash. Also he didn't seem to have a regular job or apprenticeship like most lads of his age. He seemed to spend a lot of time in Woolwich market helping out as he called it. When they questioned him about his future he'd always been vague and muttered something about being in business on his own. This meant nothing to her parents as they had the idea that businessmen were a totally different breed to people who moved in their circles. Then came the war and John was called up to join the army. This gave her a lever as he was now serving his country which her father approved of and slowly her parents grew to like the rather brash young man. They became engaged on her eighteenth birthday and Marion constantly planned for the wedding. Her so-called bottom drawer was full to bursting as she put together everything she thought she a would need for their future together.

The wedding was fairly quiet as her parents didn't have a lot of money and John's parents were unwilling or unable to contribute very much. After a brief but successful honeymoon in Margate they moved in to their first home – a glorified bedsit in a large Victorian house. They had a small area with a sink and a pre-war Baby Belling for cooking at one end of the room and shared a bathroom with another couple and an elderly man who never cleaned up after using the facilities. John swore that it would only be a temporary home as he would make enough money after the war to buy a house for them to live in and not have to share any more. Marion wasn't sure he would manage to make such a momentous event actually happen but in less than two years, despite still being in the army, he carried her, heavily pregnant with Jude, over the threshold of a small house near Plumstead Police Station. She was very happy and busied herself with ordering furniture from Cuffs department store and making curtains using cloth bought from a stall on Woolwich market. Marion never asked John where the money came from as she knew his army pay couldn't have been enough on its own and that set the pattern for their married life. He gave her a housekeeping allowance and she never delved too deeply into his various schemes.

Now, she thought, was I in denial or just happy to take the money he makes? She knew that some of his exploits were probably outside the law and she wasn't too happy with some of his associates that he'd occasionally brought home. The club was a place she'd always detested as, to her, it was seedy and attracted the sort of people she would normally avoid. When they went out she much preferred virtually any restaurant to the club especially if the menu included prawn cocktail and her favourite black forest gateau. Blue Nun or Mateus Rose were her choice of wine although John stuck religiously to beer and scotch. As the children grew up they were included in the restaurant visits and eating out as a family became a strong tradition. A small place in Welling was always their favourite partly because one of the waiters did a rather good Elvis impersonation. They also patronised a very good Chinese restaurant in Eltham High Street which did an excellent crispy duck with pancakes. As John's income steadily rose they became quite comfortable, as her mother would have put it, and they moved to the big house near the Common. Sitting there now Marion felt a glow of pride that they had done so well. So much better than all her family and friends. That, she considered, was probably why so few of them ever called or invited them to their homes. It must be jealousy.

Marion hoped that Jude and Art would get married. She knew they were hopelessly in love with each other and Jude needed a man with a brain and a kind heart to look after her. She had been rather spoilt growing up and took a lot of the things bought for her for granted. Jude was already older than she had been when she became engaged to John so Marion hoped an announcement was in the offing. John might be a problem. He wanted the very best for Jude but Marion thought that he might think he knew better than all of them and would try to steer Jude towards a richer catch in the matrimonial stakes. Oh well, she thought, there's not much I can do about it so we will have to let it take its course. She pushed herself up from the chair and went to the kitchen to make a snack for Paul who always arrived home ravenous and then prepare the evening meal. There was just enough time to cook a beef casserole with dumplings which always went down well with John although Jude preferred something lighter.

*

Paul came crashing into the kitchen shedding his bag, books, coat and shoes as he skidded across the tiled floor.

'Guess what,' he spluttered.

'I can't,' replied Marion,' give me a clue.'

'It's about Art, er, Mr James.'

'What about Mr James?'

'He's taking us to a Roman Villa. Isn't that great?'

'It's very good of him. When is it? Your Dad might be able to help.'

'Not sure, I'll find out tomorrow.'

Paul grabbed a handful of biscuits from the tin, picked up the glass of orange squash Marion had made for him and dashed upstairs to his room. Soon the sound of a Beatles' hit played on Paul's record player drifted down to the kitchen. Marion smiled to herself and was pleased that her son was so happy. Life for him was still uncomplicated and she hoped that would last for ever but deep down she knew that he would change as he reached his teens. She wasn't sure if a life in his father's business was the best plan for him. He wasn't as driven as John and had too kind and gentle a nature. She hoped he would go to university and make a name for himself in a way far removed from John's world. Possibly Art could have a good influence on the boy as he grew up. After all, Paul worshipped the ground he walked on and might see him as a more appropriate role model than his father. Marion felt a little guilty about such a thought as she knew John wanted the best for his family. But was he always right?

*

Jude and John arrived home together and sat in the kitchen while Marion finished cooking the dinner. Paul was called down and told to lay the table which he did without any complaint. The family sat down and Paul told Jude and his dad about the proposed Roman Villa outing for the class. John said he might be able to help if he knew the date of the trip and Paul, yet again, promised to find out. Jude was smiling to herself.

'What's the Joke?' asked John.

'It's probably the one Art took me to when we went to Otford for the day at Easter. I was just thinking how much I'd enjoyed the day.'

'No Idea how anyone can get so excited about an old building,' John replied.

'There was more to it than that,' Jude said quietly, almost to herself, as she relived the day and how it had ended.

'I hope it's as good for me, I'm going to take my camera and make a record of what we see,' Paul said.

'I'm sure you'll have a great time,' his sister added. 'But maybe not as great as I did.'

Marion butted in, 'Please can we get on with the meal? 'Jude, you can tell Paul all about it later. Did you have a good day John?'

'So-so, not everything went to plan but I sorted it out.'

111

'As you always do. Now, who's for some apple pie and ice cream?'

Chapter 8

London, July 1964

Summer term was nearing its end and there was a holiday mood in Art's class. The children had mixed feelings as they were pleased to be breaking up for the long holiday bur all had niggling worries about the big move to the secondary school they had either chosen or been allocated to by the local divisional education office in Woolwich. A few of the boys, including Paul, had been accepted for a place in one of the nearby grammar schools. He had gained a place at Colfe's which was the most prestigious of the schools in the area. Other boys were off to John Roan or Shooter's Hill Grammar but most were going to Woolwich Polytechnic or Charlton Boys. It was a similar picture for the girls and it meant that friendships built up over six years in primary school were suddenly going to be pulled apart. It was a time of uncertainty but they did their best to hide their emotions until the last day of term when the leavers' party would be held in the school hall. They all knew that the party would be an emotional affair as it always had been for their older siblings. It was somewhat of a school tradition to end their time in Vicarage Road in tears. Art knew little about this so he just carried on as usual and didn't give it much thought. His mind was on the upcoming holiday to Minehead. Two whole weeks with Jude. He still couldn't believe it.

Since Easter he'd had to force himself to focus on his school work and only saw Jude at weekends. Having Paul in his class was a constant reminder of her and he found himself thinking of Jude every time he looked at her young brother. Paul had proved to be very diplomatic about Art's growing relationship with his sister. He had successfully fended off the questions from other children and they had given up trying to quiz him about their teacher and what he did after school. The girls in the class had been the most interested in Art's private life and wanted to know all the details but they were destined for disappointment. None of them would have dared to question Art so the whole affair soon became old news.

At the start of the new term Art had found himself in charge of the cricket team despite having only a scant knowledge of the game. One of the parents offered to help and soon they had put together an enthusiastic first eleven. They relied on accurate bowling and close fielding to try and prevent the opposition scoring many runs in their twenty over matches. One boy was a fearless player and became the wicket keeper. He enjoyed staying as close to the wicket as possible to stump any batsman who strayed from the crease. The batting prowess of the team left a lot to be desired and in many matches a score of forty runs was hailed as an achievement. The other schools from Plumstead they played against on the rough grass of the Common were equally inept and it was only when they came up against a school in the

114

knock-out competition from the leafy suburbs of Eltham did they realise that there were some very good primary school cricket teams in the borough. The team they played all wore immaculate whites and each boy had his own bat and equipment. Vicarage Road won the toss and opted to bowl. In the twenty overs the other school lost only three wickets and scored over a hundred runs. In reply Art's team scored eight runs all out. Art was upset but the boys all took it in good part. It appeared they were used to losing to Eltham schools in all sports including the girls' netball and rounders.

The last week of term came soon enough and the excitement was building up. The school didn't send formal written reports home to parents but did hold an open evening so parents could meet their child's teacher and discuss their progress and behaviour. Nearly all the parents of the pupils in his class attended and it took over three hours to see them all. Art had tried to have an appointments system but it soon fell apart when he realised he needed to give some parents more time than others. When the evening ended it was nearly ten o'clock and all the Staff went to the Rose Inn for a winding down drink. Art would have preferred to go to his local but didn't want to appear aloof or unsociable. The staff swapped stories about the parents they had seen and the questions they had been asked. It appeared that most of the parents were very grateful to the teachers and held them in high regard so there were very few negative incidents reported.

On the last day of term the children were allowed to bring in quiet games so that the teachers could concentrate on clearing up their classrooms and returning books to the storeroom ready for the next term. Art was surprised to be given many cards and presents by his class. The presents were not of great value but were personal and Art was touched by the kindness of families who didn't have much themselves. There was a card from Paul with a bottle of aftershave. Art opened the card and quickly closed it again before anyone could see it when he read Paul's message. It read, 'Thank you for a great year and please marry my sister soon as I want her room.' Art blushed and put the card in his drawer as he didn't want the other children to read it. It did, however, make him think seriously about the future. The last event of the school day was an assembly when the headmaster said goodbye to those leaving, both staff and children. He then told those children who were moving up a year in the school the name of their teacher for the following term. There were a few muted groans when the name of one of the more unpopular teachers was mentioned and some cheers when the head announced ones that were more favoured. Art was flattered when he came in the cheers category but felt a bit sorry for those awarded boos as he knew all the teachers did their best and children often mistook strictness for unfriendliness.

The fourth year leavers' party was in the evening so Art went along to the school at six o'clock to help the volunteer band of parents set everything up. The parents had already arranged tables and chairs and were putting up bunting to make the hall look more festive. The school record player was in position and was connected to the tannoy system so that music could be played for the inevitable games of pass the parcel and musical chairs. All the parents of the leavers had sent in food which was being spread on the trestle tables used for school dinners. It was a veritable mountain of sandwiches, cakes and crisps with numerous bottles of fizzy drinks. Paper plates and cups had been bought to save on the washing up at the end and it looked to Art that there was little left for him to do.

John and Marion were there helping and Art went over to chat with them. As he reached them he overheard a woman say to the man with her, 'I don't think a teacher should mix with such people. It isn't good for the school. And he's seeing their daughter.'

Art didn't know what to do. Should he ignore it and pretend he hadn't heard anything even though it had been said loud enough for everyone to know that he must have heard the comment? The only other option was to confront the woman he now recognised as one of the school governors and a parent of a girl in his class. But this was fraught with danger as she had the ears of the other governors. He turned and smiled at her as sweetly as he could and said so everyone could hear, 'Good evening, so pleased you could come and help. It means such a lot to the children when all their parents turn up and work together. I'm sure it will be a great party. Oh, and by the way, who I choose to mix with in my own time is nothing to do with the school and certainly none of your business.'

She glared at him but said nothing and turned away to put out even more crisps. The other parents who had stopped and watched the unfolding situation went back to their jobs and indulged in muted conversations with each other. John clapped Art on the shoulder and said, 'Well done lad. I know we aren't the most popular of families round here but some folk are very jealous. We'll be off now and bring Paul back with us for the start. Jude will probably want to come as well if you don't mind.'

'No, of course not. You know I'm always pleased to see her. Tell her I can't wait.'

After John and Marion had left the deputy head sidled up to Art and took his arm. She steered him towards her classroom and shut the door. 'What was that all about? You might have made an enemy of Mrs Newman by speaking to her like that in front of the other parents. I know, as does everyone in the school, that you've been seeing Paul's sister but didn't realise it was serious. How much do you know about the family?'

'Quite a lot,' Art replied. 'They've been very kind to me and Jude's a wonderful girl. I know John owns a club in Eltham and also a security company and a minicab firm but I can't see why that would make people dislike the family. Is it really jealousy of their wealth? I'm going on holiday with them next week so I'll be with Jude for a fortnight. Between you and me I'm hoping to propose to her. Anyway, do you know why so many people seem to hate them?'

'Yes, jealousy is part of it but it's more about how they became wealthy in the first place rather than just envy. Mrs

Newman's husband owns a shop and probably has no choice but to use Mr Hayes' so-called security firm. That might be the reason she is against him. Please make sure you know what you're getting into before you commit yourself.'

'I still don't get it,' Art puzzled. 'He's only a businessman. And why the "so-called" bit? I thought it was a proper business.'

'Some of it probably is but I've heard that some shops and other concerns pay to prevent damage to their businesses. And the damage only tends to happen if they don't pay their dues to Mr Hayes' men. Be careful what you're getting yourself into with that family.' She walked off without further comment leaving Art standing open-mouthed.

It was outside his experience and he still couldn't believe that the family he liked so much was involved in anything illegal. Then he remembered what his friend Tony had said about John Hayes and wondered if he'd been blinded by their kindness and his love for Jude. What could he do? He didn't want to lose Jude or fall out with her father. He determined to tread carefully and see how events panned out.

Art returned to the hall with his head in turmoil. The children had started to arrive all dressed up in their best clothes. They greeted him warmly and some of the girls gave him a hug. He felt a little better and forced himself into the party mood. He didn't want to spoil the occasion for the children he'd grown to love over the year.

The leavers' party ended with the traditional tears and declarations of undying friendship. The parents' committee had bought all the children a leather bookmark with the school's name on in gold print and the date they left. A large cake was also cut and distributed to all those present. Art stood with the Hayes family. Not, he thought, as an act of defiance but because they were now his closest friends in the neighbourhood. It was duly noted by a number of the parents but no further comments were made. After clearing up John asked Art to join them at home to discuss the upcoming holiday in Minehead. The car was outside so they all clambered in and went to his house where Art and John settled down in the large lounge as Marion and Jude made tea in the kitchen. Paul had gone up to his room to change out of the shirt he'd had autographed by all his classmates.

'Sorry about earlier,' John said to Art. 'Some people admire me for making a go of my life but others think I've somehow betrayed my working class background. As far as I'm concerned I'm still working class despite having a nice car and house. You can't win against the narrow minded people who think everyone should know their place.'

'It's not a problem,' replied Art. 'But I have heard that some folk aren't happy with the way some of your business associates conduct themselves. I'm sure you don't condone what they do.'

'That's true, but in business you sometimes have to be tough to stop others walking all over you. It can be a fine line to tread and sometimes it goes wrong. People always judge you by your mistakes rather than your successes. I know I've rubbed some locals up the wrong way but usually I had no choice.'

'That's understandable,' Art added thoughtfully, 'so long as no one comes to any serious harm.'

'Have to break some eggs to make an omelette,' replied John with an enigmatic smile.

Marion and Jude came back with a tray bearing the usual tea things and a plate of assorted cakes. When the tea was poured they all discussed the upcoming holiday. John had booked the hotel on the front at Minehead and the car had been serviced by one of his friendly garages so he felt that he'd done his bit. Marion and Jude had bought their new outfits suitable for all weather and occasions. Art told them he had been researching the area and had planned a number of possible outings they might all like to go on together. He'd thought up a few more just for him and Jude but didn't mention these.

'It all seems to be working out well,' Marion said. 'I'm sure we'll have a great time and it will be nice to explore the area. Usually Art we just go back and forth from the hotel to the beach with the customary breaks to the pub near the harbour and the occasional cream tea.'

'I hope you haven't planned any long hikes,' John said. 'I want a restful break not a route march over Exmoor.'

Art laughed, 'I had planned a walk to Dunkery Beacon but if you think that's too much like hard work then leave it to the youngsters.'

'Bloody cheek,' retorted John, 'I'll out-walk any of you, Just wait and see.'

Paul slipped into the room and curled up on a sofa.

'What was that about Dad?' he asked. 'Did you say you were a good walker? I think Mr James is better than you. He can certainly run fast when we have football training.'

'It's not Mr James now,' said Art. 'You've left junior school so now you can call me Art like the rest of your family.'

'Can I really? Is that okay Dad?'

'Yes. That's fine,' John said. 'But I'm still Dad to you.'

Jude looked across at Art and grinned. 'I suppose You'll have a new load of kids after the Summer. I wonder if any of them will have a sister as pretty as me?'

'Not possible,' Art replied. 'Lightning never strikes twice.'

Marion sighed, 'Well it's also the end of our long connection to Vicarage Road. It only seems like yesterday I was dragging a very reluctant little girl to her first day in the infants' school.'

'Me reluctant?' Jude exclaimed. 'I always liked school.'

'Not on your first day,' replied Marion. 'I could barely disentangle you from me to push you into the playground.'

'What about me?' asked Paul.

'Oh, you were no trouble. You seemed pleased to get away. But you had the advantage of knowing more about school from Jude so it was much easier.'

Art got up and said he was going home as he had to pack to visit his mother in Liverpool. Jude saw him to the door and kissed him.

'I can't wait to go away together even though we're in separate rooms. I'm sure we'll manage to have some time alone together.'

'I hope so, I'm also excited about the holiday. You know, it's actually the first one I've ever had apart from occasional trips to the seaside at New Brighton or Southport. My mother being a widow she didn't have cash to spare and my grandparents weren't much better off.'

'Well, as it's your first we'd better make it memorable.'

'I'm sure it will be. Just being with you for two weeks is fantastic.'

They kissed again and Art set off down the hill to his house. After he'd packed, he thought a visit to the pub would be a good way to end the day.

*

Art's trip by train to Liverpool was uneventful. He left Mossley Hill Station and walked up Rose Lane to his mother's house. It held many memories for him and he still felt at home as soon as he crossed the threshold. It was a warm feeling of security and simplicity. He'd had a happy childhood despite never knowing his father and his mother and grandparents had done as much for him as they could afford. Without the student grant from the government and a little extra from Liverpool Corporation he knew he would never have had the opportunity to go to college and become a teacher.

His mother was sitting in her favourite chair dozing and only stirred when he called out to her that he was home again. She took a moment to focus on him and to gather herself together..

'I thought you were coming home tomorrow,' she said tremulously. 'You've given me quite a start.'

'Don't worry Mum. I might have given you the wrong date in my letter.' Art knew he hadn't but didn't want his mother to think she was wrong.

'I've nothing in for tea,' she replied.

'No problem. I'll pop to the shops after we've had a cup of tea and a chat.'

Art went out to the kitchen and made a strong pot of tea. He couldn't find the sugar when he looked in the cupboard but there was half a bottle of milk on the shelf. In the fridge he found the sugar bowl. Strange, he thought, Mum's usually very pernickety about putting things away properly. Maybe she'd been in a hurry and got a little muddled.

He took the tea things on a tray with a few biscuits he'd discovered into the sitting room.

'Here we are,' he said, 'just as you like it.' He poured out two cups and passed one to his mother. He noticed her hand shaking as she took it. 'Do you want a biscuit?'

'Have we got some? I couldn't find them yesterday. Things keep moving around so I can't find them and I spend ages looking.' She sipped her tea gratefully. 'It's good to have you home. It'll make my life so much easier with a man about the house again.'

She thinks I'm back for good mused Art. He was worried that she was becoming forgetful but thought it might be a temporary lapse. A visit to the doctor to see what was wrong might be a good idea.

'When did you last see the doctor?' he asked with as neutral and expression on his face as he could manage so he didn't alarm her.

'I've no idea love. It must have been last year.'

Art knew that was wrong because she'd had the flu during his Easter visit and that was only a couple of months ago.

'I think you should go again as your memory isn't as it was. I'll make an appointment after we've finished our tea.'

'You do fuss over me,' she grumbled but actually looked quite pleased at the prospect.

The next morning Art and his mother went round the corner to the doctor's surgery in Queen's Drive. They sat in the bleak waiting room until the doctor called Art into his consulting room. It was Doctor Wilkie who had known Art since he was born. He was a dapper man with steel-rimmed spectacles and thinning white hair. Art suddenly remembered the car the doctor drove many years ago. It was a Triumph Mayflower and was all straight lines and angles. Art, as a small boy, had thought at the time that he would buy a car like that when he grew up. It looked posh and expensive. However, he knew now that on his teacher's salary there was no chance of buying a top of the range vehicle in the foreseeable future. He sat down and the doctor looked at him.

'Good to see you Jack. What can I do for you?'

'It's not about me but Mum. She's becoming a little forgetful and I'm concerned she's not really looking after herself properly.' Art told the doctor about the sugar in the fridge and a few other odd events.

'Send her in to me,' said Doctor Wilkie.

Art went back to the waiting room and told his mother the doctor would see her. She stood and went into the consulting room. About ten minutes later she re-emerged looking flushed.

'The doctor said could you go back in. I've no idea why he asked me all those questions about the date and the Prime Minister.'

Art returned to the doctor and sat down again. The doctor looked serious.

'I'm afraid it's not good news,' he began. 'Your mother appears to have developed senile dementia despite only being relatively young and it will become progressively worse over time. Are you back here permanently now and able to look after her?'

'No, I'm teaching in London and can't leave my job without at least a term's notice.'

'Do you have any family who could help?'

'You know I'm an only child and Mum has no other living relatives. What can be done to help her?'

The doctor paused for a moment's thought. 'My cleaner, Mrs Carr is a very caring woman and could do with some extra income. She could possibly pop in and help your mother every other day for a few hours and keep an eye on any adverse developments. If you like I'll give her your phone number and you can arrange a meeting.'

'Thanks a lot. I'm very grateful and I'm sure Mum would like a little company.'

'Can you afford to pay her?'

'It'll be a bit of a struggle but I'll manage somehow.' Art suddenly had a sinking feeling about his own future. His plans were disappearing fast. No new house for him and Jude. But what could he do?

The doctor hadn't finished. 'You must be aware that this disease progresses at different rates in different people. It's impossible to predict how long it will be before your mother becomes totally dependent on help. She'll almost certainly have to go into a nursing home when she's in the later stages.'

'We'll cross that bridge when it comes,' replied Art. 'I'll do what I can and if I have to move back home then that's what I'll do.'

Feeling shattered Art took his mother home. She still seemed unaware of why they had gone to the doctors and asked Art if he was ill.

'I'm fine,' he replied,'but it does no harm to have a check-up now and then. By the way the doctor said that he knew a lovely lady who would like to help you with the shopping and housework. Won't that be nice?'

'Yes, I'd like that. Things have been getting on top of me recently and a friendly face would be a tonic.'

Mrs Carr phoned that afternoon and Art explained to her what was required. She said the doctor had told her a little about his mother and she was looking forward to meeting her.

Art asked when she could come round and it was arranged for that evening.

Mrs Carr was a large and buxom woman who had a no nonsense look about her. Her meaty arms hinted at her capability for hard wok and her iron grey hair pulled back into a bun gave her a rather formidable appearance. Art welcomed her and they went to sit in the front room where the better furniture was kept for more formal occasions. She spoke softly and had a warm smile that made Art feel a lot better disposed to her. Never go on first impressions he reminded himself. It was exactly the same with a class of children in school. They discussed duties, hours and pay and then he took her to meet his mother. The two women hit it off immediately and were soon chatting about old times and found they had a few mutual friends. As they were such a compatible pair Art decided immediately that Mrs Carr would be ideal to keep an eye on his mother and help her manage the house. He made them all a cup of tea and after this when Mrs Carr was leaving Art gave her his school's phone number explaining that he hadn't a phone at home but could be contacted on that number during school hours.

'I suppose that means you'd like me to start?' she asked on the doorstep.

'Of course,' replied Art. 'As soon as you can. Mother really needs some help and I'm too far away to return to Liverpool at short notice. I'm sure you'll contact me if there are any problems and I'll send you your money every week.' He handed her the key to the front door which she stored safely in her voluminous handbag.

'That's fine then.' She gave Art a piece of paper with her details on it. 'I'm looking forward to knowing your mother better and being of some use to her. I know that she will probably become more dependent on me as time goes by and I'll tell you if I think she needs more help. My aunt had a similar complaint and she eventually had to go into a home.'

'It's good you have some experience of her condition. I know you'll be just what's needed to help her through these troubling times.'

Mrs Carr left and Art returned to his mother in the sitting room. She smiled at him and he felt a lot happier that things were sorted out for the immediate future.

*

A few day's later Art was on the train returning to London. The visit home had left him with a great deal to think about. He was satisfied that his mother would be in safe hands but was well aware that the future was uncertain. He worried how he would cope when the inevitable happened and she need to go into a nursing home. He wasn't sure if they were free on the National Health or he'd have to pay. He knew his mother couldn't afford much so the bill would be down to him. All of this had wrecked his plans to move as the cash for Mrs Carr would prevent him saving to buy a house or even an old car. Would Jude still want to go out with him if he still lived in squalor? He had serious plans for their future together but these were unravelling by the minute. There seemed to be no way out of the dilemma. He read a book he'd bought in Liverpool to pass the time and to forget his problems. It was a collection of poems by John Betjeman and the superb atmospheric descriptions of places and perceptive depictions of people and their innermost thoughts took Art out of himself for an enjoyable hour until the train rolled in at Euston Station. Art left the train and went by underground to Charing Cross to catch the Dartford train which would take him to Woolwich Arsenal Station. It was then only a ten minute walk to Pattison Road and home.

Nothing appeared to have changed in the few days he'd been away. He unpacked his small case and put his dirty washing in the laundry bag ready for a visit to the laundrette. Sitting down on the sofa he went though all the possible permutations of his situation again. He wanted to see Jude and tell her about his mother. He hoped she'd understand that his duty lay in helping sort out the future care that his mother would require. Jude was the bright star in his life that made the future bearable and he never wanted to lose her whatever the circumstances. It had dampened his enthusiasm for the trip to Minehead but he hoped a couple of weeks with her family would help to cheer him up a little. He went out to the nearest working telephone box and called Jude at work. Without telling her the full story over the phone he said that they needed to meet as he had something to discuss with her. They agreed that he would visit her house that evening at around eight o'clock when they had finished dinner. As he put the receiver back on its cradle he hoped he hadn't made Jude concerned by his serious tone during their talk. Usually he was very cheery and positive. He didn't feel like that now.

That evening Art sat with Jude and her parents. He explained the situation he was in and how he had to focus his time and resources on helping his mother. They were all very sympathetic and agreed he was doing the right thing. They wanted to know if was still going with them to Minehead and he immediately said he was and was looking forward to the holiday. Jude was quiet and Art wondered if she was considering their future together. Eventually she spoke.

'You're a good man Art and I would think far less of you if you didn't support your mother at this time. Don't worry about me. I will wait for as long as it takes for the situation to be resolved. There's no need for anything to come between us.'

Art's heart raced at this. He was close to tears as he realised that Jude thought as much of him as he did of her. He couldn't find the words to express his feelings so he just reached across to her and gently squeezed her hand. She looked in his eyes and he knew that everything would be fine. John and Marion smiled at the couple and John cleared his throat. 'Art, I know you're worried sick but we'll sort something out for the best. Give me a little time to think about it and I'll try and come up with an answer that suits everyone, especially you mother.'

'Thank you,' Art said simply, 'You're now my family in London. I value your help and support. Let's make our plans for Minehead.'

Chapter 9

Minehead, August 1964

The drive down to Minehead had taken them six hours with a short stop on the A4. Even though it was all on 'A' roads there had been numerous hold-ups in the many small towns and villages they passed through on the way. During the journey Art had played the game 'arms and legs' with Paul and Jude to help pass the time. They took it in turns to count the arms and legs mentioned in the pub signs they passed. The King's Arms scored two for Jude and Art had a zero for The Castle. After a time the scores were fairly even until Paul hit upon The Cricketers and was declared the outright winner. The last part of the journey on the A39 had been the worst and they were all relieved to see the hill rising behind Minehead and park outside their hotel. Art and John carried the cases into the hotel lobby where a porter took the luggage from them and stowed it all on a trolley ready to be delivered to their rooms. At the reception desk John explained who they were but the receptionist just smiled and said she remembered them from the year before. After John had filled in the requisite paperwork she gave him the keys to the four rooms and asked if they wanted to be booked in for dinner. After a brief discussion they said they would and set off for their rooms. They were all on the first floor and their luggage was waiting for them. The porter hovered around so John tipped him a half-crown and he shambled off looking pleased.

Art's room was next to Jude's and Paul was in a room opposite them. John and Marion were further along the corridor as they had booked a suite with a sea view and private bathroom. The rest of them had to use the shared bathroom at the other end of the corridor. Art soon unpacked his clothes and toiletries as he hadn't brought a great deal. Actually he'd brought most of his clothes and hoped he wouldn't look too shabby when they went out of an evening. Daytime wasn't a problem as it was a holiday resort and he could wear any old shirt and shorts for trips to the beach or the moors. He'd planned a few excursions to cover all eventualities, especially inclement weather. Trips to Wookey Hole caves, Selworthy Village and Dunster Castle were high on his agenda as was a hike to Dunkery Beacon on Exmoor if the weather wasn't sunny enough for the beach. From his window he had a view of the car park but he could just see over the rooftops to North Hill rising up steeply to the edge of the moor. There must be a path up to the top, he thought, and then we could probably walk to Selworthy or even Porlock. He'd have to chat to the others about this as he didn't want Paul thinking he was being too much of a schoolmaster. He must relax more and go with what the rest of them wanted. He locked his room door and knocked on Jude's. She opened it and he asked if she'd like to go for a walk along the seafront.

'Give me half an hour,' she replied, 'I'm still unpacking my dresses. Go down to the lobby and I'll meet you there. I'd invite you in but Mum and Dad might get the wrong idea.'

Art went down the stairs and sat at a small table which had a number of magazines on it. He chose one and leafed through it but it was all about country pursuits and he soon put that down and picked up one about cars. He suddenly felt tired and closed his eyes for a moment. Jude found him slumped fast asleep in the chair with the magazine in his lap. She touched his shoulder and he woke with a start.

'What? Who?'

'It's me,' Jude said leaning forward to kiss him. 'I thought we were going for a walk. Paul wants to come as well. Do you mind?'

'Course not, he'll be lonely if we don't include him.'

She kissed him again, took his hand and pulled him out of the chair spilling the magazine on to the carpet. 'Come on, the holiday's just begun. let's make the most of it.'

Paul came crashing down the stairs. 'Good, you're still here. I thought you might have gone without me.'

'No chance,' laughed Art, 'we wouldn't dare.'

They walked along the sea wall to the harbour and stopped to admire the small boats resting on the mud.

'How do they get out to sea if there's no water?' asked Paul.

'They have to wait for the tide to come in,' answered Jude.

Art added, 'As this is the Bristol channel the tides can be very high and the water in the harbour will come right up to near the top.'

'Wow,' Paul said, 'can we wait to see that happen?'

Art explained, 'The tide only comes in twice a day so, as it is now out we would have to wait about six hours for the next high tide. I think your mum and dad would wonder where we'd got to. And we'd be very hungry.'

They walked on and looked at the Lifeboat Station. The door was closed and nobody was about so they went on past a small car park where the road ended. Art noticed a path going up the hill through some bushes.

'I wonder if that leads up to the top of the hill and then on to Selworthy?' he asked no one in particular. And no one answered so they turned and retraced their steps back to the hotel where Art went to phone his mother and then Mrs Carr to make sure all was well. To his relief there were no problems and Mrs Carr reassured him that his mother was coping well and they'd had a right good chat about life in Liverpool before the war.

*

John was in his room and was also telephoning. He kept daily contact with the club and always spoke to his second in command. This was Mike, a tough, heavily tattooed and intimidating man in his forties who had been a sergeant in the army and served in Malaya. He had been lost in civvy street until John had met him in a pub and hired him as an enforcer to make sure his business deals went through without a hitch.

Mike's experience fighting communist guerrillas in dangerous areas made him the ideal man in South-east London's urban jungle. He had proved to be very effective. He was good at organising men and soon became one of John's most useful and valued employees. John was always straight with Mike and hoped his trust would be returned and his interests well looked after in his absence. They made a formidable pair and were feared by all the local ne'er-do-wells in Woolwich as well as legitimate business men such as shopkeepers who came under John's protection or insurance as he preferred to call it.

Mike had nothing serious to report to John. There had been a minor incident at the club with a disgruntled member who claimed to have been short changed by the barmaid but Mike had sorted it out by throwing the man into the street and telling him not to return. John was pleased that his holiday could continue without any worries. Apart from Art. John was well aware that the relationship with Jude was heating up and he was concerned that Art's mother was now taking up all his spare cash leaving him with the bare minimum to live on. John resolved to try and find a solution to the problem which would please everyone involved, especially Jude.

After a very fine dinner in the hotel which had pleased Marion in particular as prawn cocktails had been on the menu they all went for a coffee in the spacious hotel lounge. The talk led to making a plan for the next day. The weather forecast was good so they decided to stay in Minehead and spend some time on the beach. Marion and Jude wanted to explore the shops in the main street named The Avenue and the men just wanted to relax and have a beer or two. Paul was happy just to be able to have a swim and poke around the harbour looking for crabs.

The day went just as planned. Marion and Jude spent some money on garish sunglasses and bought silly summer hats for the menfolk. John and Art investigated a couple of the local pubs and tried out the Somerset cider. It was stronger than the beer they were used to in London so they'd had a nap on the beach before the women returned. When they were all together again they set out walking along the promenade away from the harbour and stopped at the railway station. John had a glance at the timetable and saw that it would be quite quick to go to London by train. Further along they came to the Butlin's holiday camp that had opened in 1962. It looked rather basic with rows of wooden chalets and some larger buildings which they presumed housed the restaurants and bars.

'Don't much like the look of that,' said John. 'It reminds me of an army barracks.'

'I'm sure the people who stay there have a good time,' Marion said thoughtfully. 'Otherwise they wouldn't return. I know some families in London who swear by it and go year after year. They say it's good value and very friendly with loads of things to do during the day and every evening.'

As they stood and looked through the fence they heard the tannoy blaring out. 'Hello campers. It's time for the kiddies' talent competition in the theatre and old time dancing in the ballroom so put on your dancing shoes and join in. Tonight we have the Red Coats' cabaret evening so come along for the fun.'

'Not really what I'd like on a holiday,' Jude said looking at Art,' I don't like being told what to do when I'm trying to relax.'

'I'd noticed. Each to their own,' replied Art with a smile. He was thinking how much some of the regulars in the Star and Garter would love such a holiday. 'At least the families don't have to do their own cooking and I've heard the drinks are cheap.'

'Don't knock it Jude,' chipped in John. 'I never had a holiday at all when I was a lad. A great day out for us was to go backwards and forwards on the Woolwich Free Ferry. My mother used to tell me about the trips her family made to the Kent countryside to help with the hop picking. Hers was a real East End family. We never went as my father didn't want us away leaving him at work in the Arsenal. He didn't want to have to do his own cooking and cleaning as well. Then the war came and I was called up.'

Marion looked thoughtful and added, 'My parents took us to Margate on the train for a few days each summer. We stayed in a small boarding house and weren't allowed back in until six in the evening so, If the weather was bad, we had to huddle in a shelter on the prom. Luckily the weather was usually okay.'

'This is just like a history lesson,' said Paul tucking his thumbs in the sleeves of his t-shirt and doing a jig while singing a verse of "Knees up Mother Brown".

They all laughed and John tried to clip him round the ear but he moved quickly away and danced off down the pavement.

Art tried to persuade them to go further along the coast towards Dunster but was outvoted and they turned back to the hotel to change for dinner. They'd decided earlier to eat out that evening and Marion had noticed a small café near the top of The Avenue. As they strolled past the shops Jude pulled Art towards a jewellers and they admired the rings and watches. She pointed out a ring she particularly liked and Art looked with horror at the price tag. He then noticed a piece of paper stuck on the window which gave a weather forecast for the coming week. He pointed it out to Jude who prodded him in the ribs and accused him of trying to divert her attention away from the jewellery.

'Not at all,' he said, 'I just thought you might like to plan your outfits for the week if you knew what the weather would be like.'

'Don't be alarmed,' she replied linking her arm through his. 'I wouldn't want you wasting your money on an expensive ring. I'd be happy with a brass curtain ring so long as I was with you. I suppose that's a bit of a mangled proposal.'

Art bent and kissed her. 'If it is I accept but I'll have to ask your father's permission.'

'He'll say yes if I tell him to,' laughed Jude taking his arm as they went on to catch up with the others. 'Can we marry next year? I don't want to wait any longer than that.'

'Yes.' Art grabbed her by the waist and swung her around. 'Next year it is.'

*

The food was excellent and they all agreed that they would eat there again. It was only a small place but the owner had cooked everything from fresh and had made them most welcome. He told them he was a local man who had once owned a moorland sheep farm but it had become more and more difficult to eke out a living on the thin soil. He did, however, insist on all the food he cooked coming from farms nearby as he wanted to support his farming friends.

John, with his family and Art, walked back to their hotel on the seafront. It was still daylight and quite early so Art suggested to Jude that they could go for a walk to the harbour and a drink in the pub he had noticed by the lifeboat station. She readily agreed and wishing the others goodnight they set off arm in arm.

'I'm really enjoying this holiday,' said Art. 'It's just what I needed after the problems with Mum. It's sort of putting everything into perspective.'

Jude looked at him thoughtfully. 'I'm not sure I know what you mean but if coming away with my family cheers you up then I'm more than happy. Do you ever miss Liverpool and all your friends there?'

'Not really. Most of my friends have moved away from the city and I was never part of a strong social group. I had a few friends at school but after four years away we seem to have little in common any more. It's much the same in London as I

141

never really mixed well with the college crowd. I found them a bit superficial and silly so I chose to live near real people who have to work hard to make ends meet. I know quite a lot of the men and a few of the women in my road who use the pub but only one is a real friend and he doesn't seem to like your dad very much.'

'That's interesting. It's the same with my friends. I used to think it was because we had a bit of money but it seems more than that. I know Dad sometimes rubs people up the wrong way and is probably involved in some shady deals now and then but he's always been kind to us and I've never seen him lose his temper even when Paul or me have done something stupid. I must admit I don't like some of his friends. They're quite rough and I wouldn't want to cross them. Actually I wouldn't want to meet any of them on a dark night.'

Art swirled the beer around in his glass and thought about the confrontation in the school hall. 'I like your dad but when we went to his club I felt a bit uncomfortable. Like you I didn't take to some of the people there. I suppose being in the sort of businesses your dad runs means he has to mix with all sorts. Anyway, let's drink up and go back. If it's all quiet we might be able to spend a little time together. My room or yours?'

'Your room would be best as neither Mum nor Dad would think of disturbing you so we should be left alone.'

The hotel was quiet when they returned so Art took the opportunity to phone his mum. She seemed a bit confused but soon recovered her composure a little and asked him if he was still in London. She had obviously forgotten about his holiday. Gently he reminded her he was in Somerset and she seemed to understand. After a few exchanges about the weather and her health he put the phone back on its cradle and went up to his room. After a few minutes there was a light tap on the door and he opened it to let Jude in. She had showered while he was on the phone and was only wearing her dressing gown. They sat on his single bed and Jude laughed, 'One day we'll find a bed big enough for both of us to lie down comfortably.'

'The sooner the better,' replied Art.

'Is that another proposal?'

'What would you say if it was?'

'Yes,' she breathed and kissed him.

Art was a bit carried away by how quickly the prospect of marriage was progressing and could only say, 'Now I'll definitely have to speak to your dad.'

*

The next day was a little dull so Art suggested a hike up to Dunkery Beacon. He explained that they could drive to Luccombe, park the car and then follow a footpath to the Beacon and return by another route. Marion asked if she would be able to manage the walk and Art reassured her that it was only around six miles in total and they could take it easy up the hill to the top. He promised them magnificent views over Exmoor and towards the sea. The hotel provided them with packed lunches and after gathering together all they thought they would need they piled in the car and set off.

John found a place to park near the church in Luccombe and they set off through the woods and up onto Exmoor. It was quite steep and hard going in places and the path was uneven where it had suffered from water erosion. Paul had found a stick to help him walk and took a few photos with his birthday camera. At last they reached Dunkery Beacon and they sat down to rest. All agreed that Art had been right about the view and Paul used up some more of his film recording it.

The packed lunches were broken out and they ate in companionable silence until Paul said, 'This is better than the beach. We've seen much more interesting things and I've never been up a mountain before. I thought we'd need ropes.'

Art let him down gently, 'It's only a hill I'm afraid. A mountain is more than two thousand feet high and this is only around one and a half thousand.'

'That's okay,' Paul replied, 'We can walk up again next week and that will add up to a mountain.'

'Your maths is improving,' his father joked, 'but you can think again if you expect me to climb up here again.'

After lunch they made their way downhill back to the car. John then drove them down the narrow lanes until they reached the main road. He turned towards Minehead and Art suggested they could go and see the quaint village of Selworthy on their way back to the hotel.

'What's there?' enquired Marion. 'I don't feel up to another six mile hike.'

'It's just a very pretty village, ' Art answered. 'And I think there's a tea room there which just might sell cream teas.

'Good,' Marion replied, 'A cream tea would be just right. Good idea John?'

'Sounds great. I'll watch out for the turning and we'll have a look.'

They found they could park in a lay-by near the village and walked through a gate onto the village green which had a number of thatched cottages round it. Above the treetops they could see the white castellated tower of a church with the flag of St George flying from its flagpole. One of the cottages had been made into the Periwinkle Tearoom and Marion headed directly for it. The rest followed and they went in through the low door to the comfort of a chintzy room with tables and chairs set for tea. Ordering was left to Marion and soon the makings of their cream teas arrived. After a brief discussion about jam before cream or vice versa they all tucked in and Jude declared it heavenly. Marion claimed it was two minutes in her mouth but two months on her hips which amused John who gave her a squeeze and declared that he liked to have something to get hold of. Paul told him not to be so disgusting and everyone laughed. It was a very happy time and, not for the first time, Art wished it could last forever. It was really the only time he'd ever felt part of a complete family and he found the feeling rather uplifting. He looked at Jude and she smiled back. Art knew he would have to try and have a word with John about the future and determined to do so that evening.

*

It didn't happen. On arriving back at the hotel John was told there'd been a call for him form London and that it was urgent. He phoned the club and spoke to Mike who told him that there had been a major problem with the Lewisham firm. They had raided the minicab office, smashed it up and injured the controller who was now in Greenwich General Hospital. He asked if John could return as soon as possible as it appeared Stevens knew he was away and was taking advantage of the fact. John said he'd be back that evening. He went and spoke to Marion and said he had to return as there were a few problems to sort out. John then told Art and Jude. He gave Art the keys to the car and said he was going back by train and that Art had to look after his family while he was away. He couldn't tell them when he'd be back but promised to phone daily and keep them in the picture.

After kissing Marion goodbye he left the hotel and walked to the railway station to catch the five o'clock train to Paddington where he had arranged with Mike for one of the minicab drivers to meet him.

Chapter 10

London, August 1964

The minicab picked John up as arranged and took him straight to the office in Woolwich where he was met by Mike and a couple of his men. The place was a complete mess with broken windows and furniture and the small toilet wrecked so badly that the water had had been turned off until a plumber could fix the devastation. John took a deep breath while he calculated his next move.

'How do you know it was the Lewisham mob and not a gang from somewhere else such as Hackney?' he asked Mike.

'Because the controller recognised one of them. He said it was that nutter Joe who's the main enforcer in Alan Stevens' gang.'

'Have you done anything about it?'

'No. I wanted to wait for you to return before doing anything hasty.'

'Good,' said John looking again at the state of the office. 'I want it put about that we don't know who did this and think it must be a customer with a grudge. It will then be up to Stevens to decide what to do next. He might do nothing but

I'm sure he'll want us to know it was down to him. He's obviously trying to take over our patch. We'll be ready for him as he'll almost certainly go for the club next as I doubt he'd risk mixing it with the security guards in our Plumstead depot. All the time the club's open I want at least four men in the back office waiting to act if there's any trouble. I'll warn the staff, especially the bar staff, to keep out of the way if anything kicks off.'

Mike went to use the phone then realised it had been ripped from the wall. 'I'll go to the shop next door and call from there. By the way, a passer-by called the police and they came to investigate but we said no one was hurt so they just recorded it as vandalism and went away.'

Mike left the office and John decided to check that his house hadn't been targeted. Using one of his minicabs he went there and to his relief it was still undamaged and Jude's car was still parked outside. He dismissed the driver and went indoors to make sure everything was okay. He made a sandwich and had it with a bottle of beer before going to bed.

The next morning after a quick coffee he took the keys to Jude's Mini from a drawer in the hall table and went outside to drive to the club. During the drive he thought about the situation he was now in and how to deal with it. In the short term he could probably manage to discourage Alan Stevens from doing any further damage to his business interests but knew that Alan was unpredictable and could decide to escalate the violence until one of them capitulated. John knew that it was now at a critical point and that if he showed any

148

weakness he could lose all his hard-won assets and possibly be left with nothing. He was realistic enough to know that most of his employees would happily work for the Stevens' gang if they gained the upper hand. It might, he considered, be better to take the initiative and deliver a crippling blow to one of Stevens' enterprises and hope that it would either sort the problem or cause an uneasy truce to break out. Stevens, apart from his own protection racket, was heavily involved in the betting game and was running a string of illegal gaming establishments in and around South London. John knew where some of them were and reckoned he could send in some of his boys to close a couple down. He had no idea how Stevens would react but it might just be sufficient to show him that he was still a force to be reckoned with.

At the club he nursed a large whisky and reassured the bar staff that all would be well in the event of a visit from Stevens' men. They looked a little doubtful and this made John decide that he was right about which side they might support if push came to shove in the power stakes. Immediately he made up his mind to act quickly and decisively. He gave one of the staff they key to the mini and told him to drive to Woolwich and bring Mike to the club picking up a couple of other men on the return journey. Another whisky ordered he sat back and made the plan to be executed that evening.

When Mike and the men arrived John ordered drinks and they discussed how best to hit Stevens where it would hurt most. After a lengthy chat and numerous drinks they decided that they had enough muscle to simultaneously raid three of the gambling dens. They would cause damage to the properties but more importantly frighten off the customers who were regular punters. This would damage Stevens' income as well as his reputation. They all agreed it was a risk but hoped that their show of force, being larger than Stevens would expect, might cause him to think again about attacking any of John's interests. With all the details discussed and the personnel required for the raids sorted out John asked Mike to take complete control of the operation and to report back to him when it was over. He didn't want to wait in the club as that might implicate him if the police were involved so he arranged for Mike to phone him at home. He had considered returning to Minehead straight away but thought that might look as if he was bottling out and wouldn't go down well with his men. John never involved himself in the more violent aspect of his firm even though in the early days he had had to prove himself to be tough in his fight to reach the top. He now regarded himself as a businessman and not a thug. He was proud of what he had built up from nothing but now, becoming older and with a family to look after, wanted to become both respectable and respected in the eyes of the local community. Art, he thought is well educated and bright so might just be the man to help him achieve that aim. He would have to figure out how that could happen when he returned to his holiday.

*

Mike orchestrated the raids with his usual military efficiency. He was indebted to John who had dragged him up from a life in despair about his future in civvy street. Mike was well aware that the men he organised were little more than mercenaries who would work for the highest bidder and had no loyalty to either him or John. They had to be controlled through a mixture of fear and promise of a good life with money in their wallets. So far he'd had no problems as John paid them well and was ruthless in how he dealt with any man who had his hand in the till or was unreliable. A few had turned out to be in the pocket of rival firms and these had been sent back to their bosses with a variety of painful injuries. The scale of the injuries was commensurate with the amount of damage John calculated they had caused his business with a little extra added on for annoying him. Mike was the one usually responsible for these disciplinary measures. He wasn't always happy to hurt people, some of them he had known for a while and quite liked, but regarded it as necessary to keep the others in line. Also, he had hopes that John would make him a partner in the not too distant future.

He led the raid on Alan Stevens' largest gaming club called The Black Cat because it was in Catford, a seedy part of Lewisham. A couple of doormen tried to stop them entering the club but these were soon taken out of the equation by a few well aimed blows with iron bars and knuckle dusters. They were left on the pavement and watched over by one of Mike's gang in case they recovered sufficiently to try and stop the raid.

Once inside Mike realised that there was no other security to stop them so he led the men in a spree of gratuitous violence to the furniture, staff and any punters stupid enough to try and stop them. Once the club had been thoroughly trashed and any money they found removed as their own bonus payment Mike spoke to the manager who was discovered cowering under his desk in the office upstairs. Mike hauled him up and punched him hard in the stomach.

'Tell Stevens this is only a taster of what will happen if he or any of his gang ever show their faces in Woolwich again. Mr Hayes was very upset about the minicab office but now regards the matter as settled unless Stevens wants an all out war which he would lose as we're much bigger than his tinpot outfit.'

The manager was visibly shaking and Mike could see a wet stain spreading round his groin. He couldn't speak so just nodded his assent and Mike turned and left him scrabbling for the phone to tell his boss what had happened.

They returned to John's club and waited for the two other groups to return from their visits. There was an air of celebration and drinks on the house were ordered. When the others returned they reported that their raids had also been successful so Mike went to the office and called John to give him the good news. Both of them were well aware that there would probably be some fallout from the evening and discussed how best to guard their own interests from any likely revenge attacks. John asked Mike to up the security at the club on a permanent basis and to have work done on the minicab office to prevent another attack. He asked for bullet-proof glass in the windows and door and steel shutters that could be operated from inside to stop anyone entering. As before, he wasn't too concerned about the security firm's office as there was no money kept there and it was only used by the security guards who were more than a match for any of Stevens' men who were stupid enough to think they could take them on. He was a little worried about his house so he also arranged for an alarm to be fitted as well as stronger doors front and back. Marion and Jude would have to be warned never to open the door to strangers but he didn't want to alarm them to the point where they would be afraid to live in their own house. It was a difficult balance to find but he knew that he would consider any way that would keep his family safe. It might even mean moving away from the area he had known all his life and finding a more secure place deep in Kent. Jude had enjoyed her day out there with Art and had regaled them with how peaceful and beautiful it was so it was an option worth considering.

The next morning John waited for any reaction to his raids on Stevens' premises. At lunchtime there was a call from his club telling him that Alan Stevens was there and wanted to see him. Apparently he was on his own so John said he would go straight there. He was concerned that Stevens might have some of his men waiting nearby to storm the club on a prearranged signal after he had gone inside. He spoke to Mike and mentioned the possibility and Mike promised to send a couple of the staff out to scour the neighbourhood for possible trouble. With that in place John jumped into the Mini and set off to find out what Stevens wanted.

After parking a couple of streets away John walked to the club keeping an eye on all parked cars just to be sure all was safe. He saw Stevens' MG outside the club so went in to find his rival sitting at the bar with a beer. He looked nervous and that pleased John.

'Welcome to my little club,' he said as Alan Stevens swivelled round and came down off the bar stool to meet him. He was a tad taller than John but not as well built and his bulbous red and blue nose was clear evidence of his prolific alcohol intake. He was definitely going to seed and John reckoned he would be lucky to live another ten years even though he was only in his early forties.

'I think we need to talk,' Stevens muttered and walked to a table ignoring the hand that John had extended.

They sat down and John signalled for his usual drink. After it arrived he looked hard and long at Stevens and said,' That was a very stupid move of yours to destroy my minicab office as it's a legit business and the police are involved.' He didn't say that the police had been sent away without any charges being made.

'It wasn't my idea,' pleaded Stevens, 'It was one of my associates and I knew nothing about it.'

'Just like the shop in Charlton Village,' John replied. 'You don't seem to have much knowledge of what your men are up to so I can only presume that you are not in control of them. Time to give up?'

'No way,' Stevens said with a little more spirit. 'It's just that a few of them are rather too enthusiastic about expanding our interests.'

'If they, or you, think that's possible by muscling in on my manor then you'd better think again. The raids on your gaming clubs were a warning and only minimal damage was done. If there's a next time it will be a lot worse. Understand? I've no intention of moving in on Lewisham so you can stay clear of Woolwich.'

Alan Stevens took a long pull of his beer and smiled at John. 'Crystal clear. I'll tell my lot that we are keeping out of each other's way. There'll be no more trouble from me.'

'Problem solved,' John answered. 'Another beer before you go?'

Stevens shook his head and stood up. This time he held out his hand to John who shook it firmly. They looked each other straight in the eye and then Stevens turned and left the club.

John beckoned Mike to join him. 'Hopefully that will be the end of the matter for now but if Stevens really is losing control then it might flare up again. We'll have to keep a close watch on how things develop.'

'You're right there boss. Some of the younger men in Stevens' gang are looking to make a name for themselves. I think it will calm down for a while but, as you say, we must stay vigilant.'

'I'll go back to Minehead later today. Obviously you'll keep me in the picture.'

John went back home to collect his few things and phone the hotel in Minehead telling his family he would hopefully be joining them for dinner that evening. He then called for one of his cabs to take him to Paddington Station.

Chapter 11

Minehead, August 1964

News of John's impending return greeted Art, Marion, Jude and Paul as they arrived back at the hotel from a day out at Wookey Hole. It had, of course, been Art's idea to go and visit the famous limestone caves. Paul could hardly contain his excitement and constantly regaled anyone who'd listen about the wonders they'd seen. He speculated about the Witch of Wookey and made up stories about her supernatural powers. His main disappointment was that she'd failed to appear to him during their walk through the underground caves and passages. Marion had bought him a pointed wizard's hat and a magician's wand so he wandered round the hotel waving the wand and muttering his own versions of what he thought magic spells would sound like. Other, often elderly, hotel residents looked at him with benign amusement as he pulled grotesque faces and pointed his stick in their general direction. Marion eventually rescued them from his attentions by dragging him back to the bar where they waited for John to phone and tell them when he had arrived so Art could take the car and pick him up from the station.

The night before Art had taken Jude to a nearby pub that had a local band playing for the evening. They'd been quite good and the room in the pub that they played in was big enough for dancing. Most of the songs the group played were taken from the hit parade so it was an evening of Beatles and Rolling Stones with a sprinkling of less well known northern groups thrown in and a few American hits. At the end of the evening they played the latest Beatles' song 'And I Love Her' which had been released the month before. It was slow and dreamy so Art and Jude held each other close as they shuffled round the floor. They both listened rapt as the words unfolded.

As they swayed gently along to the music Art whispered in Jude's ear. 'This is our song. It's been written just for us. We'll keep this memory for ever.'

'It's perfect,' Jude murmured, 'It will always be a part of us and our love.'

The song ended and they kissed passionately not caring about the other people present. After the dance they walked back to the hotel holding hands and singing some of the words they could remember. Art decided that he would go and buy the single as a present for Jude when they returned to London. He didn't know that Jude had decided to buy it for him as well.

*

It had turned into a memorable evening and it was with regret that they had to sleep in separate rooms that night. Jude didn't want to upset her mother who was missing John and might want to knock on her door for a late night chat. She was sure her mother knew that she had been to Art's room but it was best to keep up the pretence that nothing like that had actually happened. If Marion had found her room empty it would have brought it out into the open and her father might have found out. He would, she thought, have probably been rather angry and it might have caused a blazing row that could have ended their romance. How much better it would be when they were married.

*

John arrived back in time for his dinner with them in the hotel. After dinner while they were having coffee in the lounge they naturally they wanted to know about his problems in London but he fobbed them off and downplayed the seriousness of the situation he'd had to deal with. He told them it was just a small problem at the taxi office which he'd sorted out straight away. Art thought about John's explanation and asked him why his employees hadn't dealt with it themselves. John replied that they needed him there to give them support and confidence. Art wasn't too convinced but wisely decided not to press the issue. In any case, Paul was bursting to tell his father about Wookey Hole and the stalagmite that was supposed to be The Witch of Wookey turned to stone by a priest from Glastonbury. He told the story in great detail and then explained how they'd also been to the paper mill and seen paper being made from old rags.

'You seem to have had a great time while I was away. I hope you've left some exciting things for me to do now I'm back.'

'You bet,' said Paul. 'Mr..er..Art says he'll take us fossil hunting tomorrow at Doniford Beach. You can come as well if you want.'

'Thanks very much,' grinned John.' Very kind of you to ask me. Now Art, do you fancy a look round some of the local hostelries? There must be quite a few we haven't visited yet.'

'Okay,' replied Art. 'Can Jude join us?'

'No thanks,' answered Jude quickly as she had guessed correctly that her dad wanted to speak to Art privately. 'The last thing I need is to spend a boozy evening spent with you two talking about football. I need to wash my hair and then I'll have an early night.'

Art was a little disappointed as it would be the first evening he'd not been out with Jude but he was diplomatic enough not to make a big deal of it. 'Right,' he said,'shall we go now?'

 In the first pub they sat near the window and chatted about the holiday and how it was going.

'Nearly half way through already,' Art commented. 'It's been the best holiday I've had. Not that there's really been any to compare it with. Sorry you had to miss a couple of days but presumably you'll now be able to stay until we go back.'

'Yes. I can't see any other problems coming up which would necessitate another train trip.' John downed his pint and stood. 'Let's go to that pub near the harbour.'

Art finished his drink and they left to walk along the promenade. As they walked John gave Art his opinion on the forthcoming football season and how he thought Charlton would fare enduring yet another season in the second division. He went on at length about how they had always been in the top division when he was younger and how he missed games against Arsenal and other famous teams. He told Art that those games were watched by up to eighty thousand people at The Valley, Charlton's home ground. Art had been to a number of games but rarely had the crowd been more than fifteen thousand. He couldn't imagine what it must have been like with such a large crowd on the massive east terrace.

Art bought the drinks and they sat in a secluded corner of the bar. John sipped his pint appreciatively, turned to Art and said, 'It's obvious that you and Jude are really keen on each other. Virtually engaged. All I want is for her to be happy but I'm worried that she is used to a standard of living way above that you can offer her. Initially everything would be all right as love has a way of making people blind to their circumstances but given time she would hanker for the things she was brought up with and this might lead to resentment. Please don't take this wrong. I respect you for being such a dedicated and excellent teacher but as a profession it's very poorly paid and it could take twenty years or more before you became reasonably well off as a headmaster. Also, your mother is ill and will probably be an increasing drain on your finances. It's to your credit that you look after her so well but what sort of future can you offer my daughter?'

Art was shaken and had turned very pale. He saw his whole future falling apart in an instance. It was just as he'd thought it might turn out in Liverpool when his mother was diagnosed with dementia. Well aware that his financial situation wasn't good he'd hoped that somehow things would work out. He didn't want to lose Jude but the way John had presented his argument left him with little doubt that something would have to change. And soon. Gathering his thoughts he replied, 'I'm sorry that I can't promise Jude the luxuries she deserves. She's never made any demands on me or even suggested that she would prefer a richer suitor. You're right about our relationship. Although not officially engaged Jude has said she wants to marry me if you give her your blessing. My mother is also very important to me as she is my last living relative and I will look after her as best I can until she is gone. Please don't ask me to choose between her and Jude. That would be cruel and I think Jude might be as upset as I am now.'

John looked compassionately at the young man next to him and thought back to his own time as a tearaway in Woolwich when everyone had written him off as a bad lot who would never make anything of himself. After a moment he spoke quietly to Art. 'There is one possible way out of this which would leave you able to support both your mother and Jude.'

'What's that?' Art asked eagerly, clutching at the possible lifeline being thrown to him.

'Come and work with me. I need someone with brains to keep an eye on the books and to help develop my business interests. I can pay you five times what you're earning now with the chance of even more if you make a success of it.'

'What would the work entail?' Art asked warily as he thought of the stories he'd heard about John's businesses.

John laughed, 'I have to hold up my hands and admit not all my ventures are squeaky clean but I would never involve you in anything illegal. Actually I want to put all that behind me and become a respected tax-paying citizen. You could help me achieve that.'

'How?

'Because you are already well thought of in the neighbourhood and, as you are a teacher, I presume you have no criminal background. That's a great asset when dealing with banks and other reputable companies. You could start by fronting the security firm and making it a more upmarket and reputable concern. I know it probably won't be as fulfilling as a career in teaching but I think you might grow to like it and should consider it carefully. It could solve all your problems in one go as well as helping me.'

Art took a long slug of his drink before answering. He loved teaching but knew his salary was too small and he'd had experience in other jobs during his college holidays. At last he spoke, 'That's very kind of you but I'm not sure if I can leave teaching without giving a term's notice. I might have to work until Christmas. Even if I could I wouldn't like to leave them in the lurch at such short notice as they've been very good to me.'

'Most commendable. But couldn't you help me out on a part time basis getting to know what's what?'

'I suppose so. I have most weekends free.'

'That's settled then. Let's go back and break the news to the others.'

As they returned to the hotel Art wondered how Jude would react to John's suggestion. She might not want Art to be too involved with her father's various enterprises. As it turned out he was wrong and Jude was enthusiastic about the plan. Art wondered if that was because of the money they would get to help set them up in married life or did she really see him as a small cog in John's empire. He was well aware she was a daddy's girl who worshipped the ground John walked on but hoped she wouldn't be blind to his somewhat risky ventures. He wanted her to accept him as he was and not as an embryonic clone of her father. He sighed to himself and thought that in time she might love him as unconditionally as she did her dad.

Soon after ten they all trooped off to bed and Jude stayed in her room. Art was a bit put out but soon fell asleep.

*

The next morning was bright and sunny so they packed their beach clothes and Marion went to the shops to rustle together a picnic. Art, John and Paul took everything they thought they might need to the car and stowed it all in the boot. When Marion returned they added her bags to the others and they set off along the coast road past Watchet to Doniford Beach. On the beach they stopped for a while for a swim and then went up the cliff to a little stall for coffees. On returning to the beach Art took them to the bottom of the cliff where they started hunting for fossils. It didn't take long to find some

164

broken ammonites just lying on the top of the shingle. Marion and John sat on a picnic rug and started to prepare lunch. Paul wanted a whole one to take back to London so Art showed him how to split the shale rocks taken from the cliff face to try and expose a brand new fossil. Jude stayed on the beach wearing her new purple bikini and found a number of belemnites which looked like little grey torpedoes. Paul asked Art how old the ammonites were and was astonished when told they could have been living two hundred million years ago.

'That's ridiculous,' he scoffed, 'they would have rotted away by now.'

Art spent some time explaining that a fossil wasn't the actual animal but sediment that had replaced the shell over time and hardened into rock. Paul still looked doubtful but accepted the explanation for the time being.

Suddenly he split a large piece of slate like rock and discovered a complete ammonite inside. He whooped for joy and the others came running to see what he had found. It was much admired and John managed to break off a little more off the edge of the rock to make it a more manageable size. Marion found some paper tissues to wrap it in and it was carefully transported back to the beach and put in a box that had contained the pork pies and scotch eggs she had bought.

They all sat round the veritable feast that Marion had bought and chatted about the holiday. Paul was the most voluble and went on at length about how much he'd be able to tell the boys in his new school. John said that he was pleased they were all having a good time and Marion nodded agreement. Art repeated that it was his first real holiday. Jude gave his arm a squeeze and said it was definitely the best holiday she'd ever had.

Paul grinned, 'That's because you've got a boyfriend this year. Last year you just moped around the arcade looking for one.'

'Cheeky little rat,' exclaimed Jude. 'I did no such thing.'

'Well, you didn't find a boy.'

Art butted in. 'And I'm glad about that. Now, when our lunch has gone down who's for a swim?'

Paul and Jude agreed to the suggestion but John and Marion thought they would prefer to stretch out and catch some sun. Some time later Art and Paul went behind some convenient rocks to change into their swimming trunks and returned to drag Jude to the water's edge. The waves were small and it was easy to push her into the sea. Naturally she then splashed them and a water fight broke out. When they were all wet they ventured deeper into the sea and started to swim. It was cold but very refreshing and Art showed off by doing handstands and back flips. Paul tried to copy him without success until his sister helped hold and steady him. He soon mastered the handstand with a little support and a round of applause broke out from his parents on the beach. He looked pleased and went to join them. Marion engulfed him in a large soft towel and he sat down to watch what Jude and Art were doing. They were now swimming parallel to the beach using a variety of strokes. Jude kept her head out of the water so she looked like a turtle while Art swam with his head down and was much more streamlined. Eventually they succumbed to the cold water and joined the others to get dry and warm up.

'Should have brought a Thermos of soup,' Marion said. 'That would have been a good idea. I'll try and remember one next time you go swimming.'

Jude and Art wandered off down the beach until they were out of sight of the others. Art turned to Jude and pulled her into his arms. They kissed ravenously and both were aware what would happen next if they continued. Reluctantly they prised themselves apart and sat, still holding hands, on a large rock just below the cliff. Art gently stroked Jude's tangled hair and ran his finger down her jawline.

'You really are the most beautiful girl I've ever met,' he whispered closely. He licked her ear and enjoyed the taste of the sea. She put both her hands behind his neck and massaged his upper back and then to his shoulders.

'And you are the man of my dreams. I'm so glad I was dragged reluctantly to that swimming gala. I'd probably never have met you otherwise.'

'You never know,' Art said quietly. 'I think fate would have brought us together anyway.'

'It doesn't matter. It happened. I'm so glad it did.'

Art looked serious and asked, 'Are you really pleased that I'm going to work with John? Or is it just for the security and lifestyle I can't offer you as a lowly teacher?'

Jude pulled away from him and glared, 'How dare you say that. I just want you to be happy and that seemed to be a good way of achieving it. I wanted you to be able to look after your mother and marry me without worrying about where the cash would come from. It wasn't for me it was for you that I was pleased. How could you think I'd be so selfish?'

She stood up and strode off down the beach with Art trailing miserably behind. He was upset and realised he'd misjudged the situation. Now, if he could, he had to think of a way to make it up to Jude and hope she'd forgive him.

Their row had put a bit of a damper on the afternoon and the mood was picked up subconsciously by the rest of Jude's family. They knew something had changed but didn't know what it was. Paul tried to lighten the mood but it didn't work so he returned to the base of the cliff and continued his search for fossils. Marion and John packed up the blankets, plates and boxes of remaining food and made to go back to the car. Jude followed and Art went to fetch Paul. They drove back to the hotel in an uncomfortable silence. When they arrived Art went straight to his room and Marion pulled Jude aside into the lounge. There were no other guests in there so she sat her down on a sofa.

'What's happened?' she asked gently.

'Oh, just a bit of a tiff,' said Jude.

'It seemed more than a tiff to me. Can you tell me what caused it? It's not like Art to upset you.'

'It was about him working with Dad. He thought I might have wanted him to give up teaching just for the extra money it would bring. I don't care how much he earns. I want to spend my life with him even if it means living in Pattison Road and having a bath once a week. I wanted him to have money to look after his mother as well as marry me. I think Dad had suggested he wouldn't let us marry unless Art joined him.'

'You're probably right. John likes to get his own way and thinks that money is the answer to all problems. Don't worry, Art loves you and it'll soon sort itself out for the best.'

'Thanks Mum. I'll clear the air in the morning.'

'No you won't. You'll go up and do it now before more damage is done. Never go to sleep on an argument.'

Jude smiled at her mother and went up the stairs to Art's room. She knocked gently on the door.

'Yes. Who is it?'

'It's me. Who else were you expecting?'

The door opened and Art pulled her into the room. 'I'm sorry,' he said as she fell into his arms, 'I was stupid. I know you only want the best for me. Please forgive me.'

She kissed the tip of his nose. 'All forgotten already. Now we have to plan for the wedding.'

'I suppose that means we're now properly engaged or at least we will be but I haven't yet asked John formally for your hand. He could say no.'

'He wouldn't dare. I'm his favourite daughter.'

Art burst out laughing. 'You're his only daughter.'

Jude joined in the merriment and, still entangled, suddenly they found themselves on the bed.

*

An hour later Jude crept quietly back to her room hoping no one would see her. She made it safely and lay down on her narrow single bed. Was she doing the right thing? She so wanted to be with Art that she'd forgotten her father's sometimes unorthodox ways of doing business and now Art was going to be caught up in the whole thing. Art loved teaching and she wondered how he would take to the admittedly seedy world her father sometimes inhabited when he was out of the family home. She knew more than her parents realised about John's businesses. It had been impossible at school to avoid the comments and insults from the other girls when they realised her dad was the well known head of a criminal gang. She'd tried to explain that he was just an ordinary businessman but they'd laughed in her face. Some of their parents had been intimidated by John's men in the shops they ran and warned their offspring to keep clear of the Hayes'. It meant she'd had few friends in school which was one of the reasons she'd left as soon as she could without even considering going into the sixth form and on to higher education. She knew she was clever enough to continue to college or even university but couldn't stand a moment longer in the catty environment of the all girls school. Refusing all help from her father she'd found the job with a local dentist who was ignorant of where her family's money came from and had been extremely kind and generous to her.

Now she was embarking on another adventure but was concerned that it was too close to home and hoped it wouldn't end badly. She sort of wished Art had a more lucrative job so they could set up home without her dad's support but realised that Art probably wouldn't have been the man she wanted to marry if he had been a boring banker in the city. Maybe the job with John would turn out to be temporary and they could eventually move out of London and set up home in a country cottage. Somewhere like the village of Otford they had visited at Easter would be just right. Jude continued with her daydream of a simple but idyllic life with Art and a couple of beautiful children as she slowly dropped off to sleep.

*

John gave his blessing to the marriage when Art asked him formally for his daughter's hand and all too soon the holiday came to an end. They packed the car ready for the long drive back to London. Art had regularly phoned Liverpool to speak to his mother and receive progress reports from Mrs Carr. It seemed nothing much had changed but he'd decided to visit again before the new term started. He'd have to go to the education office in Woolwich before going home and hand in his notice. It would also be polite to tell the headmaster he was leaving the school after Christmas so he'd do that the next day. Three years at college, he thought, and I'm leaving teaching after only four terms. Was it a waste of the taxpayers' money? It probably was but no more than if he'd gone to university and studied ancient Chinese literature. He grinned at that thought. After all he was now a fully qualified teacher and could always go back to the chalk-face later if he wanted. He rather liked the idea that he now had options in his life. It made him feel rather grand and grown-up. He must remember to tell Jude what he thought. He thought she'd be pleased with his sensible approach to the future. To their future.

*

John had also been busy phoning before they left. All seemed quiet at the club and in the Woolwich area. He hoped that there would be no more problems but was ready to act decisively if the occasion demanded it. With Art now on board, or nearly, he had great hopes for the next step in his ventures. That of making his work legal and above reproach. It might prove difficult at first but it was what he wanted for his family. Particularly Paul. He sincerely hoped Paul would join him and then take over the firm when he was old enough. By then he wanted to be running a completely legitimate business. He ruefully thought that would mean paying tax on all his earnings. But that was a long way away so his plan was to take it slowly and deal with any difficulties as they arose. The biggest problem would be other local gangs. They would be ruthless in taking over his patch if they could. It would be messy if he didn't judge the time right. By now he was resigned to losing the protection side and focussing on the minicabs and the site security. Reluctantly the club would have to go which would put some of his most loyal employees out of work. He'd have to be upfront with Art and explain exactly how he operated. That would be hard as he wasn't sure how Art would react to knowing some of the less salubrious details of his past and the details of how he made some of his money.

A few days after arriving back in London Art packed again to go to Liverpool and see his mother. He wondered exactly how much he should tell her about what was happening in his life. As he wasn't officially engaged to Jude and hadn't yet joined John on a permanent basis he decide it would be best not to say anything and just let her think he was carrying on teaching as originally planned. He wouldn't be lying as he'd already arranged to teach at Vicarage Road until Christmas.

He was shocked when he saw his mother. She wasn't her usual neat and tidy self. Her hair was unkempt and her clothes looked in need of a good wash and iron. It wasn't the mother he remembered. She greeted him warmly but seemed a little unsure about why he was there and constantly asked if he had just arrived and was staying the night. She fretted about where he would sleep and said she had no food in the house. Art went and checked in the kitchen and found the fridge and the cupboard full of food. He was worried that she wasn't able to look after herself properly so he phoned Mrs Carr and asked her to come and see him.

She arrived half an hour later and told him that she hadn't wanted to worry him about the situation as he was on holiday. She said that his mother had deteriorated rapidly in the past few weeks and she was as worried as he was about her coping on her own. Art made an appointment to see the doctor the next day so he could find out more about his mother's condition and what could be done about it. It was incredible that she had gone downhill so much in less than a month but the doctor had said it affected people differently.

Doctor Wilkie was very sympathetic. He told Art that his mother was almost certainly suffering from rapidly progressive dementia which caused the patient to deteriorate very quickly in a matter of weeks or a couple of months. The medical profession was unsure of the cause and there was no way to cure or treat it. He said the disease would have to run its course and added that life expectancy was severely reduced. Most sufferers died within a couple of years at the most. He arranged for her to be admitted to hospital for further tests but stressed to Art that she couldn't remain there permanently. A home would have to be found as soon as possible so she could receive the care required to help her through the terrible disease. Doctor Wilkie phoned Broadgreen Hospital and, after he had explained the urgency of the situation, and appointment was made for the next day to assess Mrs James. Art was distraught and didn't know what to do for the best. The new term was starting in two weeks and he couldn't let the school down. He would have to act quickly and find a suitable place for his mother. The extra money for working with John would help the situation despite only being part time. He was sure John would be sympathetic to his situation.

The hospital performed cognitive and other memory tests on Art's mother and the specialist came to the same conclusion as Doctor Wilkie. She explained the various stages the disease went through and said it was quite rare but had possibly been triggered by an undiagnosed minor stroke and reiterated that the disease would now progress rapidly and that his mother would have to move into a home as soon as possible because it wasn't safe to leave her unattended. She was already in what the specialist called stage four and that she would soon reach the next stage when full time care would be essential. Art was given a list of nursing homes in the area and was advised to visit those nearest to his mother's house straight away. On arriving home Art spoke again to Mrs Carr and explained the situation. He asked if she could look after his mother the next day while he did the rounds of the nursing homes and she kindly agreed. When she arrived Art went off with his list of homes and a heavy heart.

The first two homes were rather disappointing. They were local authority homes and Art found them dark, sterile and depressing. One had been a workhouse and still had the old forbidding façade and barred windows. Not all patients had their own room and when he explained the speed his mother's illness would progress he was met with a stony silence. They said they had limited time to deal with the symptoms of severe cases and seemed reluctant to take such a demanding patient. The third nursing home was privately run in South Mossley Road, only a ten minute walk from his house. They were really sympathetic and not at all phased by the prospect of a rapid degeneration of his mother's condition. After looking round and finding the place warm, clean and comfortable Art asked about the price. The figure quoted was higher than he'd expected but he had to make a quick decision and said he would be pleased for his mother to become a resident. The relevant papers were completed and it was arranged for his mother to take up residence on the following Monday. They gave Art a list of the clothes and toiletries his mother would need and stressed the importance of packing a few things that she would find familiar such as family photos and any ornaments that would remind her of home. It all felt very sad and final to Art and he went away with mixed emotions. He was pleased that his mother would be looked after well but very upset that she was so ill and would never return to her home again. As her disease was progressing at such a fast pace he decided to keep the house In Rose Lane so he had somewhere to stay when he visited her. What he would do with the house when she died he had no idea. He supposed he could sell it and buy a place in London but that was all for the future and he put it to the back of his mind. Funding the nursing home was his top priority for the moment. Back in the house he told his mother she was going on holiday but from her blank reaction he realised that she was totally unaware of her condition and he supposed that was for the best.

On the Monday Art packed his mother's things in a couple of suitcases and remembered to include the personal items to help her feel more at home. With a heavy heart he ordered a taxi to take them to the nursing home and left her in their care with the minimum of fuss. He didn't want to upset her further so he departed as soon as she was installed in her room with a promise to see her later. He walked back home and phoned Mrs Carr to tell her that his mother was now in the nursing home and that he would try and visit her every weekend. As she had been so reliable he asked her if she would look after the house in his absence and she said she would be happy to and that she would try and visit his mother when she had the time. Art agreed a small fee for her services and was pleased that the house would be kept clean and safe while he was in London.

On the train he had time to think about his new situation. He'd promised John he would work for him at weekends but was now having to go to Liverpool instead. He hoped John would understand if he spent some of his weekday evenings learning about the business. It was, he thought, a bit of a mess as there were so many imponderables to consider. How long would his mother live? What about the house in Liverpool? Would Jude want to live there? Could he afford the nursing home fees without help? It was all rather overwhelming. He sat back in his seat and closed his eyes.

When he woke from his doze the train was pulling in at Euston Station so he picked up his bag, alighted down to the platform and made his way to the underground to take him to Charing Cross and then a train back to Woolwich. It was mid afternoon when he eventually arrived back to Pattison Road. He had called in at the local shop on the way home and bought some milk and a loaf of bread. A few tins and a bag of apples completed his shopping and he put on the kettle as soon as he got in and made a cup of tea and some toast. After putting his few things away he went out again to phone

Jude at work and arrange to see her that evening. She agreed and asked him to meet her outside the dental surgery and walk her back to her house.

He was so pleased to see her that when she came out of the surgery he hugged her to him so hard she squealed.

'What's that for?' she complained. 'You've only been away a few days.'

'It's been a lifetime. I've so much to tell you and it's not good news. I've missed you so much. Everything seems so much better when I'm with you.'

'I'm pleased to hear it. But what's gone wrong? I presume it's your mother. Is she worse?'

'A lot worse. I'll tell you the whole story when we reach your house.'

Later they sat on a sofa in the lounge and Art explained to Jude the seriousness of his mother's condition. As he'd desperately hoped she was very supportive and praised him for the action he had taken. When Marion and John came in Art went through the tale again and they were equally sympathetic. John made it clear that Art could take as much time as he wanted to visit Liverpool and finding his way around the business could be put on hold. When Marion heard about the cost of the nursing home she nudged John and he told Art that his new salary would continue to be paid anyway. Art thanked him and the talk went on to lighter topics such as discussing how the holiday had gone. Paul came in with a pile of photos he had taken and they all enjoyed reliving their time in Minehead. Some of the snaps were a little wonky and out of focus but nothing was said to hurt Paul's feelings as he was obviously so proud of his efforts. They all laughed at the picture of Jude on a donkey and at Art on a belly-board trying to surf when the waves were only about a foot high.

John asked Art if he could spare an hour or two the next morning so he could explain about the various business interests he would be helping with in the future. Art said that he didn't have to go into school until the following week to prepare for the new term so he had time to spare. John said he would call round in the morning at nine. Jude saw Art to the door and he walked back down the hill home.

Chapter 12

London, September 1964

John knocked on Art's door and was invited in.

'This is taking me back,' John said looking around. 'I'd forgotten how small these houses are. Some families had four, and often more, kids to squeeze in. Not much room for privacy in those days. I suppose it's still like that for some of your neighbours.'

'Yes it is. But they seem to manage and some of the houses have been done up and have bathrooms and power points upstairs.'

John laughed. 'What luxury. Where do you intend to live in the future?'

'I've no idea. The house in Liverpool will be mine eventually but I don't want to move there as my life is now in London. And I don't know Jude's thoughts on the matter. I think she'd prefer to stay round here and be near her family. I'm sure that's what you and Marion want as well.'

They went into the sitting room and sat down. Art asked John if he'd like a coffee but John declined the offer and came straight to the point.

'I want you to know exactly what you are letting yourself in for if you work with me. I'll be straight with you and not gloss over any of the more unsavoury details. I'll begin by telling you how I got started and where I am now.'

'Thanks. I'd appreciate that,'

'Well. I left school without any serious qualifications and started doing odd jobs in Woolwich Market. I met some interesting and some rather dubious characters there and eventually I started working with a market trader who wasn't averse to cutting corners. I learned a lot from him and got to know all the ne'er-do-wells in the area. Most were just petty crooks and worked independently. There were no organised gangs at that time as in America but that was to change after the war. I was called up and joined the army. Luckily I was put in the Royal Artillery and was based locally manning the anti-aircraft guns which were sited around London looking out over Kent for enemy aircraft. I even made sergeant before the war ended. I spent most of my time on top of Shooters Hill. I'd met Marion just before the war and we married in 1942 and rented a small bedsit to live in. Jude came along in 1945 and then I was demobbed. The war had taught me a valuable lesson. I'd used my local contacts to make a fair bit on the black market and this had paid for a small house and a few luxuries for Marion and the baby. I'd also come to appreciate how useful army discipline and organisation could be. I thought that if I could transfer the army's methods to civvy life then there would be a good chance of making real money. My opportunity came after the war when there were a lot of unemployed ex-servicemen looking to make a living by any means.'

Art interrupted, 'But why didn't you just start a proper business?'

'Easier said than done I'm afraid. During the war many owners of businesses made a fortune and after the war it was very difficult to find a way of breaking their hold on commerce. They had many ways of closing down any opposition through their contacts in local government and the old boys network. Unless you were invited to join the Masonic Lodge you stood no chance of success. The only way to make money was by being more devious than they were. Anyway, where was I? Oh yes, the servicemen. A few of them wanted to make money by the easiest route and they'd heard about other gangs terrorising local shopkeepers. They were very disillusioned when they were demobbed and went back to find their old jobs gone and old workmates who hadn't been in the armed forces promoted. It seemed to them a good way to use their newly acquired combat skills to pretend that they were looking after the shopkeepers' interests by protecting them from damage by rival gangs. The owners of the shops knew full well that it was just a front and that their businesses would be in danger from the very people they were paying if they refused to cooperate. The problem they had was what to do with the money they extorted and that was where I came in. By opening the club I could bank the money and claim it was legitimate takings. It was a good way for me to finance other businesses and somehow I ended up in charge of the whole operation. You probably noticed that the club wouldn't be a particularly profitable enterprise on its own but it's the ideal way to bank cash from other sources.'

Art looked a little bemused. 'I can see that was the case then but now it's the 1960s so why can't you just drop that side and build up the rest of your businesses?'

'I'd love to. But there are a lot of people involved. The club would have to close and all the staff lose their jobs. The men who run the protection game would be very unhappy and would probably move their allegiance to one of the other firms operating in London. I could end up losing everything if they turned on me.'

'Surely they'd leave you alone if you pulled out?'

'Possibly. But it's a risk I don't want to take just yet. When the taxi business is fully established and I've more companies wanting properly organised site security then I'll be in a more secure position. I'm hoping that with you as the front man for those concerns that they''ll become more successful. As I said in Minehead, you will be the respectable face of Hayes Limited.'

'You know, if you become a proper limited company then the law will be fully on your side.'

'That's true. It will mean paying a lot more tax but that'll be worth it. At least I'll be able to hand over to Paul a real business free from suspicion of underhand practices. Oh, and I'm not forgetting you and Jude. I hope you'll stay with me in the firm for a long time and Jude will be free to give up work and be a housewife and, hopefully, a mother.'

'Well, I'm not too sure how Jude will react to that idea. I know she's a very independent woman who wants to do things her way. Anyway, we haven't discussed the future in great detail. I've got to sort out my mother before anything else can happen.'

'That's another very important thing,' John added. 'I know that you are fully stretched trying to finance your mother's care so I'll take you on the payroll straight away with a starting salary of a thousand a year going up to three thousand when you start full time and I'll also sort out a company car to help you with the trips to Liverpool. I know I can get hold of one of the old minicabs for you to use until a better motor comes along.'

Art gasped out loud. 'That's far too generous. I won't be making you much money until I know the business better. Are you sure?'

'It's not just for you. I'm thinking of Jude as well. I guess you'll be thinking of a wedding sooner rather than later?'

'We'd sort of put that on hold but thanks to you we can now start planning.'

'Great. You know I want the best for my daughter.'

'So do I.'

Chapter 13

London, November 1964

It was Friday again. Art was preparing for another long drive to Liverpool. He'd packed a weekend bag and went out to the old Ford Popular that John had given him. It was a bit of rust bucket but the engine was good and it had done the trip a number of times without any problems. He could drive from Watford to Birmingham on the M1 motorway but after that he would be on the old trunk roads to Liverpool. The journey would take at least six hours and he was already tired from a day's teaching. But it had to be done. His mother had, as the doctors had indicated, gone downhill very quickly. She no longer recognised him and he wondered if she would be any the wiser if he didn't visit her at all. Only a month ago she had still known that 'her Jack' was by her bedside but now he was a stranger. She even looked a bit scared when he went into her room and this saddened him. He knew she would never know Jude and obviously she would be unable to attend their wedding.

On arriving at his old home just before midnight he turned on the electric fire in the sitting room, went to the kitchen and made himself a cup of tea. The house looked clean so he knew Mrs Carr was still looking after it. He must remember to pay her for the next month with a little extra for Christmas to thank her for being so helpful. He sat down on the familiar brown sofa and sipped his tea. It still seemed strange to be alone in the house which held so many memories of his childhood. He remembered fondly the Christmases with his mother and grandparents when he had been the only child. Now there mightn't be another happy Christmas for him in the house. He was sorry he'd not been home so often after going to college but his mother had seemed to be invincible and there for him for ever. He had to face up to the fact that her death would be the next milestone in his life. It probably wouldn't be long before she passed away and that would leave him alone in the world. At least he had his new family in London and that was a comforting thought. He had a life to forge for himself and Jude but he still couldn't come to terms with the emptiness his mother's death would bring.

After turning the fire off Art washed up the cup and left it on the wooden draining board. He went up to bed in his old room and, despite the cold, lay on top of the eiderdown feeling empty of emotion. After a few minutes he roused himself and went to wash his face and brush his teeth. In the mirror above the sink he saw how grey and miserable he looked. He leaned on the edge of the sink and stared into the mirror. It was, he thought as he faced his reflection, time to stop feeling sorry for himself and try to make a positive effort to take control of his life and make a new start. Suddenly he grinned and the face in the mirror smiled back at him. He thought that this made him look more like his old self and laughed out loud. He realised he had been coasting for too long and let himself be carried along by events without realising it. Feeling more cheerful he turned out the light and returned to his bed. He slept well for the first time in many weeks.

In the morning Art went to the nearest shop to buy the basics for his breakfast. The shopkeeper recognised him and she asked after his mother. He said he was going to visit her later that day and would then know more about her condition. She asked Art to pass on her best wishes and this he promised to do knowing it would be a complete waste of time. After breakfast he walked to the nursing home and sat with his mother for an hour. He talked to her but it was a one way conversation. She spent most of the time looking out of the window and ignored Art. He was used to this now and it no longer upset him as much as it had the first time she failed to recognise him. On his way out he sought out the matron to discuss the future. She was honest and told him his mother was now doubly incontinent and needed a lot of care. He asked what he could do and she told him that there was very little but to continue coming as she seemed calmer after his visits. At least, he felt, his trips were of some use. He asked the matron how long before his mother would succumb to the disease and was told it wasn't an exact science. She could die in the next few months or hold on for a year at best.

That evening Art visited the pub down the road. He didn't recognise any of the customers and was quite glad that he could sit alone with his thoughts. The last thing he wanted was to have to explain to an old schoolmate the problems he was now having to deal with. He had a second pint and then went home to bed.

He visited the nursing home again the next morning prior to the drive back to London. There was no noticeable change in his mother's condition so he didn't speak to any of the staff and just left after what he considered to be a decent time for a visit. The concentration required for driving safely took his mind off his worries and he was quite relaxed on arrival at Pattison Road. He decided to see Jude that evening before work the next day. After phoning her he spent an hour or so finalising his teaching plans for the coming week. For his Sunday dinner he had toast and tea.

He met Jude on Plumstead Common at the old bandstand which had become a regular meeting place as it was roughly equidistant between their houses. As soon as he saw her his spirits lifted and they kissed passionately for a couple of minutes before sitting down on a nearby bench. Art kept his arm round her and she laid her head on his shoulder. Eventually Jude sat up and turned towards him.

'How was your mother?' she asked quietly.

'No real change. I don't think she'll be with us much longer.'

'I'm sad about that. I would have loved to have met her. She could have told me all about you and what you did as a little boy. Now I'll never know because you'll never tell me. Like most men you'd just dress it up to make yourself look good.'

Art laughed, 'You're right. But I had a very boring childhood. No guilty secrets to hide. I'll bring back some photos from my next visit to Liverpool so you can have some idea of my early years and see my mother and grandparents.'

'That'll be nice. But I won't be showing you any snaps of my childhood. Although I'm worried Mum might drag them out one day. I was such a spoilt little girl. Nearly all the photos of me are in various costumes for dancing school productions and plays that I was in at school. I'm not sure you'd find them at all interesting.'

'Anything to do with you interests me. Please ferret them out when I'm next at your place. Fancy a drink? We could go to The Prince Albert if you like.'

'Good idea. I'm getting cold sitting here.'

They stood up and crossed the Common to the pub. Jude sat down while Art went to buy the drinks. When he returned he told her what her father had said to him during their chat in Art's house before he left for Liverpool. Jude wasn't surprised at her father's generosity as she had been the recipient of it all her life. She was delighted that Art could now afford to look after his mother and help plan for their wedding as well. After a sip of her gin and orange she looked at Art with a quizzical expression.

'So, when are we getting married?'

'As soon as you want,' replied Art. 'How about next Easter? That'll give us time to sort out what needs to be done. It's sad but I'll be visiting mum less often now and will be able to do more work for your father. That'll put me in a better position to afford a decent place to live.'

'Too true. I've no plans to live in your hovel in Pattison Road,' Jude exclaimed vehemently. 'I'd rather live in the bandstand.'

'I'm sure that can be arranged,' Art answered with a grin. 'But I was thinking of a place in Welling or even Bexleyheath in Kent. With two salaries we'll be able to get a mortgage.'

'I'd better start working out what we'll need for a move. I know Mum and Dad will help us out and will pay for the wedding so you've no need to worry about the cost. Dad will want a pretty big wedding with all his pals as guests. What about you?

'The quieter the better as far as I'm concerned. I only know a few people to invite. Without my mother I've no family so it'll just be a few friends I've made at college and some of the staff from Vicarage Road school. I've a feeling that the people I know from the Star and Garter wouldn't come if I invited them. Sorry Jude, but that's probably because of John's reputation.'

'I know. I've always been an outsider myself because of what others thought of our family. Are you sure you know what you're letting yourself in for being associated with us?'

'I love you and think your family are fantastic. I don't care what people whisper behind our backs. I know your father only wants the best for you and that's good enough for me. He's also told me his plans for the future and how he intends to make his interests all aboveboard. And I want to be part of it. We can soon make our own circle of friends when we're married.'

'I can't wait.'

Chapter 14

London, December 1964

It was the end of term and Art's last day at Vicarage Road school. He was sad to be leaving as he'd enjoyed teaching but also excited about what lay ahead, especially the wedding. There had been a noticeable change in how people spoke to and regarded him since he had announced that he was marrying Jude Hayes. Some were supportive but many were now a little wary in their dealings with him. This applied to the staff as well as the parents. As usual, he got on very well with the children and they responded to him as positively as ever. His trips out on the occasional Saturday continued and he'd even managed to take a small group to watch a Charlton match at The Valley. As he was leaving before the end of the school year he'd not had a class to take for the term but took small groups for remedial work and filled in for other teachers when required. He'd not really enjoyed that very much as he liked having his own class to look after but knew it was good experience to teach children from all the different year groups. The end of term was punctuated by the carol service and the usual class parties. Without his own class there were few cards and presents for Art so the term ended on rather an unhappy note.

After his usual trip to Liverpool and finding his mother had stabilised somewhat after her rapid earlier decline Art returned to London to spend Christmas with Jude and her family. Art was still living in Pattison Road as, even with John's generous pay, he still couldn't afford anywhere better to live. He knew that in the New Year he was going to be full time on a larger salary and then things would become easier but he had no idea where he and Jude would live after the wedding and honeymoon. Well aware that there were only four months to the big day it was a problem that wouldn't go away. He knew he must discuss it with Jude but decided to leave that for the moment.

Buying presents had never been one of Art's strong points. He'd no idea what he should buy John and Marion never mind Paul and Jude. In the end he settled for the simple expedient of buying books. The latest football league year book for John, a cookery book by a TV cook called Fanny Cradock for Marion, the latest Guinness Book of Records for Paul and John Betjeman's Collected poems for Jude. He knew she liked poetry and hoped that the anthology that he'd read earlier would be well received. All he had to do now was have a bath in Woolwich and make sure he had clean clothes to wear on Christmas Day.

On Christmas Eve Art thought he'd spend and hour or two in the Star and Garter. Tony was there and they played darts and chatted about life in general. Tony's partner June stayed at home to look after their baby daughter so it was just the two of them standing at the bar when the door opened and a stranger walked in. He came straight to the bar but didn't order a drink. It was clear he'd had a few drinks already by the way he unsteadily clung on to the bar. He turned to Art and after struggling to focus on him he said, 'You're one of Hayes' mob aren't you? I've seen you with his daughter.'

He picked up Tony's glass and swung it towards Art's face. Before it could make contact Tony had grabbed the man's wrist and knocked the glass from his hand. In one movement he twisted the stranger's arm behind his back and forced him to his knees. Ted, the landlord, came over to find out what was happening as Tony pulled the man to the door and threw him out on to the pavement. He followed up by kicking him between the legs as he lay on the floor and then hauled him up by the collar and asked him what his problem was.

'It's your mate,' slurred the man. 'He's ruining my dad's business. He makes little enough as it is selling flowers without paying those thugs. I just wanted to make him feel the way my Dad does every time they pay him a visit. I'm not a violent man but I wanted that lot to know we can't all be treated like doormats.'

Art had come out of the bar with Ted and stood in the doorway. He'd heard what the man had said to Tony and felt ashamed. Tony pushed the man away and told him to go home and sober up.

Then he said to Art, 'I think you'd better go home as well. I'm sorry but your connection with the Hayes family isn't good news round here. I tried to warn you ages ago.'

Art turned away feeling very unhappy and went home without saying a word but promised to himself that he'd have to discuss the incident with John. He knew it would be the last time he went to the Star for a drink.

Tony also went home and told June what had happened. They both agreed it would probably be for the best if Art moved away from Plumstead.

'He's out of our league now,' said June. 'And once he's married he won't want to know us anyway.'

'Not so sure,' replied Tony. 'He's a good man and I think he'll change things if he can.'

*

On Christmas morning a rather subdued Art carried a bag of presents and made his way towards the Hayes' house up the hill. He was still upset and embarrassed about the previous evening. Not wanting to spoil the festivities he decided to change his mind and not tell Jude or John about what had happened in the pub. Still, it was difficult to force himself into the party mood when he'd had such a bad experience. It was thanks to Tony that he'd not ended up in hospital. And he hadn't even thanked him. In the New Year he'd start looking for a new place to live away from the friends he'd made in Pattison Road during his time at college and teaching in the nearby school. When he reached the common he stopped and sat on a bench to try and clarify his thoughts and be more positive about the future. Was he so much in love with Jude that he was blind to her father's faults? Did he really want to be seen as John's assistant in activities that seemed to cause so much anger to ordinary working people? At the moment he could see no way out of the position he found himself in as he needed the money to look after his mother properly and John was the only way he could manage that situation. He hoped that Jude would understand if he eventually went back to teaching when his mother died and he no longer needed John's support. But he didn't want to upset John who had been such a help to him although he was aware that the help he'd received was solely because of Jude. Art knew Jude could do no wrong in John's eyes. What next? He had no idea so tried to put on a festive face and carried on to meet his adopted family.

Paul answered the door and as soon as Art he stepped into the lounge his worries evaporated. Jude was standing by the fireplace dressed in a lemon sheath dress with a circle of green and red tinsel on her head like a halo. She looked like an angel and Art's heart melted as he gazed at her. To think he was going to spend the rest of his life with her. The feeling of love consumed him as he crossed the room and took hold of both her hands as he kissed her.

'Is that it?' she complained giving his hands a squeeze. 'I expected more than that for Christmas. What's hiding in your bag?'

'Not much. Just a few small presents. They're what my mother calls Christmas tree presents to be opened in the evening after dinner. I suppose you and Paul will already have had all your presents earlier this morning. Paul, what did Father Christmas bring you?'

Paul blushed to the roots of his hair. 'I'm a bit old for Father Christmas. Mum and Dad bought me my own record player and Jude gave me a chemistry set. I'm going to have fun trying out he experiments. The box says there are over fifty to try.'

'Well, don't blow us all up,' laughed Art. 'But I'm pleased that you're interested in science. It would be a good career for you one day.'

'No chance of that. Dad wants me to join him in the business. I don't think I've much choice.'

Jude turned to him. 'You mustn't think you always have to do what Dad says. It's your life to live as you choose. Don't you want to go to college or university like Art?'

'Don't know. I'll just wait and see. Anyway we've got dinner coming soon, Can't wait.'

'You see,' Jude said to Art, 'his stomach is more important than his future.'

'So's mine at the moment,' answered Art. 'I've not eaten since last night.'

'I'll get us all drinks,' said John as he came in and shook Art's hand. 'What's your poison?'

'We can leave the poison to Paul now he has his chemistry set,' said Jude. 'I'll have a gin and orange please. What about you Art?'

'A beer would be just right. Thanks.'

John went and made the drinks bringing them on a tray with a glass of lemonade for Paul. 'I've given Marion a G and T to keep her going as she finishes the dinner. She says we

197

should be able to sit down at the table in about two hours. Jude, why don't you go and see if there's anything you can do to help? It's about time you learnt more about cooking for when you're married.'

'I expect Art to do all that,' she replied. 'I want a modern man who shares all the household chores. You agree don't you dear?'

'Of course,' answered Art. 'You will really enjoy my one pan meals. And I can cook eggs in the kettle while it's boiling to make my tea.'

'Yuck,' Paul said pulling a face.'That's horrible.'

'I can see married life for you two is going to be very entertaining,' John said. 'Just don't invite me round for dinner.'

Jude went out to the kitchen and the men sat down in the comfy chairs. Paul turned on the television. A Christmas carol service was showing so he turned to the other channel only to find that it was also showing a church service. As he thought the carols were festive he went back to them but turned the sound down a little so it was just background music. John refreshed their drinks and, with a long sigh, stretched out his legs.

'I suppose this will be the last Christmas we spend together,' he said ruefully. 'Next Christmas Jude and Art will probably want to have Christmas in their own house. It'll just be the three of us.'

'Great,' exclaimed Paul. 'I'll get all the presents.'

Marion poked her head round the door to the lounge.

'Dinner's ready,' she called.

They eased themselves out of the chairs and trooped into the dining room. Art stood in astonishment at the table laden with food. He had experienced fairly frugal Christmas dinners in Liverpool, especially in the years after the war when rationing was still in place. His mother had usually been able to find a scrawny chicken as a once in a year treat and a change from the beef or lamb they normally had for a Sunday lunch. But this was something else entirely.

They sat down and John poured out glasses of champagne. He even let Paul have a small glass so he wouldn't feel left out. Raising his glass he called for a toast to Jude and Art and to their forthcoming wedding. They then drank to Christmases past and present and to remember family who were no longer with them. Art thought sadly about the father he'd never known, his grandparents and his mother who probably didn't know it was Christmas. His thoughts then turned to the future and how meeting Jude had changed his life in so many ways.

After battling their way through the massive turkey and mountains of vegetables they sat contentedly for a few minutes until Marion brought in the flaming pudding and brandy-butter sauce. That soon went and it was time for coffee and mince pies as they pulled the Christmas crackers and read out the corny jokes. Art asked if he could help with the clearing up but was roundly put down by Jude and her mother and told to go and sit back in the lounge. Paul was allowed to go to his room and play a few singles on his record player while John and Art returned to the chairs they had vacated earlier and sat down folding their arms over their stomachs sighing as they did so.

'Well,' said John, 'that's it for this year. It'll soon be 1965 and we'll have to wait and see what that brings. You'll now be working full time and I thought it best if I gave you my office at the security firm. You'll be able to oversee the operation and ensure it all runs smoothly on a day-to-day basis as well as drumming up new trade from nearby factories and offices. There are business developments springing up all over this area who will house companies who will need to have their premises protected by an efficient and well regarded security company. I want you to be in charge of hiring and firing suitable security guards and giving them the relevant training. I've already weeded out a number who have criminal records and want all staff in future to be trustworthy and reliable. The success of that operation will depend on us having a spotless record and using men of the highest calibre.'

'I was thinking of introducing a proper uniform with a company badge,' said Art. 'It would look a lot more professional and the clients would be pleased, especially those who wanted daytime security when their offices might be visited by other company directors.'

'Good idea. You can work out a design and show it to me. If I think it fits the bill you can go ahead and put in an order. Don't forget, it must be practical as well as smart.'

'I was thinking about using battledress blouses as a basic design. We might be able to buy some from army surplus sources and dye them blue or black with a woven badge on the chest. Black trousers and either a military style cap or a beret could complete the look.'

'Sounds just right,'

'I'll get on to it straight after Christmas,' Art enthused. 'We could have it all in place by the end of January. We'll certainly look a cut above the opposition and that should help with orders for our services.'

He was pleased that he was now becoming more involved in the business and glad that John agreed with his ideas. It was a lot different to teaching forty eleven year olds but there were some similarities. He knew it wouldn't work without discipline and organisation. Being in charge of a gang of adults brought its problems but he was confident that he would be able to manage running the firm without too much trouble.

When the women returned from the kitchen Marion announced that it was time for the adults to swap presents as Paul had already had his in the morning.

Art went first and gave the other three their books which he had wrapped up in festive paper bought in Woolwich indoor market. They all seemed pleased with their tomes and made the right sort of appreciative murmurs. Jude had bought her parents a joint present of an oil painting. It was of a country scene reminiscent of Exmoor and they both loved it immediately. Marion received a sparkling necklace from John and in return she gave him a gold set of cuff-links with his initials engraved on them. John then reach into his pocket and took out a small box. He told Jude and Art it was for both of them and handed it to Art. Jude came across the room as he opened it carefully and they were surprised to see it only contained a not very new Yale key.

'A key?' queried Jude. 'What's that for?'

'Your house,' John smiled broadly. 'You'll need somewhere to live when you're married and although I lived in a house similar to Art's current one I'm not letting my daughter live like that. Your house is a chalet style one in Welling. Art can move in as soon as he likes and then you can join him after the wedding. It's all basically furnished and ready to go.'

Jude jumped up and ran to her father, kissed him and gave him the biggest hug she could manage. 'It's fantastic. Thank you so much. When can we go and see it?'

'Tomorrow. We've all had too much to drink to go today. Are you happy Art?'

Art wasn't too sure because he'd hoped to find a place for them himself and John had rather taken the wind from his sails with the announcement. All he could manage was a rather subdued thank you and a smile in John's direction. But when he saw how overjoyed Jude was he decided it was really a very generous offer and it would be churlish to be lukewarm about it.

'It's a fabulous present,' he said putting on the most enthusiastic voice he could manage. 'I can't wait to go and see it.'

'And I'll be able to sort out the curtains and all that we'll need for the kitchen,' added Jude. 'I'm sure you'll help me with that won't you Mum?'

'Of course. I'm really excited about it.'

Art wanted to show his appreciation so he chuckled, 'And I'll be able to have my own bath for the first time in over four years. That'll be fantastic.'

They all laughed and settled down to watch the Christmas offerings on the television. There was a variety programme on the BBC which they all watched. It had a lot of their favourite acts in it such as the Black and White Minstrels, Dick Emery and the Likely Lads. It also featured a special edition of Top of the Pops which Jude and Art enjoyed. Paul liked the slapstick comedy of Benny Hill best and laughed until he cried at the comedian's antics.

After a supper of mince pies and port wine Art left the Hayes with a promise to return in the morning and returned to his little terraced house. It was cold and unwelcoming but held a lot of fond memories. Not the least of these was the times he'd made love to Jude in the confines of his single bed. Now, he thought, we'll be able to enjoy each other in a little more comfort but that didn't take away the early excitement of when their love first grew. He went to bed and pulled the covers up to the tip of his nose and settled down into a dreamless sleep.

Woke by the alarm clock he reluctantly put his feet down on the cold linoleum, pulled on his dressing gown and went downstairs to wash in the kitchen sink. After a cup of coffee and a slice of toast he returned to his bedroom and dressed. As it was a bright day he decided to leave the car outside the house and walk up to meet Jude and the others to go and see the house in Welling. Soon they were all piled in John's car and went over Shooters Hill to the railway bridge where John turned right into Westwood Lane. He slowed the car at a bend in the road and stopped just after it. they all got out and stood looking at a semi-detached house with a sign outside boldly pronouncing 'sold'. It was painted a canary yellow and looked bright and cheerful. It had a driveway and a gate that presumably led to the back of the house and a garden. The house itself was one of the many chalet style houses in the area. There were two bedrooms upstairs with the living room and dining room on the ground floor together with the kitchen and bathroom. There was also a small room at the front which could be used as a study or spare bedroom.

Jude gazed at it all with an amazed look on her face. 'This is ours,' she breathed and gave Art's arm a squeeze, 'I can't believe it. Dad, you're the most wonderful Dad in the whole world.'

John beamed, 'If it makes you two happy then I'm happy. You deserve a better start in life than your mother and I had. It's your house now so make it a real family home.'

'We will,' chorused Art and Jude.

Paul, who had been doing his own inspection of the property came bounding downstairs two at a time. He skidded to a halt in front of them and pronounced, 'I've decided which room is mine when I come to stay and then I looked out of the window and saw where I can build a den in the garden.'

'Not so fast young man,' his mother remonstrated. 'I think you'd better ask Jude and Art first.'

'Can I?' pleaded Paul.

'Yes,' Jude replied, 'so long as you don't have the biggest bedroom. That's for Art and me.'

'That's okay, actually I wouldn't mind the small room downstairs. I can make it really cosy like an indoors den.'

The adults laughed and John added, 'It'll also be near the phone I'm having installed next week so you can be the answering service.'

'A phone?' asked Art. 'That'll be very useful if I need to contact you about work now that I'll be full time.'

'Actually it's so I can contact you,' said John.

'Can we come back during the weekend to measure up for curtains and decide what else will be needed?' asked Jude.

'Of course you can. Marion might be able to join you to help.'

Marion smiled, 'I'd love to. It will remind me of when we eventually managed to buy a house of our own. It'll be good to be busy again.'

Jude locked up the house and they returned to Plumstead where Marion provided a cold lunch of leftovers and, after watching the football results as it got dark John, Paul and Art watched a live match in the evening on BBC2.

*

With the house sorted out all Art had to do was move in and wait for the wedding day in May. He already knew that going full time with John would be a lot different from school but was determined to make a success of it. He was a little concerned about Mike, John's right hand man, who had been running the club and the protection side of the business. Art was very

205

keen for both to be dropped as soon as possible but guessed that there would be quite a lot of opposition when John decided to tell his employees. It might go smoothly but that was unlikely and there would no doubt be a power struggle both within the firm and with other interested parties from neighbouring boroughs. He desperately hoped John could sort it without losing the rest of his interests, especially the security firm Art was working hard to build up as a respectable enterprise and the minicabs which provided a steady and legal income.

He looked around the house to see if there was anything from his four years in the place that he would take to the new house. Apart from his clothes there was nothing he could remotely consider to be useful. It was rather depressing to think that he'd accumulated so little during his time in Pattison Road. Not a picture, ornament or piece of furniture would be going with him when the new house was ready for him. He'd thought he would be sorry to move but after the altercation in the pub he was now glad to go. A new beginning. Such a pity that his mother would never know anything about it. Possibly that was for the best as he couldn't see her really liking John and Marion. She would have regarded them as a bit common and called them "johnny-come-latelies" in her best Townswomen's Guild voice. He sighed. Sometimes things did work out for the best even though it wasn't immediately apparent.

He'd be moving in a couple of days and wondered if Jude would come and visit him on his first night there. She wouldn't be able to stay the night as that would not be allowed by her parents. Funny, he thought, Paul could stay the night but Jude couldn't. Never mind it didn't have to be dark for them to get together and there was something quite romantic about making love in daylight. He smiled at the thought and couldn't wait to share it with Jude. He was sure she'd feel the same. They'd been taking precautions since their first encounter and would continue to do so until the wedding.

After a last look round he left the house and locked the door. He went for a walk which took him to the school where he'd been so happy. Another final look. He hoped he wouldn't regret his decision. You are being morbid he remonstrated with himself as he went back home to prepare for the coming months in his job and all the plans for the wedding. He'd wanted Tony from the pub to be his best man but now felt that, after the problem in the pub, it might be impossible and he didn't want to embarrass his old friend who might refuse him. He didn't really know anyone else of his age so wondered if he could ask if Paul could do the job. After all, he reasoned, he wouldn't have met Jude if it hadn't been for Paul. He was sure Jude would approve but he'd have to ask John and Marion for permission. And, of course, Paul. He would probably like the idea as he'd already firmly stated that he wouldn't be a page boy under any circumstances. There was a lot to plan, do and think about over the next few months and Art hoped he would be up to it.

Chapter 15

Liverpool, July 2017

Louise looked at the screen again and then at her sister Ellen. It showed the Facebook open group page for Vicarage Road School where their dad had taught. She read aloud what they had both seen. She hoped it might make more sense that way.

'Anyone remember Mr James?' she read. 'He was the best teacher ever and he took us on visits to the Science Museum. I know he married Paul Hayes' sister – the very pretty blond girl. I wonder where he is now?' The post was from someone called Chris Steggles.

The first reply was from Brian Border so Louise read that one. 'Yes, he was a great teacher. The wedding was in the local paper – quite a big do but then the Hayes always had pots of money. I think Paul is still around.'

Next she read one from Christine Nuttall. 'Mr James was lovely and ever so kind. I seem to remember people called him Art even though his first initial was a J. My mother wanted to take me to the wedding but my dad wouldn't let her. He didn't want people to think we were friends with Paul's family although Paul was a nice quiet boy. I fancied him at the time'

They trawled through all the posts about the school but that was the last mention of their father and no photos had been added. It was, to say the least, a bombshell for the sisters.

Ellen scrolled back to the top and said to Louise, 'It can't be right. If it is it means that Dad was a bigamist and that makes us illegitimate.'

'I always said you were a bastard,' said Louise as she tried to make light of what they'd found out. 'I suppose that could cause all sorts of problems as Dad never left a will. How can we find out exactly what did happen in London at that time?'

Ellen looked thoughtful. 'One of the posts mentions that the wedding was in the papers. If we can find an archive from the local papers at that time then we might know more. At least we know the family name of the girl he married so we have some useful information. We could try and contact the people who wrote on Facebook but they don't seem to know much about what happened after the wedding. But first I'll do a search for the nearest libraries to Woolwich and try and find the titles of the papers and if there are any records kept.'

'No wonder Dad never wanted to take us to London. He was probably worried we might bump into his first wife,' said Louise. 'I'll leave it to you to try and find out more. I'm not sure if I'm really upset about this news or just fascinated about the fact that Dad wasn't at all as we thought he was.'

'I'm not sure what we find out will be good news,' Ellen said. 'But now I want to know the full story. At least Mum isn't around any more. This would have devastated her. We can cope with what we unearth as, apart from the possible legal tangle, it doesn't really mean that much to us. Give me an hour and I'll try to track down some information on newspapers around at the time.'

Louise left Ellen's house as she had some shopping to do and promised to return later. Ellen tried a number of searches on her laptop and found the phone number of Woolwich Library. She called and a helpful lady, after being briefly filled in on their search for a wedding, told her that the main local paper in the 1960s was called The Kentish Independent but that it had been closed down for many years. She thought that there might be an archive of back editions in the Bexleyheath Library as that was the borough in which the paper had been based. She gave Ellen the number to call and wished her good luck in her search.

Ellen called Bexleyheath Library straight away and was answered by a very efficient sounding man who, to her delight, said that they did indeed have a microfiche archive of the newspaper and it was free for the public to view.

'Can I access it online?' asked Ellen.

'Sorry,' came the reply, 'We haven't got round to doing that yet and, with the cuts, probably never will. You're very welcome to come here and look for yourself. We're open Mondays, Tuesdays, Fridays and Saturdays from nine to five.'

Ellen thanked him and asked for address of the library which she jotted down.

The doorbell rang and she let Louise in. After making a pot of tea they sat in the lounge and Ellen told Louise what she'd discovered.

'It looks as if a trip to London is next,' she added after telling her sister about the archive. 'There's no other way I can think of to find out about the wedding. Do you want to come with me?'

'No, it doesn't need the two of us. If there are any other leads to follow up or people we could meet then I'll certainly join you for another visit. let's keep it low key for the present and you can fill me in on your return. It might all be a big mistake or just a joke by his ex-pupils.'

'I don't think so. Dad must have married the girl. Pity we don't know her full name. I'll go next week on Monday when the library is open. I'll phone them again to see if there's anyone who'll help me with the search or might remember what happened at the time. It's along drive for one day so I'll go by train from Lime Street if you can give me a lift there.'

'No problem. I hope you can sort it all out and we can forget about it. Why couldn't Dad have been as straightforward as we'd always imagined?'

'We'll find out soon enough.'

Chapter 16

London, February 1965

Art had immersed himself in helping to improve the efficiency and image of the security company. He'd had to tread on a few toes to do it and this hadn't endeared him to Mike, John's right hand man. A number of the guards who were friends of Mike had been sacked by John because of their criminal records and unreliability and Art had recruited a number of new guards who had clean backgrounds. He'd also appointed a retired police sergeant to be a mobile supervisor who travelled round the sites ensuring the men were performing their duties correctly. Having such a man working with him just antagonised Mike even more and he complained to John that having a copper on board could jeopardise his own arm of the business or at least make it more difficult to operate successfully. Unbeknown to John he had taken on some of the men sacked by Art and they were willing to work with him to try and oust Art from his favoured position within the firm. Art was oblivious to all these machinations and blithely continued with his focus on pleasing John and building up the security side. The less he knew about Mike and what he got up to the happier he was.

There was no way it could go on as if nothing was happening and John could sense the animosity and did his best to keep the two men apart. He only saw Mike in the club and Art in the security office. He took more personal control of the minicab business which was growing at a rapid rate as people realised they were cheaper than black cabs and easy to order. There was more money around than in the 1950s and phoning for a minicab became a regular way of returning home from nights out in the area. Black cabs were few and far between in south-east London despite many of the drivers living in Welling and Bexleyheath. They preferred to work the West End and the mainline stations than run drunks home from boozy nights in the pubs. With the business thriving and Art doing well John wondered if it would be a good time to lose the less salubrious part of his empire. Not yet, he thought, with the expense of the upcoming wedding it would be better to continue as things were for a few more months. He could rethink the business later in the year and make any decisions then. The problems with Stevens and his mob seemed to have settled down so there was no need to rush things.

*

Meanwhile, Jude and her mother were busy preparing for the big day. They'd spent a lot of time at the house in Welling and had it looking good with matching curtains and cushions and all the latest appliances in the kitchen. They knew Art probably wouldn't use them but Jude reckoned they were essential for when she moved in. Jude was very happy sorting everything out but was seeing less and less of Art as he seemed to be either working twelve hours a day, seven days a week or visiting Liverpool. They'd hardly been out anywhere since the New Year party in John's club and she was missing their late night chats as well as the more intimate moments. She hoped that after the honeymoon when they were living together he might find more time to be with her. There were no doubts in her mind about getting married so young and was more than happy to be Art's wife and, hopefully, the mother to their children. She was already planning the décor for a nursery in the smaller upstairs bedroom but hadn't yet expressed her ideas to her mother and certainly not to Art.

The wedding itself would be one to remember. She knew her father was keen to make a big show of it to all his friends including some from the world of show business and some of the Charlton footballers he'd got to know over the years when he'd sponsored games. The wedding itself was to be held in St Nicholas' church in Plumstead with the reception at the nearby Conservative Club. Jude knew her dad was a member of the Conservative Club but rarely went there as he regarded it as a bit old fashioned and stuffy. But the connection meant that he could hire the function room for the reception and the dance in the evening. The catering would be done by a company from Old Bexley Village which specialised in such events and supplied everything from tablecloths and decorations to the food and serving staff. It would, thought

Jude, give her mother a day off to relax and enjoy the occasion.

Jude wasn't really concerned about having a big wedding but knew that was what her parents wanted as they'd not had much of a do themselves. It was the honeymoon she was looking forward to the most as they'd booked a week on the Greek island of Corfu and it would be her first trip abroad. The wedding dress and the dress for her solitary bridesmaid, an old school friend – actually her only school friend – were being made in a bridal shop in Woolwich. She had chosen a white satin A-line dress for herself with small seed pearls as decoration. It was simple but she hoped it would look smart and modern. She definitely didn't want a dress with loads of petticoats and a train as she thought that was too much of the fairy princess type and she wanted to look adult and trendy. Her bridesmaid was to wear a similar style dress but in blue. John had wanted the men to wear morning dress and top hats but her mother had vetoed the idea as being too pretentious for a Plumstead wedding so it was agreed that the men would wear smart lounge suits. Without no family on Art's side and very few on her own it would be mainly up to her parents to provide the guest list. She'd loved Art's suggestion that Paul should be his best man and her father had agreed it would be a nice touch. Paul had been delighted when Art had asked him and was forever asking questions about his role on the day. Jude had teased him about making a speech and having to dance with her bridesmaid but soon relented and told him that he would just have to read out any cards or telegrams and the dancing could be left to the adults.

*

Mike, now sidelined from the family, was counting the day's collection in the club and working out how much he could salt away for himself without raising John's suspicions. Since Art was apparently now the one who was second in command Mike had decided to forge his own path despite some residual loyalty he still felt for John because of what he had done to help him out when he was down. He had harboured thoughts of taking over the whole business when John eventually stood down but that was now an unlikely scenario as Art was obviously in line to succeed John and then Paul would inherit when he was older. Mike was becoming a bit fed up with taking a back seat and regarded only as useful in extracting cash from unwilling shopkeepers and small businessmen. He knew the men he used to collect the money were toe-rags who would work for whoever paid them the most and would change their loyalties with as little regard as they changed their socks.

But Mike had his eyes on the future and was finding out about new opportunities. Primarily these were to do with various narcotic drugs which had been slowly gaining momentum over recent years starting with purple hearts and then on to cannabis and now LSD, the drug of choice among the rich and famous. LSD was legal and he knew how to get his hands on it. It could prove to be very profitable if he could stay ahead of any opposition. He was very aware that other gangs in London would soon jump on the bandwagon so he had to move quickly and guarantee his supply. Naturally, he didn't want John or Art to know. John was too old school and wouldn't have anything to do with drugs, legal or otherwise and Art was too naive. That was why he was building up a bankroll of his own to finance the operation. But John mustn't find out he was siphoning off cash before he was ready to go it alone.

*

On Valentine's Day Art sent Jude a huge bouquet of roses with a card expressing his undying love. She hadn't sent him anything and he worried that she was cooling off about their relationship. He was still rather insecure and amazed at his good fortune in meeting such a wonderful girl. He constantly expected it to go wrong and find himself on his own again. He went home after work feeling down and turned the key in the lock. The house was in darkness even though it was only five o'clock. All was quiet until he heard some music playing. It was coming from the lounge so he listened at the door. When he realised it was their Beatles' song that was playing he opened the door and saw Jude reclining on the sofa without a stitch of clothing on. She smiled and said, 'Happy Valentine's Day.'

Art stood mesmerised, 'I thought you'd forgotten as I hadn't heard from you. Not even a card.'

'I thought this might be better than a card,' she whispered silkily as she stood up and went to him. 'Let's dance like we did on holiday.'

Art held her close and they swayed around the room trying to avoid the furniture. When the record ended he took her hand and they went upstairs. Art considered that it was definitely the best present he could have ever wished for as he frantically pulled off his clothes and joined Jude on the bed.

*

Jude stayed for a couple of hours but then had to go home so as her parents wouldn't know she'd been with Art when they thought she was at work. She'd left the surgery early so as to surprise him and had told the dentist she wasn't feeling too good. As she'd recently passed her driving test she'd come in her car which she'd parked in a side street so that Art wouldn't see it when he arrived. As she slid behind the steering wheel she felt so full of happiness that it was almost overwhelming. She'd never known life could feel so good and fervently hoped it would never stop. Taking a deep breath to compose herself she switched on the engine and carefully drove off home.

Her mother was in the kitchen preparing the evening meal and Paul, as per usual, was in his room.

'Had a good day?' asked Marion. 'I thought you'd be seeing Art as it's Valentine's day.'

Jude blushed as she thought of how much she'd just seen of Art. 'I might go round to the house later and see if he wants to go out for a drink. We hadn't planned anything as he's been so busy recently.'

'Yes, your father says he's really making a difference and is delighted that he took him on. It will make both your lives easier as he's now earning good money.'

'Why does everyone think life is just about money? I'd happily live in a tent with Art rather than lose him.'

'Not sure your father would be happy with that. I know money isn't everything. After all, John and I struggled in the early days. But it certainly makes things easier. At least you and Paul have had most things you want as you've grown up and look at this lovely house. Never in my wildest dreams did I ever think I'd live in a place like this. And I didn't marry John thinking it would happen so we're really just the same as you and Art.'

'Sorry Mum. I just can't help feeling we're getting everything too easy. Anyway, what's for dinner?'

'Corned beef hash, beans and pickled onions. Your father's all time favourite meal. I think it reminds him of being in the army during the war. He says it's very good for soaking up the whisky.'

'It's also a favourite of Art's. He calls it dry hash. I think that's a Liverpool thing. Have we enough? I could phone him and ask him round.'

'There's plenty. You go and ask him before he cooks his own meal.'

Jude went to the telephone in the hall and called Art. She was just in time as he was starting to put a tinned meat pie in the oven. At the mention of the hash he said he'd leave immediately and buy a bottle of wine on the way.

John arrived home before Art got there. He took one look at the roses Art had sent Jude and exclaimed to no one in particular, 'For me? I didn't know anybody cared.'

'Idiot,' laughed Marion. 'They're for Jude. Art sent them.'

'So, nothing for me? Didn't you think of buying me anything?'

'I'll do that the day you remember any of our anniversaries without a lot of hints and prompting. I suppose you've conveniently forgotten that it's February the fourteenth?'

'Ah. Valentine's Day. Tell you what I'll make you a large gin and tonic to celebrate.'

'Wow, thanks. I was going to have one anyway.'

The doorbell chimed and Jude went to let Art in. They joined the others in the kitchen and John took their drinks requests and went to the lounge to make them. Marion called up to Paul and he came down for the meal. They ate in the kitchen as it was the warmest room in the house and soon all the hash had gone. There was no cooked pudding so Marion went to the lounge and returned with the fruit bowl so they could each choose between an apple, banana or orange. After he'd munched his way through an apple John wiped his mouth, sat back and looked around the table at Art and his family.

'I've got some news about who's coming to the wedding. You knew I was asking some of the Charlton directors and a few of the team. Well, they've all said yes so I've also asked the manager and he's coming as well.'

Art's eyes lit up. 'The manager's coming to our wedding? That's amazing. Anyone else famous?'

'I'm working on it,' John grinned. 'I might have a few showbiz people as well. Not Tom Jones or anyone that well known but a few who have minor parts in some TV shows.'

'How do you know these people?' asked Jude.

'Oh, I have a some business contacts in the West End and occasionally they bring them to my club. It's amazing what free drinks can do. They like the attention and the club members make them feel special. All I do is shake hands and make sure they have everything they need.'

'And what would that be?' Jude came back at him.

'Don't ask. It's better you remain ignorant. Anyway, It'll be good to have those people as we don't have a lot of family and Art has none at all to invite. Sorry Art, I know you would have wanted your mother to come but from what you say that'd be impossible.'

Art grimaced, 'Yes, it's a pity but that's they way it is. She's not getting any better and probably won't be with us much longer.'

'At least you've done the right thing for her,' Marion put a hand on his arm. 'I'm really sorry I'll never get to know her. I'm sure she could have told me lots of tales about your childhood. Do you have any photos of her and you? We could blow some up and display them at the reception.'

'That's a brilliant idea Mum,' Jude enthused. 'And I'd like to see how Art looked as a little boy. Is there one of you on a sheepskin rug wearing only a smile?'

Paul pulled a face. 'Nobody wants to see someone in the nude.'

'Wait a few years,' Jude replied with a smile.

Chapter 17

London, May 1965

Jude woke early to a bright spring day and it came to her in a sudden wave of mixed emotions that today was the day. It was her wedding day and she sat up and swung her legs out of her single bed. Last single bed I'll sleep in she said to herself as she rose to have a shower and prepare for the day ahead. There seemed so little to do now everything was arranged. All that was now required of her was to look her best and say 'I will' at the right moment. Her hair was to be done by a friend of her mother who had a salon in Eltham High Street and after that all that was left was to dress and go to the church with her father in the white Rolls Royce he had booked.

After showering she put on her dressing gown and went downstairs for breakfast. Marion was already up and in the kitchen having her first mug of tea of the day. She smiled at Jude and said, 'Well, this is it. Are you excited?'

'Not as much as I thought I'd be. It all seems so natural now to marry Art. It's both the end and the beginning. I'll probably be a bit more nervous when I walk down the aisle with everyone looking at me. I hope I don't let anyone down after all the effort that has gone into making the day so special for me.'

'Don't be silly. You'll look stunning. I'll bet there are loads of girls who'll be very jealous when they see you. And Art will complete the picture. It'll be the happiest day of your life.'

'Too late. I had that day when Art asked me to marry him. Nothing can beat that.'

Marion turned to the sink and filled the kettle. She plugged it in and reached for another mug. 'Tea or coffee?' she asked.

'Coffee please.'

The kitchen door opened and Paul entered looking half asleep. He'd stayed up late the night before full of the excitement of being Best Man for Art. He'd asked time and time again what his duties were and practised taking out the ring to give to the vicar until everyone was thoroughly fed up with him.

'Morning dear,' said his mother. 'Before you have breakfast I think you should have a shower.'

'But I had one the other day,' complained Paul. 'I won't need another for at least a week.'

'Upstairs now and shower before I take you up and give you a shower myself.'

With that threat of embarrassment hanging over him Paul soon scooted out of the kitchen and up the stairs.

John was next to enter the kitchen. 'Heard the noise so I thought I'd better get up,' he grumbled. 'Why can't a man have a lie in now and again? It's not as if we've anything important to do today.'

Jude jumped up, ran to him and threw her arms round his neck. 'Stop teasing. You know exactly what day it is.'

'Must be a Charlton fixture.'

'You know the season's finished. It's my wedding day.'

'Oh is that all it is. You could have said and then I'd have made an effort to be up earlier.'

'Tea or coffee?' asked Marion.

Paul came down with his wet hair slicked back. 'Now can I have some breakfast,' he grumbled.

'What would you like dear?' asked his mother. 'Cornflakes or porridge?'

'Cornflakes please. With lots of sugar and milk. Then some toast and marmalade.'

'Is that all?' John queried. 'How about a fry-up as well?'

'Yes please. I'll need that to keep my strength up. Being best man will take up a lot of energy.'

'Cheeky sod,' grinned his father. 'You're lucky to get anything as your mother is very busy sorting out everything for Jude. Anyone would think you were getting married and not her.'

'No way,' Paul grimaced. 'You won't catch me marrying. I don't know why anyone with any sense would want to marry a girl. They're soppy.'

Jude laughed at her brother's comment. 'I've told you before, Wait and see.'

*

The wedding was quite well attended given the lack of family on both sides and Art not having very many friends. To Art's

225

surprise, Tony from the pub and his wife June were there with their baby daughter. He hadn't invited them as he was scared they'd refuse. Now he felt guilty and wished he had. Most of the teachers and staff from Vicarage Road school were there as well as a few of Art's ex-pupils with their parents. The footballers and the minor celebrities were only expected to attend the reception but a few, including Charlton's manager, had made it to the church.

The service went off as expected with Paul producing the ring when asked and then, after Art had kissed Jude, they went to the vestry to sign and witness the relevant documents. It was soon all completed and it was time for the photographs to be taken in the church grounds. As well as the photographer they had booked there was one from the local paper who asked for the details of the main participants so he could include them in the article he was directed to write by the editor. He also made sure he took photographs of the football players, the manager and the couple of minor local celebrities John had invited. But most of the interest was on the singer Dorothy Squires who lived in Old Bexley and knew John through her club work. She had separated from her second husband Roger Moore a few years earlier and was keen to have as much publicity as possible for her faltering career so an invite to a publicised wedding had proved very tempting. After the photos the cars took them along the road to the Conservative Club where the steward and his wife were waiting with trays of sweet sherry to greet the wedding party and their guests.

The meal went ahead and at the end it was time for the speeches. John made a short speech and Paul read out the cards and telegrams. The guests stayed on in the club after the meal and were joined by others who had been invited to the dance in the evening. John had paid for a free bar until nine o'clock so the guests made the most of it and soon everyone was very merry. Art and Jude had to start the dancing and, of course, danced to 'And I Love Her' their own Beatles song which they had told the emcee about earlier. Dorothy Squires feigned reluctance when asked to sing but did so to much applause. The dancing continued and when the evening refreshments were brought out Art and Jude slipped away to change out of their wedding finery.

When they returned there were even more people enjoying the dancing. Art was pleased to see that everything was running smoothly as he had been a little concerned that some of John's employees who had been invited might cause trouble if they drank too much at the free bar. But Mike was there to keep an eye on them so all was well. He had stayed in the background throughout the wedding almost as if it was none of his business. At ten o'clock the emcee called for silence and announced it was time to say goodbye to the newly-weds as they were leaving for their honeymoon. The usual ribald comments followed the announcement and then everyone trooped outside to see Art and Jude on their way. Naturally, Paul had tied various cans to the bumper of the car below the just married sign he had made. The car clanged off to cheers and Jude relaxed into Art's arms and they headed to the house in Welling for their first night together as man and wife. They were leaving for their honeymoon to Corfu the next day. Art carried Jude over the threshold and put her down on the sofa.

'Welcome to your home Mrs James.'

Jude stood up and kissed him. 'Now we can spend our whole life together as a married couple. It already makes me feel old.'

'You'll never be old to me.' Art said. 'I love you so much I don't care what the years do to either of us. We'll make a very good couple.'

They kissed again and Art led his wife by the hand and up the stairs where they could make love for the first time without worrying if someone found out. As they undressed Art looked a little sad.

'What's the matter?' asked Jude.

'Nothing really. It's just that my mother would have loved to have been at the wedding. Now she'll never know we're married and never even meet you. It's such a shame.'

Jude kissed him and looked deeply into his eyes. 'I know it must be hard but it's your life and you must live it to the full. I'm sure that's what she would want.'

'You're right. That's exactly how she would have felt.'

They lay in bed with their heads together and felt totally relaxed and at one with each other. Art caressed Jude's arm and down her side until she shivered in expectation and put her hand on his chest making little circles with her fingertips as she traced a path down his stomach to his groin. He was more than ready for her and their lovemaking that night was the best they'd ever experienced and both fell asleep feeling complete.

Chapter 18

London, July 1965

Mike was in the club feeling fed up. After the wedding reception he'd evaluated his future as he realised that now he would definitely be sidelined with Art married to the boss's daughter. He had continued to build up his cash without raising suspicion because Art was totally focussed on the security business and John on the minicabs. So long as there was a regular stream of income going into the club's account he knew John would leave him to get on with it. He'd been busy building up contacts in the murky world of legal and illegal drugs and felt that in a couple of months he'd be able to go into that in a big way alone or possibly with a partner or two taken from the gang of heavies he controlled. Any guilt he had felt about cheating John had dissipated that day when he'd seen how happy the family had been at the reception. They'd virtually ignored him and he'd left early saying, as an excuse, that he wanted to check on the club. John had just grunted, 'Fine.'

So Mike was trying to work out the best way to make the break. He could just walk out but that would make John suspicious and he might delve a little deeper into the club accounts. That would lead to the sort of retribution he didn't want to think about. He knew John could still be a violent man if pushed too hard. What he didn't know was that John was seriously trying to work out how to disassociate himself from the protection racket without losing face in the eyes of the other gang leaders. One possibility for Mike would be to join forces with Stevens which would offer him a modicum of protection. That came with a great deal of risk as he wasn't sure how Stevens would react to any suggestions from the man he regarded as John's lieutenant. It could backfire badly. He eventually decided to keep his head down and wait for a month or two and see what transpired.

As it turned out he didn't have to wait for more than a week.

*

Art had been puzzled for some time that the money from the club didn't appear to add up properly. There seemed to be a discrepancy in the amount banked and the amount he'd expected to be collected from the local tradesmen. He didn't think that the club takings had changed much as a glance at the stock ordered and the salary slips were much the same as in the previous year. It could only mean one thing. That someone was hiving off cash before it was banked with the club takings. And that pointed to one man. Art knew John wouldn't be at all happy if Mike was implicated but he felt he had no option. His main worry was that John might see it as sour grapes on Art's behalf as there was no love lost between him and Mike. If John took Mike's side it would be very awkward. So Art decided to just leave the figures on John's desk and hope he came to the same conclusion without any prompting. This he did and then waited nervously to see what ensued.

*

John looked at the papers Art had left on his desk. He went through the figures three times before he sat back and thought about what he'd deduced. Cash was definitely missing. It had to be Mike and something had to be done swiftly. It upset him to think the man he'd trusted had betrayed him but knew he would have to be decisive or other employees could take it as a signal that he was a push-over and would also try to cheat him. On the other hand, he thought, this might turn out to be a good way of backing out of the protection business. He summoned Mike to his office.

Mike sat down and glanced at the papers on John's desk. Although they were facing away from him he could see the columns of figures and guessed that he'd been rumbled.

'What is it Boss?' he asked.

John looked at him with no expression on his face. 'I think you know. I'm very disappointed. Firstly of myself because I thought I'd judged your character correctly and secondly that you thought I wouldn't find out. Thanks to Art I have the full picture. Why did you do it? Are you that short of cash? You know I'd always help you if you were in debt or in trouble.'

'I'm not in any bother. I just wanted cash to finance a deal of my own. I was going to pay you back when it was all sorted out.'

'That's rubbish. You would have come to me if you had a good idea. What was your plan?'

'I had a good offer to buy a consignment of LSD. I could have made a bomb.'

'Drugs.' John looked aghast. 'You know my feelings on drugs. No wonder you never told me. I'd never finance anything like that.'

'I know. But I think that's the future.'

'Not for me. Now, I'll be generous. If you pay back what you owe by tomorrow I'll take no further action. But if you don't.....' John reached into his desk drawer and took out the service revolver he'd liberated from the army in the war. He just put it in front of him on the desk without saying another word.

Mike stared at it in surprise. He hadn't expected John to react like that. He stood up and turned to leave. As he reached the door John spoke to him again. 'After I've got my money back you're no longer welcome here and barred from the club. I have a good idea who you'll be working for next and hope you find him as amenable as me. I doubt it.'

Mike turned and said, 'Stevens is wanting part of the drugs game and knows there's good money to be made. You'll get your money but I'll take my men with me and you'll lose out on the protection cash. We'll work for Stevens in future.'

John smiled to himself. It was just what he'd hoped. Word would get round that Mike had been caught with his hand in the till and been dismissed. John would then spread the word that he was retiring from the protection business as he was making more than enough from his other enterprises. He would also put a word in the ear of his pet police inspector about Steven's intentions to enter the drug market. He hoped that would sort him out for good.

'The protection racket's had its day,' he said to Mike. 'It's old hat and will soon end. The police no longer turn a blind eye as much as they used to and the new breed of coppers are too straight to bribe.'

'I don't need or want your advice. You've gone soft since you took Art on. I'll show you how to make real money.'

With that Mike left the office and the club.

*

Mike was furious. He was annoyed with himself for getting caught and embarrassed now that others would know what he'd done. He hoped he could rely on his heavies to support him and with John losing interest in the protection game he could go to Stevens with a proposal to work with him and share the profits. Of course he'd have to pay John back at least some of the money he'd taken as it would be the end of him if he didn't. There was still some honour even in the crime business and he would be hung out to dry if he failed to pay his debt.

After paying John he would move on and try to make his fortune with the Lewisham mob. He didn't actually know Stevens attitude to drugs but guessed he'd be willing to become involved unlike John so he could use his contacts as a bargaining chip in negotiations. But he was determined that he would get even with John one day to pay him back for the humiliation he had suffered in the office. It would be good to also take that educated son-in-law down a peg or two at the same time. he'd have to think of how best to do that. But for now he had to focus on negotiations with Stevens.

*

John sent for Art and told him what had gone on with Mike. He explained about his ultimatum for the return of the cash and the fact that Mike was now sacked. Art asked about the future of the protection side of the business and John told him he was letting it go. Art was naturally delighted with this news as it had been a thorn in his side since he'd started working for John. The work he'd done building up the rest of the firm now seemed a lot more worthwhile now that the possibility of prosecution was lifted. That could have destroyed all the businesses if John, and possibly himself, had gone to prison.

John told Art that he was still a bit concerned about how Stevens would react but surmised that with the extra income he would gain that he'd probably leave John alone to follow his new legitimate path.

'I've some further news,' he told Art. 'A couple of local entrepreneurs in the entertainment business are interested in buying into the club and upgrading it by adding on a restaurant to make it a venue where we could hold dinner dances. It seems that those dances with a cabaret thrown in are becoming very popular in the West End and they think there would be a market for one locally. People would prefer not to catch a train up to town if they could experience the same level of food and entertainment on their doorstep. It would also mean not having to close the club down and stop any staff losing their jobs.'

'That's fantastic,' enthused Art. 'How much are they willing to invest and what percentage of the business would they want?'

'They're willing to pay for the whole upgrade for a fifty percent interest in the venture. Plus they have all the contacts for the acts we'd need for a quality cabaret including a dance band. I'll hold on to the freehold of the club itself.'

'Sounds like a good deal. I can't see how we'd lose. When and where are you seeing them again?'

'Here, tomorrow lunchtime. I'd like you to be present to check all the figures. I don't want to sign anything until we've checked all the details.'

*

Jude was at home. She had settled into married life in a state of constant joy. She loved looking after Art and keeping the house spotless. They rarely went out and had spent most of their time away from work in the garden which was shaded by a couple of Victoria plum trees. One of these had a tree house in its lower branches that Art had built with Paul who had helped with the fetching and carrying of the tools and materials. He loved spending time up the tree and had asked if he could spend the night up there. John had agreed but Marion wasn't too sure and was worried he might fall out of the tree in his sleep. He'd eventually spent a night there without mishap but, as it was light very early, he'd returned to the house and wakened Art and Jude at five in the morning. They weren't too pleased.

Jude was looking forward to harvesting the fruit and had been to the library to find out about jam making and preserving fruit. She cooked simple but tasty meals which Art devoured with obvious enjoyment. As she'd never had many close friends the fact that they rarely went out didn't bother her. An occasional trip to the pub and to her parents was the sum total of their social life. She'd never been happier. Now they had their own bedroom their sex life had blossomed and both derived great satisfaction from giving each other pleasure. She'd met the neighbours a couple of times but they were middle-aged and she found them a little too formal. She would have liked to invite a few people round for dinner but, apart from her brother, had very few visitors. They'd made no plans for a summer holiday as they'd only been back from their honeymoon a couple of months and Art was working hard for John. Jude had continued to work at the dentist's and went there each day in her little red car. Art was still using the car John had given him so they both had a measure of independence. He had suggested a trip to the coast or the Isle of Wight for a short break and Jude intended to ask the dentist when it would be convenient to take a few days off. August would be a good time as the weather was usually hot and there was little rain. She decided to talk to Art about it again when he got home from the security office.

After Art had cleared up after dinner they sat in the lounge drinking coffee. Jude decided it would be a good time to talk about a break if they could find time off from their work. Art was very pleased with her suggestion of a visit to the Isle of Wight as he'd never been there and had read good reports about how quaint it was. August was a problem for him as many of the guards were on holiday then because it was the school holidays and the rota was a nightmare to organise. September might be better but, of course, his mother's condition was always a factor in any plans they made.

'If Mum is okay then September would probably be better than August when all the kids are on holiday. I think the island is probably very busy and will quieten down when the schools go back. It will also be easier for me to organise the security rotas as all the men will be available.'

'Suits me,' replied Jude. 'September weather is often good and the sea will be warmer by then. Let's do a bit of investigating to find hotels and things to do. I noticed a book in the library about holidays in England. It might give us a few ideas. And I'm sure there will be a tourist board we could phone who might be able to send us some information. I'll call directory enquiries to see if they know the number.'

'Good plan. It'll be a sort of second honeymoon. Do we need to take our passports and change money to go to the island?' he joked.

Jude didn't fall for the bait. 'Don't be silly. You know full well it's part of England. Although having to go by boat will make it seem like a trip abroad.'

With the holiday plans in place they settled down to watch the news on the television. Later in the evening Art told Jude about her father's decision to sack Mike and renovate the club. She was delighted with the news as she'd always been a bit concerned about the way Mike organised his part of the business and thought it reflected badly on her family. Without his influence she hoped that Art and her dad would make a good living in an honest way. She might eventually make more friends if they were just another pair of businessman and not involved in any shady activities.

'We can do much better without Mike,' she said, 'He wasn't good for Dad. I hope it's the last we hear of him. He always frightened me.'

'Me too. I wouldn't want to cross him. It's good riddance as far as I'm concerned. The further he goes from this area the better.'

But Mike hadn't gone very far.

Chapter 19

London, September 1965

Mike had been to see Tony Stevens as soon as he could after paying back John some of the money he had salted away for his drug enterprise. Without the cash he had hoped to use to finance the venture himself he had to persuade Stevens to back him. Stevens had been fairly impressed with what he heard but wasn't going to tell Mike that. Not until he had worked out what it could mean to his bank balance. He had a few reservations about Mike's plan to sell drugs to the rising stars in the entertainment world. The first was that he had no contacts in the rarefied atmosphere of the burgeoning West End scene of dolly birds and pop stars. He knew there would probably be plenty of competition to make the stars and starlets part with their easily earned cash. Some of the people involved would be unscrupulous and wouldn't care who they crossed, even the police. Stevens thought it might be a step too far for his South London outfit. Mike had come across as plausible but had refused to give many details about how he would run the operation. He had, however, been crystal clear about the fact that he would need backing. This meant muscle as well as cash. He picked up the phone and summoned Mike to join him in his office at the back of one of his gambling dens.

When Mike appeared he offered him a drink from his cocktail cabinet. Mike chose scotch as he knew that was what his previous employer would have gone for. As he cradled his drink Tony Stevens looked at him over the rim of his glass.

'I've been considering your proposition,' he said. 'It seems to be workable if you can persuade me that we'll have the jump over any other suppliers and that you have a reliable source of pills at a reasonable price for us to deal in. Without such assurances it's dead in the water. I'm not in the habit of throwing money away.'

'Didn't ever think you were,' answered Mike. 'I can give you my word that there are no other firms with control of either the supply or distribution. We'll have a clear field to work in and it could only mean big money.'

'That's another thing. It's another cash business. How can we launder the money so's not to arouse the suspicion of the fuzz or the revenue?'

'That's were you come in. Hayes used to funnel cash through his club. I thought you might have a similar set-up.'

'I have some outlets for spare cash but not big enough to launder the amounts you've been talking about. That'll take more thought. How soon can you set up this operation and what cut do you want from me?'

'Tomorrow. And fifty-fifty.'

'Tomorrow's good. But I want sixty-forty in my favour or it's no go.'

Mike grinned. That was what he'd expected all along. 'Okay, it's a deal.'

They shook hands and Stevens opened a draw in his desk. From it he took a large wad of notes and handed them to Mike. 'Get started. Here's five grand. Buy as cheap as you can and we'll see how things go. I expect you to more than double that money in a week. And keep me fully informed of your progress.'

'Will do boss,' Mike replied as he stuffed the cash into his inside jacket pocket.

*

Jude and Art had a really relaxing break on the Isle of Wight. On the last night they had dinner in a quiet restaurant in Shanklin after a strenuous day's walking over Tennyson Down and back round to Freshwater Bay. At the end of the meal Jude smiled at Art.

'I think now would be a good time to tell you that you're going to be a father. I wasn't sure until just before the holiday but the doctor said there's no doubt about it.'

Art sat stunned and open-mouthed then jumped up from his chair and went round the table to put his arms round Jude. 'That's fabulous news. I can't wait to tell everyone. When's it due?'

'Not until the New Year. It seems that our honeymoon was when it happened. Probably the first time we didn't use any protection.'

'So,' said Art. 'It's a Greek baby. I suppose we'll have to find a suitable name from Greek mythology. Hang on. Why have you been walking all over this island in your condition?'

'I'm not ill. Just pregnant. It's still early days but I'll have to take more care with what I eat. I'm sure my mother will have lots of ideas. Some of them probably Victorian.'

'That wouldn't be too bad. Queen Victoria had nine children and all of them survived. Now we must celebrate. I doubt if this place does champagne so we'll have to make do with another bottle of wine.'

They giggled their way along the cliff path back to the hotel in Sandown where they were staying. The bar was still open so they had another drink before going up to bed. As they prepared for bed Art wondered if he should try and tell his mother the good news. He decided he would try but was almost sure it would be a waste of time as she hadn't even known that he was married. She still showed no sign of knowing who he was but he thought it would be the right thing to do.

On their return to London they shared the news with John. Marion and Paul. All were delighted and Paul insisted that they must have a boy as he didn't want to be the uncle to a girl.

*

John had completed his negotiations and the plans for the club were in place. Art had proved extremely helpful by going through the financial aspects with great care. He had pronounced the deal to be sound and virtually risk free as John retained the freehold of the property. The work was to start immediately and, as it would mean closing for a few weeks, the staff were given paid leave which made them very happy. They were all looking forward to working in a more upmarket environment and John had assured them that their jobs were safe so long as they continued to work hard and make the club a success.

The builders moved in before the end of the month and, after ripping out the interior, installed a new kitchen, modern toilets and a dance floor with a small stage for a band. The decorators were next and they papered and painted until the main room which was to double up as a restaurant and club room was bright and attractive in the current angular style. It had cleverly concealed lighting that could be dimmed and have the colours subtly changed to suit the mood of the event. John was very pleased and couldn't wait to show it off to Marion. He knew she had never liked the club and thought it too dark and unwelcoming. Now, he was sure, she would be pleased with the changes.

Extra personnel were required as chefs and waiting staff to meet the demands on the restaurant. John advertised in the local press and soon had a team in place which was a mixture of youth and experience. He wondered who he should invite to the opening and contacted his partners to ask their advice. It turned out that they knew many local dignitaries from the council and the more important businessmen. John wondered if this was through their membership of the Masonic Lodge which he knew met regularly in Woolwich Polytechnic. He had never been approached to join and thought that, if he was, then it might be the final seal of approval on his position in the neighbourhood. However, he also was aware that any member could deny him membership under their secret voting system. If not him then Art might make a suitable candidate. After all, he was well respected in the community and was of a good character.

The guest list was finalised and the big day soon came. Most of the people invited had replied confirming their attendance and the evening was to be a dinner dance with a cabaret consisting of a singer, a juggler and a comedian. A dance band had been booked although the partners hoped to have their own resident band before too long. The bars were fully stocked and the kitchen staff had been working since early morning to prepare the three course meal. Marion and Jude arrived together to be greeted by their husbands and were suitably impressed with how the club now looked.

'We could be in town,' commented Marion. 'Or in Paris, although I've never been there I'm sure it's not as nice as this.'

Jude laughed. 'Neither have I but I know what you mean. It really is great Dad. I've no hesitation in coming here – it's not like it used to be.'

John and Art ushered them to a table near the front and waved to one of the waiters to bring them a drink. Naturally it was champagne and the two women sat down. John and Art had to leave them for a while to join their business partners welcoming the couples who were now arriving and show them to their seats. Before long the club was full and the band, who had been quietly playing some background music, suddenly upped the volume and John took to the stage to welcome everyone and hope they'd all enjoy the evening. He then left the proceedings under the professional care of the emcee and went to join Marion and Jude. Art was already there so they clinked glasses and sat back in eager anticipation.

The whole evening was a resounding success and John's business partners were delighted. Although it had made a loss because all the guests were invited to come free of charge they thought that it boded well for the future. A few more nights like this, they reckoned, and we'll be sitting on a goldmine. They'd also invited reporters from the local and national papers who had been plied with drinks and all praised the food and the entertainment. The dancing had continued until late and when only the staff and owners were left then the clearing up began. Art and John helped out while Marion and Jude made some coffee. At last all was ready for another night and it was time to head off home.

As they left the club John turned to Art and said, 'Well, that's been some night. I hope that we can attract some paying customers from now on. We'll have to sort out future acts and menus to keep people interested. What do you think?'

'I think it's worked out very well. I'm sure we can make a real go of it. The staff all seem very happy and worked hard. I think it might be a good idea to give them some sort of bonus scheme to keep them loyal.'

'I agree. I'll sort something out in the next few days.'

Art and Jude set off in their car looking forward to a bright future.

Chapter 20

London, December 1965

Mike wasn't happy. He'd hoped that Stevens would regard him as an equal but realised that he was just another of the underdogs on the payroll. His grand scheme to supply drugs to the rich and famous hadn't worked out as well as he'd hoped and he was now back organising the protection side of Steven's business just as he'd done for John Hayes. The police seemed to have got wind of all his plans in advance and he'd been lucky to escape being arrested for supplying drugs. His prospects were now no better and probably worse than before. He blamed Art for his current problems as he was pretty sure he was the one who'd told John about the missing cash. He was also annoyed that the club was now a very popular venue and rumoured to be making a packet and the other arms to John's empire were also thriving. He knew now that John had been right and the protection business was not going to last long and wondered what would happen to him if Stevens no longer required his services. His annoyance was slowly turning to anger and he was considering ways to get back at Art and John by harming one of their business interests. He remembered the raids he and John had organised on Stevens' gambling dens and thought that John's club would be the obvious choice of target as it was the most public and any adverse publicity to its reputation would seriously harm its future. The security firm was too much of a risk because of the trained guards and the minicab office was now too well protected. But how best to target the club?

A couple of the heavies he'd taken with him to the Stevens' firm would probably support him as they were also unhappy with how things had gone. He would have to pick a time to act which would cause the greatest damage, make the headlines and really hurt John's precious club. And to take Art down a peg would make it even more enjoyable. With Christmas on its way he hoped for a suitable opportunity.

*

Jude's baby bump was now very obvious but she continued to work despite Art fretting about it and worrying that she might harm herself or the baby. She was looking forward to their first Christmas together in their own house and had already invited her parents and Paul round for Christmas dinner. It was fun planning the menu and working out what they would need for the day and she had made long lists of what needed to be bought and what had to be done on Christmas Eve as well as on the big day itself. She'd decided to give up work after the festivities and had told her employer that he'd have to find someone else to do her job in the New Year as she had no real plans to return to work after giving birth. Art was vaguely involved in the planning but was still working long hours at the security office. He knew his Christmas would be severely disrupted by the commitments they had with the many businesses and factories that relied on twenty-four hour security. Christmas wouldn't mean much of a break for him and he hoped that no problems would crop up to prevent him being at home, at least for the meal.

John and Marion were also excited about Christmas. They were really looking forward to going to Jude and Art's for the day and had bought loads of presents to take with them. John had decided to close the club after a party night on Christmas Eve. It would open again for Boxing Day lunchtime and then continue as normal until New Year's Eve when a gala night with top class entertainment had been arranged to see in 1966. All the tickets had been sold already so he knew it was going to be a very profitable evening. They would all be going including Paul who wanted desperately to see the magician who'd been booked and he'd seen on television. Marion thought it might be Jude's last outing before the baby came so hoped she was fit enough to join them. It would be a great family evening to welcome in a New Year full of promise.

A week before Christmas and all was prepared in Jude and Art's house. The decorations, with Paul's help, were all up and the tree stood in pride of place in the corner of the living room. Art had managed a quick trip to Liverpool to spend a couple of hours with his mother but, as usual, she was unresponsive. The nursing home had called out the doctor to her just before Art had arrived and the matron told him the news wasn't good and that she could pass away very soon. It was sad but Art had been expecting it since the summer and knew it would be a kind release for his mother. Such a pity that she'd never known Jude. He'd left strict instructions to call him day or night if there was any news and returned to London with mixed feelings. Jude and the upcoming baby had to be his main concern now.

Christmas Day was a great success with far too much food and drink. John had brought a bottle of champagne and Marion had supplied home made mince pies and a huge Christmas pudding. The turkey was cooked to perfection by Jude and after demolishing large portions of meat and vegetables followed by the Christmas pudding the five of them sat with groaning stomachs on the three piece suite. They dozed and tried to watch Dixon of Dock Green followed by the Queen's Christmas Message and then Billy Smart's Circus. Paul was pleased that Dr. Who was on later and Marion said she was looking forward to watching the Ken Dodd Show which was on in the evening as his silly antics always made her laugh.

'I think we'll all need to go for a walk tomorrow,' commented Art. 'The fresh air will do us good. We'll make our way to your house in the morning and then we could walk up through to the woods to the top of Shooters Hill. I don't think the café will be open though.'

'Don't worry about that,' John said, 'the pub will be.'

True to their word Art and Jude drove to John and Marion's house in time for morning coffee and another few mince pies. They then all put on their warm coats and hats and set off through the side streets up the hill to the top. They crossed the main road and took the lane down to the café at the top of

Oxleas Meadow. It was a clear day and they were rewarded with spectacular views across south London to the North Downs. As Art had guessed, the café was closed for the holiday so they continued their walk through the ancient woodland and then round the perimeter if the meadow back to the top. Paul wanted to see Severndroog Castle so they strolled through some gardens until they reached the tall triangular building with a tower at each corner. Paul ran about fighting off imaginary foes while the adults sat on a handy bench to admire the structure.

'What was it built for?' asked Jude.

'No idea,' her father replied. 'Art, do you know?'

'Sorry, I don't know its history but I'll try and find out in the library sometime in the New Year.'

Marion smiled. 'Thinking of the New Year we were wondering if you're still going to be able to come to the gala dinner and dance at the club on New Year's Eve?'

'Wouldn't miss it,' replied Jude cradling her ever-growing bump. 'It'll probably be my last evening out for a while. And how good it will be to spend it with my family.'

'That's definite then,' Marion said. 'It should be a spectacular evening with a dinner, cabaret and dancing. Loads of well-to-do business people will be there. It'll be a great advertisement for the club. Even the local press are coming to take pictures for a special feature.'

Paul joined them after dispatching all the evildoers and perched on the bench's armrest next to his father. 'I've never been to a dance before unless you count Jude's wedding. Will I have to join in?'

'Of course,' replied John. 'I'm sure there'll be lots of very pretty young girls just waiting for you to ask them.'

'Oh. Do I have to?'

'It'd be very rude not to,' added Jude. 'I'm sure I can teach you a few steps this week so you can be the belle of the ball.'

'Ding, dong,' Art laughed.

'It's not funny,' Paul grumbled. 'I'm not so sure I want to come now.'

'Stop teasing the boy,' Marion chided. 'It's okay Paul. You can be my partner as you were at the wedding. John will be too busy talking business with the guests to bother dancing.'

They all stood up and made their way back to the road and then back down the hill towards Plumstead Common. Once at the house Art drove Jude back to Welling and then went to the security office to make sure everything was running smoothly. He'd had no phone calls so he knew it had been a quiet Christmas for the guards with no serious incidents. It had meant that he had been able to enjoy a couple of days without having to be on site. The supervisor was there when Art arrived and assured him that everything was in order and all the guards had turned up on time for their shifts. He added that the double time Art had paid them for working over Christmas had been instrumental in ensuring that all the sites were fully covered. Art drove out to a couple of the nearest sites to check for himself and to show the guards that they weren't the only ones working during the holiday. His visits were well received and he was pleased that all his hard work seemed to be paying off with an efficient and responsible set of men. The mobile patrols which utilised dogs as protection were unable to contact the office from their vans and had to rely on public phone boxes to keep in contact. This was a problem Art had been unable to solve although he had heard about short waveband radios being used in America he knew they were illegal in Britain. Meanwhile they would just have to rely on landlines and the mobile supervisor. He hoped that some of his more established clients would allow him to put a phone in a secure box on the outside of their premises so the guards could call in directly to the office or the client if there was a problem. That was something else to consider in the New Year.

*

Mike was sitting at home after a lonely Christmas in his small terraced house near Plumstead Station wondering if his plan to damage the reputation of John's club would work. The idea was to wait until just before midnight on New Year's Eve and then storm the club with his team of heavies and smash the place up. He had managed to procure a pistol which he intended to fire in the air to frighten into submission any guests who might be brave enough to try and stop the attack. The others with him would wield their customary baseball bats and jemmies. He had done some research and knew the event was to be attended by the press so, because of the photographers there, his gang would all wear masks as well as gloves. He was certain that John would probably have an idea who they were but it would be better not to leave any definite proof. He'd told the team not to speak to or physically assault any of the party-goers but just to damage the furniture and fittings and cause as much panic as possible. The reputation of the club as a respectable venue would be irretrievably damaged by the reports in the newspapers. This thought made him feel extremely happy. He would have the last laugh over John and Art.

Chapter 21

London, New Year's Eve 1965

The dinner-dance at the club was well under way and all the guests were thoroughly enjoying the evening. The bar, which had been well stocked with a wide variety of drinks and a good supply of champagne, was very busy. Olive, the barmaid, was rushed off her feet but happy to still be employed by John as they'd worked together for many years. She felt she was almost part of the family and looked fondly over to where they were sitting at a table near the stage. What a beautiful girl John's daughter is she thought to herself.

Everyone had enjoyed the meal that had been served earlier and each table had been given a complimentary bottle of wine. To start the meal John had employed a Scottish Piper and he had ceremoniously piped in a haggis to the amusement of most of the diners and the bemusement of a few. They were given the opportunity to try the delicacy but most declined as they preferred the sirloin steaks on offer.

Marion and John sat back after eating and John raised a glass.

'A toast to tonight's success,' he called as he looked at his family and they all raised their glasses.

'And to Jude's upcoming event,' added Marion. 'It won't be long now.'

'The sooner the better,' said Jude with obvious feeling. 'I can't wait to get back to my normal size and do the things I used to.'

'And you can look forward to a lack of sleep,' John laughed. 'I remember the problems we had with you. I didn't sleep for months.'

'What about me? I was the one who had to get up. You just turned over and put the pillow over your head,' Marion grumbled. 'I hope Art's more considerate.'

'I don't remember you complaining at the time. Anyway, Paul wasn't any trouble at all. He slept through most nights.'

'He's still just as dozy,' laughed Jude and nudged her brother in the ribs.

'I'm not dozy,' he exclaimed heatedly. 'It's just that my large brain needs a good rest each night. That's right isn't it Art?'

'I'm not getting involved,' Art diplomatically replied. 'We'll just have to wait and see what sort of baby we have. So long as it's fit and well I don't care how much noise it makes.'

'I'll hold you to that,' smiled Jude.

All the tables had been cleared and the cabaret was about to start. Chairs were moved around so everyone had a good view of the stage. The emcee picked up the microphone and, after giving it the customary two taps and saying, 'one-two, one-two,' announced the first act. It was a female singer who looked a little like Doris Day. She was obviously aware of the similarity as she started her act with a rendition of "Move Over Darling" a very popular song from the movie of the same name. This went down very well and she followed it with a medley of more recent hits by other female singers. When her fifteen minutes were up she left the stage to great applause and the emcee returned to announce the next act.

'Ladies and gentlemen. We are now very fortunate to have the world famous magician Ali Bongo who appeared on TV recently in The Good Old Days.'

Ali bounced onto the stage wearing his trademark sheik's outfit and proceeded to bamboozle the audience with a range of tricks. They all laughed at his catchphrase 'Hocus Pocus Fishbones Chokus' which he used instead of the more traditional abracadabra. Paul was mesmerised and his eyes never left the mad magician. Even so he was unable to work out how he did the magic.

He was followed by a comedian who hadn't really researched his audience and pitched his jokes a little too blue for the more refined folk present. He must have thought it was the usual working men's club that he normally performed at on the comedy circuit. There were few laughs and he left the stage to a polite ripple of applause. Marion looked at John and said, 'I hope Paul didn't understand those jokes.'

John replied, 'It doesn't matter if he did or he didn't. If he did then he knows more than he should for his age and if he didn't then it will all have gone over his head.'

'I know. Boys grow up so quickly these days.'

'Not as quick as I did on Woolwich market,' joked John. 'I heard a lot worse I can tell you.'

'I'm sure you did but it's nothing to be proud of.'

The next act was another singer. This time a man with slicked back hair who accompanied himself on the club's upright piano. He was a good tenor and a competent pianist so the people settled back in their seats to enjoy the performance. He had only just started his second song when there was noise of a commotion just inside the door. The singer stopped mid-song and all heads turned to see what was happening. The fracas spilled out into the room and the guests were horrified to see four masked men burst in waving weapons. The leader was brandishing a gun above his head and fired a shot up to the ceiling and people dived under the tables in panic. One man who stood up was swiftly dealt a blow to the head from a baseball bat and fell unconscious to the floor with his wife screaming beside him as she cradled his inert body. Two of the men went to the bar and started smashing all the bottles and glasses. The barmaid Olive just stood her ground and stared at them as if defying them to do their worst.

The apparent leader was still waving his gun in a threatening manner as he walked towards the stage. As he turned back to the cowering guests he caught his foot on the snaking microphone lead and stumbled forward. The gun went off as he fell forwards and more people screamed in terror. This bullet didn't go harmlessly towards the ceiling but went straight towards where John and his family were sitting. Marion screamed and Jude slumped forward. Time seemed to stand still and the room went eerily silent. John stood and rushed towards the gunman but he was too late as the man had realised what he'd done and raced to the door followed by his associates. The screaming having stopped it was replaced by a quiet sobbing as couples comforted each other. Art held Jude but noticed blood spreading rapidly across her stomach. He realised she had been hit and tried to find the wound. Marion joined him and tried her best to staunch the bleeding coming from Jude's stomach but it was too difficult. John stood in anger at the scene clenching and unclenching his fists. For probably the first time in his life he didn't know what to do. This was beyond his worst nightmare. One of the doormen who had tried to stop the gang entering the club had recovered from the blows he'd received and already phoned the police. Now he phoned again, this time for an ambulance.

One man came running forward to see how Jude was. He was a doctor and tried his best to help Marion tend to her daughter. When he realised Jude was in serious danger but was heavily pregnant he wondered if the baby could be saved. On a closer inspection he realised that any procedure would have to be performed in hospital as the bullet had passed right through Jude's abdomen causing severe bleeding and probably serious damage to many organs, possibly including her womb. The ambulance men arrived and, after more attempts to stop the bleeding and revive her, put Jude on a stretcher. The doctor accompanied the family to the waiting vehicle and they clambered aboard and sped off to the hospital. Marion held Jude's hand and John just sat and stared as if he didn't understand what had happened,

At the hospital they tried again to revive Jude but to no avail. She was declared dead on arrival. The family sat in a waiting area while the doctors attempted to save the baby but it was too late to do anything. It was the unfortunate duty of the registrar to go and inform the family of the tragic news. This they received in total disbelief until Marion threw herself at John and pounded his chest with her fists. She yelled at him that it was all his fault for running the club that had caused the death of her precious daughter and now the baby as well. John didn't try to defend himself in any way but waited for her anger to subside into weeping and put his arms round her protectively. Paul sat crying into his hands. Art was still stunned. He was numb and had no idea how to come to terms with events. He couldn't cry or feel any emotion. It was all too much. His only thought was that his life had ended as well.

The police arrived at the hospital a few minutes later to try and find out what had happened. When they found out Jude had been fatally injured they immediately realised they were now heading a murder enquiry. A swift call was put through to CID as they would have to take over the case. The sergeant commiserated with the family but was unable to interview them until the detectives arrived. He did, however, put a call through to his colleagues at the club telling them to secure the scene and take down the names and addresses of all the guests, employees and performers. He hoped that not too many had already left and that nobody had started to clear up the mess as the whole club would have to be meticulously examined by the forensic team.

When the detective inspector arrived at the hospital he'd already been given an outline of what had happened at the club. He realised it would be a waste of time to try and interview the distraught family straight away so called for a car to take them home telling them he would be round to talk to them the next morning. Art went with John, Marion and Paul back to their house. Only John spoke to tell the driver their address and then they sat in total silence until they reached their destination. John was wanting to do something to take his mind off the evening's events. He thought he might return to the club to see what was happening there but realised that Marion and Paul needed him at home for the night. He found he couldn't even look at Art and had no idea how he could comfort him.

*

Was Marion right? Had he been the cause of the night's events? John's head was in a whirl as he tried to find an answer to that question. He was almost sure the raid had been organised by Tony Stevens but had no proof. In all the mayhem he'd been unable to recognise any of the gang so hoped the police would be able to find evidence that would bring them to justice. Jude had been the light of his life and he knew that nobody could ever replace her in his heart. He felt very sad for Art but he was young and might be able to recover over time. The loss of the baby was heart-rending for all of the family but Marion in particular had taken it very badly. He wondered how it would affect Paul.

Anger and revenge were the next things to enter his conscious thoughts. If the police were unable to find the murderer he would have to take things into his own hands even if it meant him going to prison or even suffering the ultimate penalty. Capital punishment was still on the statute book although it had recently been suspended. He was unsure as to how Art would react but felt it would probably be for the best if he didn't involve him in anything he decided to do.

Chapter 22

London (Bexleyheath), July 2017

Ellen's trip to London had gone smoothly and she was now outside the library in Bexleyheath where she hoped to unravel her father's story. Worried that she might need assistance looking through the newspaper archives she'd phoned the library from Liverpool and was pleased to hear that there would be someone willing to help her.

She pushed open the door and went to the large desk. A librarian was seated behind the desk and who looked up as she approached.

'Good afternoon. How can I help you?' the pleasant looking young man asked.

'Yes, I hope so. I'm from Liverpool and I've phoned you a number of times regarding my father's time in London.'

'Oh yes, you must be Ellen Owens. We told you we managed to find someone to help. She's Mrs White and is a volunteer here at the library and an amateur historian. She was living in the area in the sixties and knows a great deal about events at that time. She's having a cup of tea in the staffroom so I'll just go and give her a call.' He stood and went through a door behind him.

He soon returned with a grey haired lady who looked to be of a similar vintage to Ellen's father. She smiled at Ellen and came round the desk to shake her hand.

'I hope I can help you,' she said quietly. 'I've only been told that your father was called Jack or Art James and lived in Plumstead in the early 1960s. You think he married a local girl sometime around 1964 or '65. I've had a trawl though the microfiche and think I've found the report on the wedding. Would you like to come and see?'

'Yes please,' replied Ellen and followed the lady to a small room where the microfiche machine was housed. They sat next to each other on two stools and Mrs White turned the machine on and scrolled through the pages until she stopped at the edition for a week in May 1965. The headline on one of the inside pages read, 'Large Turnout for Plumstead Wedding of the Year' and the text underneath a photo of the bride and groom gave the details.

Ellen looked open-mouthed at the picture. It was clearly a much younger version of her father standing next to an extremely pretty bride who, despite the picture being in black and white, was clearly a blond. The text gave the details of the bride and groom telling readers that the groom was Art James, a primary school teacher and the bride Judith Hayes, a dental assistant. The was more about the bride's family mentioning that her father was a well known businessman and that, unusually, the best man had been the bride's younger brother. Photographs and a list of the more prominent guests followed with many references to the football team, Charlton Athletic and Dorothy Squires, the famous singer. More photos of the guests at the reception completed the page.

'Wow,' was all Ellen could say initially. She recovered her composure and continued. 'We never knew anything about this. It's a lot to take in. However I do remember Dad following the fortunes of Charlton when the results came in on a Saturday.'

Mrs White added, 'I remember the wedding. I was a teenager at the time so weddings always fascinated me. It really was a big occasion although I remember my mother telling me that Judith's family were involved with some very dodgy businesses.'

'Like what?'

'Well, apparently, the father ran a number of shady concerns and was probably a bit of a gangster running a protection racket in the neighbourhood. He wasn't well liked by many people but had a number of influential friends. The girl and her brother however were really sweet. Actually, you look a bit like an older version of her.'

Ellen smiled, 'Thank you for that.' She paused for a moment. 'Was my father a bigamist then.' she blurted out. 'He married my mother in 1968 in Liverpool and nobody knew he had another wife.'

'He wasn't a bigamist,' Mrs White explained, 'Please prepare yourself for another shock. I've got another newspaper from the start of the next year that will explain all.'

She fast forwarded the machine to stop on the first edition of 1966.

Ellen looked in horror at the headline, this time on the front page of the newspaper. It read, 'Shooting in local club. Pregnant mum killed.'

'Was that Judith?'

'Yes, I'm afraid it was. Both her and the baby died that night. It was a big story for weeks.'

Ellen read the article all the way through. 'Did they catch the gunman?' she asked.

'No,' came the reply. 'He was never caught. I presume your father returned to Liverpool soon after that to start his life over again.'

'Yes he did. But we were told he returned to look after his mother who was suffering from dementia. We knew nothing about the events here.'

'Probably just as well. I'm sure your father just wanted to put it behind him. It was very sad.'

'What happened to the rest of her family?'

'I'm not sure. The parents will be dead by now. The son, Paul, was only just a teenager so he's possibly still alive. I do remember a fairly large security company locally which went under the name of Hayes and I think it's still going but I've no idea if the son has anything to do with it. You'd have to look it up to find out.'

'Not yet. I'm still trying to get my head round all this. Can you print out the pages from the microfiche so I can take them back home to show my sister?'

'No problem. I'm not sure how it's done so I'll ask the lad on the desk to do it for you. It shouldn't take long. I hope all of this hasn't been too much of a surprise. Would you like a cup of tea while you're waiting?'

'Yes please. That would be great. Thank you so much for all you've done.'

'It was a pleasure. Although the answers to your questions might not have been what you expected. Come with me and we'll sit in the staffroom.'

After drinking her tea Mrs White went to fetch the copies that had been made from the two newspapers. Ellen checked the pages to ensure they were what she wanted to show Louise back home. She folded them and put them in her bag and turned to Mrs White. 'Thank you once again. I doubt if I'd been able to find this without your help. One further question if I may?'

'Go ahead.'

'Do you know anything about Vicarage Road Junior School. I couldn't find it on google.'

'I knew it. It was just down from Plumstead Common. I used to live nearby. When they made it a primary school by combining the infants and juniors they changed the name to North Rise School. They demolished the old building in the seventies when the whole area was converted to high rise flats. It was such a waste. All those Victorian terraced houses were flattened. The could have spent the money renovating them but I'm afraid that large blocks of flats were seen as the way forward at that time. Now they're demolishing those ugly towers and, guess what, they're building houses again.'

'According to my grandmother's address book my father lived in a house in Pattison Road. Do you know it?'

'It's gone as well. In fact the whole road no longer exists. Where the houses once stood is now a bit of a dump. It was supposed to be a green and pleasant area for the children to play but it was never used. It was too difficult for parents on the twenty-something floor to keep an eye on their little ones so it soon fell into disrepair and has been neglected ever since. Apart from a the usual druggies and gangs of feral youths of course.'

'Oh well, I thought it might be nice to go and see where he lived. We never discovered any other address for him in London. So we've no idea where he lived with Judith when they married.'

'I doubt it would have been in Pattison Road. Most of those houses didn't even have bathrooms. Don't forget Judith came from a well-to-do family. Her parents wouldn't have let them live there. I think your only chance of finding out more is to try and find the son.'

'I think I'll go back and discuss what I've found with my sister. She mightn't want to take it further. We've had enough to think of recently.'

Ellen left the library and, after thanking the young man on the desk and paying for the photocopies, went along the road towards the railway station to catch the next train back to London and then on to Liverpool.

Once on the train from Euston she phoned her sister Louise and gave her a rough outline of her findings. She didn't go into too much detail as she wanted her to see the newspaper reports for herself. Then they could decide what, if anything, to do next. Ellen was keen to continue investigating her father's past but wasn't too sure how enthusiastic Louise would be. She didn't want to upset her by acting on her own and digging up things her sister might prefer to stay buried. An attendant came round with a trolley and Ellen bought a coffee and a slab of fruitcake to keep her going during the remaining two hours of the journey.

Ellen went home from Lime Street by bus and found her sister waiting in her car outside. Louise had decided that she wanted to see the cuttings as soon as possible so that the whole story could be pieced together. Ellen took her into the sitting room and gave her the first report about the wedding. Louise looked closely at the photos and then read the text.

'It's unbelievable,' she whispered. 'It's obviously Dad in the pictures but they call him Art. Why is that?'

'I think it's because his middle name was Arthur so he shortened it to Art. I've no idea why. He might have thought it was more interesting than plain old Jack. What do you think of the bride? She looks very attractive. The elderly lady in the library said I looked a bit like her.'

'Actually you do. It's strange to see Dad when he was young. The only other photos we have of him were taken in Liverpool before he went to college. The wedding seems to have been quite an occasion. To have a full page in a newspaper, even in a local rag, must have meant it was newsworthy.'

'Possibly because of what I heard about the bride's father. I'll tell you that after you've looked at the second cutting.'

Ellen handed over the report about the shooting to Louise who, as before, scrutinised it carefully before laying it down on the coffee table. She rubbed her eyes.

At last she spoke. 'That's incredible. And so sad. To think they were married for less than a year and then Dad lost his wife and unborn child in one go. He must have been devastated. No wonder he returned to Liverpool. I wonder how Judith's family took it? They must have been distraught. From the paper cuttings I'd guess that she was their only daughter.'

'I know. It must have been a terrible time. Her father owned the club where the shooting took place and the newspaper speculates that it might be connected to local gang wars. From what I was told he might have been involved in criminal activity as well as some legitimate businesses. Do you think we should try to contact the son, Paul?'

To Ellen's surprise Louse agreed. 'Yes. I think we owe it to Dad to find out the whole story. Also it's our own family history and our children should know as much as possible about their grandfather. If you can contact him, assuming he's still alive, he might be willing to answer our questions although from the wedding pictures he only looked about twelve or thirteen at the time.'

Ellen went to fetch her laptop and put in a search for Hayes Security. Among the results was a security firm of that name based in London. She accessed the website of the company and a professionally produced home page filled the screen. It had a picture of an office block with a number of vans parked outside. On the building was a large sign which read "Hayes and Son Security". Ellen scrolled down and found a message from the owner of the company.

'Look,' she said to Louise. 'The name is Paul Hayes. He must have taken over the business from his father. Obviously he would almost certainly no longer be alive as he must have been at least forty when Dad was married fifty-two years ago. Now we've found the brother-in-law what should we do next?'

Louise pondered the question for a moment. 'I think we should contact him and try to explain our interest in his family. He might just ignore us but I think it's worth a try. Is there an email address there?'

Ellen found the contacts section. 'Yes, there's an address. I'll copy it down and then we can try and compose a message that will hopefully spark his interest without frightening him off.'

They sat for over an hour deliberating about the best wording for the email. At last they were satisfied and Ellen read it through aloud.

'Hi Paul,

Please excuse us contacting you through your company but we have no other address for you.

You have no idea who we are and this email will probably come as a shock to you as it concerns events from over fifty years ago. To put it bluntly our father was Jack James. If you are who we think you are you probably knew him as Art and he taught at Vicarage Road School in the 1960s.

We're sorry to say he died this year and we only found out about his time in London by going through his papers after the funeral. After looking on Facebook and a visit to Bexleyheath library we found out about his marriage to Judith, your sister, and the tragic events that followed. He never ever spoke of these events to us or, as far as we know, to our mother who is also deceased. It was a part of his life he obviously wanted to be kept secret for some reason.

If you are not too upset by us contacting you then we'd be very grateful for any information about Dad that you feel willing to share with us. We know it might rake up some memories you'd prefer to forget but we think that both us and our children deserve to know about our father, their grandfather. We hope you can help.

Best wishes,

Louise and Ellen'

Ellen looked at Louise. 'If you're happy then I'll press send.'
'Go ahead. We can't lose anything by it.'
Ellen sent off the email.

Chapter 23

London, January 1966

Jude was cremated at Falconwood Crematorium with the minimum of fuss. Only family and very close friends attended. There was no press presence at the event. The short service was fairly impersonal although Art had insisted that their personal song 'And I Love Her' was played as the coffin slid towards the furnace. After the funeral the mourners went back to John's house for a few drinks but soon dispersed leaving John and Marion, Paul and Art to their own private grief.

'What do we do now?' asked Art.

'Nothing,' replied John. 'We have to wait and see what the police manage to find out about the raid although I don't hold out and great hopes as they found no fingerprints and none of the guests could identify them.'

'But it must have been Stevens who ordered it,' Art said.

'Possibly but I doubt it,' answered John. 'It's not the sort of thing he'd do as there's no money in it for him. This seems more personal. Meanwhile we have businesses to run. Art, could you go to the club tomorrow and see how it's doing? It will take a lot to restore the public's confidence after the shooting. My partners are worried we'll have to close.'

'Sure, it'll give me something to do. The security side is running smoothly without too much input from me.'

'That's good. So's the taxi business. Paul, you're now back at school. Is everything okay there?'

Paul looked up from the book he was reading. 'Yes Dad. Everyone's been kind and it's already ancient history.' He suddenly burst into tears. Through his sobs he said,' But I miss Jude. I can't believe I'll never see her again. I loved her so much.' He jumped up from the chair and ran upstairs to his room where they could still hear him crying even though the door was shut.

'Should I go to him?' asked Marion.

'No,' said John. ' Let him work out his grief in private. He'll come to you when he needs to.'

Art was wondering what he should do. He didn't really want to return to his own cold empty house but didn't want to impose on the family that had welcomed him into their midst. He needed to clarify his thoughts and decide what could be done to salvage his life. What he did know was that he wanted revenge on whoever had wrecked his life. He hoped the police would find and prosecute the gang members but as each day went by this seemed more and more unlikely. At last he stood and, without a word, left them and drove home to Welling.

*

Mike sat on his threadbare sofa nursing a glass of bottled beer. It had been three weeks since the raid on the club and he'd kept well out of the way. He knew that no one could have recognised him, or was unwilling to do so, because the police hadn't been round. He'd heard from one of his cronies that the trail was cold although Tony Stevens had voiced his opinion that Mike might have been involved. But there was no proof.

He knew the funeral had taken place and had even toyed with the idea of attending but decided that would be a risk too far. Best to just stay in the background for a few more weeks and then take up his life again as if nothing had happened. There was always the possibility that one of the gang who'd been with him that night would tell someone but thought that unlikely as they would also face a long prison sentence if caught. He had now convinced himself that he had got away with it.

At the back of his mind, where a small piece of conscience still lurked he was sorry for the girl's death. He hadn't intended it to happen. He'd just gone there to discredit John and ruin the club's reputation. It would have been justice, as he saw it, for the way John and that jumped up teacher Art had treated him after all the years of faithful service he had given them. His time in the army had desensitised him to violent death but that had been against men and not defenceless women. But, he reasoned, there was nothing he could do to make it better so it was best forgotten. Tomorrow he would venture out to the shops to stock up on the essentials. Bread and beer being the most important items on his shopping list.

*

Art rose when daylight came after yet another fitful night's sleep. He washed and dressed and, after a hasty cup of coffee and a biscuit for breakfast, he went out to the car to drive to the club as John had requested. He knew John had asked him to go because John couldn't face going there himself after the terrible tragedy. It was a cold morning and Art had to scrape ice from the windscreen but it was sunny and this made the world appear a little brighter. The car started first time and he set off towards Eltham. Parking near the club he got out and stood for a moment looking down the street towards it. All was quiet and deserted. It seemed impossible that only a few weeks ago it had been the scene of such chaos with police cars and an ambulance filling the road. Shaking off the thought he walked to the door and knocked. The club manager opened the door and let him in. At that time of day it was empty of punters but some of the staff were there preparing for the lunchtime session. Art nodded to those he saw and made his way with the manager to the office. He sat down in the chair usual occupied by his father-in-law and asked the manager to bring him the accounts books to see how the club was faring. When he had the books he asked him to send him up a coffee then to carry on with his own work. Art settled down to inspect the figures and work out how much the takings had been affected since New Year's Day.

After about ten minutes there was a knock on the door. He told whoever it was to enter and the barmaid Olive came in with a mug of coffee. She placed it on the desk and turned to

278

go but hesitated and turned back to face Art. He could see she was wondering if she should speak to him.

'What is it?' he asked gently.

'I'm so sorry,' she blurted out. 'I loved your wife. She was so beautiful. I've worked for Mr Hayes for many years and he's always treated me well. There's something I know but I'm not sure if I can tell you because it could mean a load of trouble for me. My children need me and my income as I haven't a husband.'

'What is it that's on your mind? I promise I'll tell no one unless you want me to.'

'It was the night of the shooting. I was behind the bar when the men burst in. The one with the gun was holding it above his head pointing it at the ceiling. He was wearing gloves but I noticed that his sleeve had slipped down his arm showing his wrist and part of his forearm. There was a distinctive tattoo that I'd seen before. It was a dragon and I saw enough of it to be sure who's arm it was. It was Mike's. I'd seen it many times when he worked here for Mr Hayes.'

'Are you sure?'

'A hundred percent. What will you do?'

'Leave it to me. I'll make sure you're kept out of it. Thank you. You've done the right thing and I'm very grateful.'

'Will you tell Mr Hayes?'

'I don't know. I'll have to think about that.'

Art left the club with the information from Olive whirling round his head. He drove to the security office and checked everything was still okay and then he went up to Plumstead

Common. He parked the car and went to sit in the bandstand which held so many happy memories of his early days with Jude. He decided not to tell John about Mike as he wanted to deal with him without involving anyone else. After half an hour he had made up his mind to go and confront Mike and find out why he had done such a terrible thing. He knew where Mike lived so he returned to his car and drove to the narrow road near St. Nicholas's Hospital. Mike's house was about half way up the road on the right so Art went past it to see if he could see any signs of life. All was quiet as he passed the house. At the top of the road he turned the car round and parked looking down the hill where he had a clear view of the scruffy brown front door. As he watched he tried to decide what to say to Mike and how he would react if he denied all knowledge of the shooting.

As he was well aware Mike could be violent Art considered taking some sort of a weapon with him in case he had to defend himself. There was a tyre lever in the boot which might fit the bill so he opened the car door to go and get it. As he put his foot on the pavement he noticed Mike's front door open and Mike emerge. Art quickly closed his car door to see what Mike was going to do.

Mike stood with his hands on his hips and looked up and down the road. There was nobody in sight and he didn't seem to notice Art's car as he set out down the road towards the shops in the High Street. Something snapped in Art's brain as he saw Mike nonchalantly stroll down the road. How dare he be alive after what he'd done and now Jude was dead?.

Without further thought he started the engine, released the handbrake and put the car in second gear. Gunning the engine he let out the clutch and the car shot forward. All he could see was the spreading red stain on Jude's dress as the car flew towards Mike's back and mounted the pavement just before it reached him. There was a thump and Mike was flung forward into the low brick wall of one of the houses and bounced back. The car hit him again and then veered off on to the road. Art stopped for a brief moment, looked back and saw that Mike wasn't moving and was twisted in an unnatural position against the wall.. Without further thought he drove off quickly and made his way back to the Common and then turned left towards his home.

He had no memory of the drive back to Welling but when he arrived at the house he got out and saw the damage to the front of the car. One headlight was smashed and there was a smear of red on the grill. He knew what that was. He went inside and phoned John. He had to tell someone what had happened and needed help to deal with the situation.

John answered the phone and listened as Art gabbled away. 'Slow down,' he said. 'I've no idea what you're trying to tell me. Is it about Mike?'

'Yes, I think he's dead. I think I killed him.'

'Where is he?'

'Lying on the pavement outside his house. I ran him over. He was the one who shot Jude. Olive told me.'

'Olive from the club?'

'Yes, she recognised him from the dragon tattoo on his arm. I went to confront him but looked so smug that I couldn't help myself. I drove the car right at him.'

'You should have told me that he had fired the shot. Never mind, it's too late now. Did anyone see you?'

'I don't think so. The road was deserted.'

'I'll come round to your house. The car will have to be disposed of as soon as possible. I suppose there's damage to it?'

'Yes, and blood.'

'Keep calm. If it's any consolation I think you did the right thing although it could have been done with less risk. I'll send one of the minicabs to Mike's road to try and find out if he's really gone.'

John made the call to the cab office and waited anxiously for news. It came after less than fifteen minutes. The controller told John what the driver had found out. He'd told him that the police and an ambulance were at the scene when he'd arrived and he'd spoken to an elderly neighbour watching the action who told him there'd been a hit and run. The man's wife had been looking out of the window and saw the car hit the man. She had told the police what she saw. According to the man she'd no idea of the make of the car or its number and had only been able to tell them it was a blue one. He'd added that the victim was dead. With that information John had to decide what he could do to protect Art.

Art was waiting at the door when John arrived. He had a bucket in his hand as he'd been washing the blood off the car. John told him that Mike was dead and that there was one witness but fortunately she was old and couldn't identify the car apart from its colour. Art went a chalky white colour at the news and John guessed that he was in shock so he took him indoors and made him a mug of hot sweet tea. Again. Art went over what little he remembered and told John he didn't care what happened to him now. John knew he had to act fast as Mike was well known to the police and they would have a good idea that the hit and run was probably no accident. They would soon be investigating all Mike's known contacts. They would include Art and himself. The first thing to do was lose the car for good. He took the car keys from Art and gave him the key to his own car telling him to drive it to his house in Plumstead and stay there until he arrived. He added that Art mustn't say anything to Marion. The fewer people who knew the better.

John drove Art's car to Bleak Hill, a scrap yard on the edge of Plumstead Common. He knew the owner and paid handsomely to have the car crushed. When he saw it reduced to a block of metal he walked quickly across the Common to his house trying to work out what to do with Art. He was pleased that Mike had received his just deserts but worried that there could be repercussions. And not just from the police. The walk helped to clear his mind and when he arrived home he'd worked out the only plan he thought would work.

Art was sitting on the sofa in the living room. Marion was in the kitchen preparing the evening meal and Paul was in his bedroom. The radio was on but no one seemed to be listening to it. John went and sat next tor Art.

'I'll say it again. You should have told me Mike was the gunman. I would have dealt with him. Now there's only one thing to do.'

'What's that?'

'You'll have to disappear. Eventually someone will work out it was probably you and then you'll be the next victim. Luckily the police have no record on you and nobody really knows your background. I think the only course of action is for you to return home to Liverpool and start again. I'll take you to your house and you can pack a bag. Take all your personal details with you and some clothes. Then I'll drive you to Euston to catch a train. We won't risk using a cab as it's best if only I know where you've gone. There's one other thing.'

'What's that?' Art asked wearily. He just wanted the whole sorry saga to end.

'You mustn't contact any of us again and never return to London. It's better if everyone, including all our employees and your friends and ex-colleagues, thinks you've probably run away in grief and possibly committed suicide. It sounds drastic but will hopefully work. Oh, and change your name back to Jack.'

'Never see you, Marion or Paul again?'

'Yes. I know that will be hard. You know we regard you as one of the family so it'll also be hard for us. But it has to be done if you're to make anything of your life. Now I've just got to get something and then we'll drive back to your place.'

John left Art looking bereft and went to his study. While John was out of the room Paul came down and sat next to Art on the sofa. He lifted Art's arm and put it round his shoulders and leaned against him. The comforting gesture was more than Art could bear so he took his arm back, leaned froward and buried his head in his hands. He was clearly distressed and Paul didn't know what to do. How do you comfort a grown man? John suddenly appeared and Art looked up. He stood and turned to Paul. 'Goodbye Paul,' he said quietly. 'Be a good boy for your parents and don't forget me.'

'I won't,' replied the boy. 'I'll see you often. If you like I could come and live with you. I know you're going to be lonely without Jude.'

Art just smiled ruefully for what might have been and ruffled Paul's hair. He went with John to the car and, as they drove off, he looked back at the house where Jude had spent all her childhood. He knew he'd never see it or any of the Hayes family again. With his mother so ill and unable to communicate he was now completely on his own for the first time in his life.

Art gathered together his clothes, toiletries and all the documents he'd kept in a folder. The most important things were his Certificate in Education from Avery Hill College, his letter from the divisional inspector informing him that he'd successfully completed his probationary period and an excellent reference from Mr Dixon, the headmaster of

Vicarage Road School. He also took his marriage certificate and Jude's engagement and wedding rings. He also took her favourite jumper. It still had a faint residual smell of the scent she wore. It would remind him of her.

He went and joined John who was sitting in the lounge. 'Will you dispose of everything you don't want to keep?' he asked.

'Of course,' John replied. 'I'll bring Marion over to sort out Jude's clothes and then we'll decide what to do with the house. It's in my name so there'll be no problem if we sell it.'

John took from his jacket pocket a large brown envelope and handed it to Art. 'Have this to tide you over. I always keep some cash in my study for emergencies and, as this is obviously an emergency, it will hopefully be useful. There's about three thousand in there.'

'Are you sure you want me to have it. After all, it's my fault that I'm having to leave London.'

'You brought Jude a lot of happiness. We'll never forget you for that. She would want you to be happy so regard it as a gift from her for your future. I hope you have a good life Art. But remember, as much as you might be tempted, never return here or you risk being recognised and that could prove disastrous for you and us. Now let's go to Euston and put you on the next train to Liverpool.'

*

Art sat in the train carriage and looked out of the window at the wintry countryside. He knew he had a lot to consider and deeply regretted having to sever his ties to the area he'd

286

grown to love. He had mixed feelings about the death of Mike. Part of him was happy that some sort of justice had been served but it wouldn't bring Jude back. Anyway, there was nothing he could do about it now so he'd just have to try and keep out of the limelight and rebuild some sort of a life in Liverpool. Focusing on caring for his mother would be his main priority and the money from John, all in used five and ten pound notes, would give him time to work out his options.

He alighted from the train at Mossley Hill Station and walked slowly up Rose Lane to the familiar front door. Letting himself in he went into the back room and turned on the electric fire. Everything was just as it always had been. It gave him the feeling that he'd never really been away and his years in London were some sort of dream. Or a life lived by someone else. He sat for hours just staring at the artificial coals until he realise it was getting dark. There was no food in the house so he had to get to the shops before they shut. Rousing himself he put his coat back on and went down the road to buy the makings of a meal and some milk and bread. He would sort out everything else he might need in the morning.

Before he cooked a simple meal he phoned Mrs Carr to tell her that he had decided to return home for good and then phoned the nursing home to ask about his mother. Mrs Carr was surprised at his sudden decision but was pleased that he would see more of his mother despite her condition. She knew nothing of his life in London and he thought it best to keep it that way. The matron at the home was able to tell him his mother was no worse but was now bed-bound and requiring total care. He promised to go round the next day for a visit.

Art, now calling himself Jack again, had a surprisingly good night's sleep considering all that had happened the day before. He was feeling a little more positive now that he was back in Liverpool and on familiar ground. A visit to his mother would probably upset him as usual but he now thought of the visit as important as she was now his only relative. He knew that Jude would expect him to do his best and he decided to wear her wedding ring to keep her in his thoughts. He took it out and tried it on. It fitted perfectly on the little finger of his left hand and reminded him of how slim and delicate her fingers had been. He put her engagement ring in his bedside cabinet. After a quick wash he went downstairs for a breakfast of toast and tea then set off up the road to the nursing home. On his way he wondered if he should use some of John's cash to buy a cheap car. He'd got used to having a vehicle and one could be useful for any number of reasons.

As he'd expected his mother didn't recognise him and looked very frail. The doctor was at the home so he took the opportunity to ask about the future. It wasn't good news. The doctor told him that his mother would probably only survive a few more weeks as her body was gradually shutting down and death would be a merciful release. He left the home feeling sad but realised that the inevitable would happen and he'd soon have another funeral to attend. On his way home he bought a couple of newspapers with his shopping and over a coffee skimmed through them to see if there was any mention of Mike's death. There was nothing so he guessed that it was of no interest to the national press as they probably considered it to be an accident rather than a deliberate hit. He decided that monitoring the news would achieve nothing and his best course of action was to follow John's advice and keep his head down and forget the past.

The phone call came a fortnight later. His mother had stopped breathing in the night and they found her in the morning. He immediately went round to the home and started sorting out the arrangements. Her death had to be registered but there was no need for a post mortem as she'd been under the care of a doctor for months. As she hadn't made a will the estate would come to Jack in its entirety. He had already decided to have her cremated and asked the funeral directors to sort everything out for him. This they did and the funeral took place in the middle of February. There was a reasonable turnout of mourners, mainly old friends and acquaintances from the Townswomen's Guild and the Cumberland and Westmorland Society she'd joined after the war. Jack was, of course, the only family mourner and he was accompanied by Mrs Carr. After the cremation he invited her home with him for a cup of tea. Once there he asked if she could continue to clean the house for him and she gratefully accepted the offer. Money was tight in her household and she'd been worrying about losing the small amount Jack had been paying her.

Easter came and Jack had fallen into a routine which required the minimum amount of effort. He went to

Calderstones Park for a walk each morning, had lunch and then read one of the books he'd borrowed from Sudley Library. After an evening meal he'd watch the television for a couple of hours before having a couple of glasses of scotch whisky prior to turning in for the night. It was an existence; but only just. One morning he looked out of the window at the garden. The grass had started to grow and some of the roses were in bud. The whole garden had been neglected during his mother's illness. He would have to do some work to make it tidy and wondered if he should think about buying some plants to make it more colourful. It would, he thought, be good exercise to dig over the flowerbeds and make the garden a pleasant place to sit in the summer. He went out to the brick outhouse his mother had called the washhouse and hunted for the gardening tools he'd need. The old push lawnmower only needed oiling and he found all his grandfather's hoes and spades as well as a pair of secateurs. It would be a good project to keep him occupied for the next few weeks. He knew he was putting off the inevitable. He'd have to find a job. John's money would only last him another six months at best so it was time to do something about his situation.

After some deliberation Jack decided to return to teaching. He'd enjoyed it in London and thought he could still make a go of it. He'd had enough of security work and didn't want to carry on in that profession. So in May he took his references and teaching certificate to the Education Office in the centre of Liverpool and spoke to one of the local inspectors. She was most impressed by his reference from the headmaster and asked what he had done since leaving Vicarage Road School. Without going into too much detail about dates he explained about his mother's condition and how he'd returned to Liverpool to look after her. She was very sympathetic and when he told her his mother had recently died and said that she was sure a position could be found for him in September. This suited him as it would enable him to take his time doing up the house and sorting out the garden before having the regular commitment of taking a class and all the other duties expected of a primary school teacher.

Chapter 24

Liverpool, July 2017

There was a reply to the email just as Louise was preparing to go to her own home. Ellen hesitated before opening it as she was scared about what Paul might say. Louise sat down again next to her sister and nudged her.

'Open it,' she demanded. 'We've got to know the truth even if it hurts.'

Ellen opened the message and read it out loud.

'Hi,

Your email certainly came as a shock to me. I had no idea what happened to Art after he said goodbye to me a couple of weeks after my sister's funeral. He just disappeared and even though I asked my parents they always said the less I knew the better. They never mentioned him again. I was very sad to hear of his death. Please accept my condolences.

I'm happy that he remarried and had a new family as he was such a good and kind man. He treated me like a brother and I worshipped him as my teacher before he met Jude (actually I was instrumental in their meeting).

I suppose, although we're not blood relations, as Art was my brother-in-law then you two must be my nieces-in-law!

There's so much I'd like to know about his life after 1966. Would you be willing to visit me? My wife and I would love to meet you and I've a few photos and things to show you.

Hoping that is possible.

Best wishes,

Paul Hayes'

Louise smiled at Ellen. 'Well, what do you think? Fancy another trip to London? I'll join you this time.'

'Can't wait. Could we go next month when the kids are on holiday? My mother would be happy to look after them.'

'Good idea. Email back and arrange a date with Paul. He sounds like a very friendly man and will be happy to share his memories of our dad. Do you think they'll be a lot different to ours?'

'Probably. He was much older when we really got to know him. He must have only been in his early twenties when he married Judith, or Jude as her brother referred to her. He was in his thirties when he married mum so he was over forty when we could start to think of him as an individual and not just a dad.'

After consulting their I-phone diaries they decided on a couple of suitable dates and Ellen replied to Paul saying how much they would enjoy meeting him and that they would come by train. This time he replied straight away and agreed to meet on one of the dates they'd suggested. He told them where he lived, his phone number, and promised to pick them up from Woolwich Arsenal station if they phoned him when they reached Euston.

With that all sorted out Louise left Ellen's house to tell her family what they'd found out and their proposed trip.

*

Ellen sat quietly for a while pleased that her sister was now as keen as her to trace their father's history. Now they knew that, although he had claimed to be a bachelor and not a widower when he married their mother Susan, at least he wasn't a bigamist with a clutch of kids and grand-kids hidden away in London. She reflected on what she knew of his life in Liverpool both before and after living in London. What could she tell Paul? There were very few photographs of him among those of Louise and her as they grew up. Apart from the usual family occasions, all of them limited to the four of them, there was little to tell. She knew he'd been a successful and well respected teacher and then headteacher but thought, if she'd been asked, that she'd be unable to start to describe how he felt or what really motivated him in his private life. His marriage to Susan had been, on the surface, a happy one. They rarely argued and seemed to get on well although she was hard pushed to remember any demonstrations of affection between them. A peck on the cheek when he left for school was about the sum total of their physical contact.

She wondered if it had been different for him with Jude. Was that a more passionate affair? Was it possible that he'd only married Susan for convenience because he was lonely?

It was all very difficult to unpick and she hoped the day in London might answer some of her questions. It would be good to meet someone who knew her father over twenty years before she was born.

Chapter 25

Liverpool, September 1966

Jack, never to be called Art again in his lifetime, had been allocated a teaching post at Edale Primary School in the Junior department. The headmistress had given him a third year junior class which pleased him as the children were only a year younger than those he'd enjoyed teaching in London. The school was near his house and he could walk there each day so he'd put off the idea of buying a car. All the staff welcomed him as the only man in the department and, of course, he was yet again tasked with teaching football, cricket and boys' handicraft. He threw himself with gusto into his work and soon built up a reputation with staff, parents and children for being a dedicated and hard-working teacher. It was the making of him and he soon all but forgot his past problems. His mother's memory faded faster than that of Jude and in quiet moments at home he would silently weep for what might have been with the woman he'd been with and adored for such a short time. Sometimes he would fantasise about having had a family with Jude and watching their children grow up. Always a boy who looked like him and a girl like Jude. Such emotional turns slowly became rarer and by the end of his first full year back in teaching he was almost free of the feelings of guilt, hate and love that had previously been uppermost in his mind. He missed Jude's family, especially Paul, but had no regrets about what he'd done to Mike. In quiet moments he still worried that his past might catch up with him and kept as low a profile as he could just in case any of Mike's cronies found him.

He went on the annual school journey to Southport with the teachers and children from the top two classes. It was a hectic week and he thoroughly enjoyed the twenty-four hour company of the boisterous youngsters. It really took him out of himself and he realised that a career in teaching was all he'd ever wanted in a job. On his return the comfort of the predictable school routine made him happier than he'd been for over a year. He decided it was time to have more of a social life and, although he hadn't bothered contacting any old school friends, he thought he could rejoin the sports club which was based at the top of the hill next to the church. He'd never been very keen on playing team sports despite his coaching the football and cricket teams at school but had enjoyed tennis and swimming as a youth. He knew the club had a bar and quite a vibrant social scene so he ventured up there one evening and enquired about membership. He was made very welcome by the club secretary who explained about fees and the various sections he could join. After paying his membership he accompanied the secretary to the bar where he was introduced to the bar steward and a couple of members.

The bar steward served him a pint of bitter, the first he'd had for ages, and the two members sitting on stools at the bar asked him about what he did and where he lived. Jack explained, without too much detail, that he was single and lived just down the road. He also mentioned he was a teacher in a local primary school. This seemed to satisfy the men's curiosity and the conversation turned to a discussion of the relative merits of Liverpool and Everton's first team squads. After another pint Jack walked back home and felt pleased that he now had somewhere to go of an evening and new people to meet. It would make a change from his usual fare of television and a whisky each night.

*

Jack's life continued to revolve around the club and school for the next six years. Thanks to his dedication and hard work he had risen to become deputy headteacher of Edale School and had taken on further responsibility for a new maths scheme he wanted to introduce as it was, he thought, better suited to teaching children of varying abilities. It was well structured and the children were able to progress at a comfortable rate according to their expertise with lots of reinforcement to give them confidence. It proved to be a success and he started searching for a similar scheme to improve standards in reading.

His social life had also blossomed and he was now a committee member of the sports club and involved in organising some of the social events which took place on a weekly basis. The darts knock-out competition was always popular and attracted a good number of participants. Jack's experience of playing darts in the Star and Garter in Pattison

Road proved useful and he often made it to the semi-finals and, sometimes, even won the final.

One warm summer's evening in June 1973 he was throwing a few darts to warm up for the competition when he noticed a young woman watching him. He threw his darts and retrieved them from the board and then went over to speak to her in his capacity as a committee member. She introduced herself as Susan and added that she was a new member and wanted to know if there was a competition for women. Jack told her there was so she put her name down to play despite, she said, never having thrown a dart before. Jack asked if she would like a quick lesson and she readily agreed. She really was hopeless to start with but eventually managed to hit the board with most of her darts.

After the competition jack sought her out again and asked if she would like to join him for a drink. He was delighted when she said she would and sat down at a table while he went to the bar. They sat and chatted for the rest of the evening and Jack found her very good company. She told him about her work in an insurance office and that she was an only child. It was soon time to go home and Jack asked her where she lived. It wasn't far from the club so he offered to walk her home. On the way he mentioned that there was going to be a dance on the Saturday and asked if she'd like to go to it with him. He was delighted when she said yes and he arranged to pick her up from home on the night.

That night, as he had a cup of coffee and a biscuit before going to bed, jack felt that it had been a wonderful evening.

He'd never actively sought out a woman's company since Jude's death but somehow it now felt right. Susan was pretty and, he guessed from what she'd told him about her work, was around his age. He found he was quite excited at the prospect of having a partner for the dance. Usually he just sat at a table inside the door and checked the tickets. This time another committee member could do that job.

It wasn't a particularly passionate relationship. They enjoyed each other's company and spent more and more time together. Inevitably, both being in their thirties, the subject of marriage cropped up. This was mainly prompted by their friends in the club who assumed it to be a certainty as they watched how well they got on. Susan had asked about the ring Jack wore but he'd lied and said it had been his mother's. When they got engaged he'd briefly wondered if he should give her Jude's engagement ring but soon decided that wouldn't be appropriate although he was sure Jude wouldn't mind. He was certain she would have wanted him to be as happy as she had been during their short time together. He bought Susan a new ring in town.

The wedding in July1975 was another quiet affair for Jack. No family for him and Susan had few relations to invite. Peter, the club secretary, was his best man and it went off smoothly with the reception in the sports club. After a short honeymoon in Windermere Susan moved into Jack's house and they started their married life. They were comfortable together and Jack grew to love and respect his wife. Susan was happy to be a housewife and soon had her first child. They named her

Louise and two year's later had Ellen. It was a happy home for the girls and they grew up to be bright and well-mannered young ladies.

Jack, however, continued to be haunted by his past. He took great care not to be in the public eye even when he was made headteacher on the retirement of the previous incumbent. London was definitely a no go area despite many pleas by Susan and the girls for a visit. He also avoided having his photograph taken especially if it was likely to be published in the local newspaper. You never knew who might see it and cause his world to come crashing down.

Susan had no idea why he was so reluctant to be in the public gaze and if she asked him about it he just said that he didn't want to take the credit for all the hard work of his staff. Avoiding visiting London was something she never understood. He was kind and thoughtful and looked after her and the girls although she always felt there was a part of him she'd never reach. She was content and when she was diagnosed with breast cancer he was very understanding and cared for her throughout the illness.

Chapter 26

London, August 2017

Louise and Ellen came out of Woolwich Arsenal Station and looked around. A tall man with thinning blond-grey hair who looked to be in his sixties came up to them.

'Hello, I'm Paul. I'm guessing you must be Louise and Ellen.'

'That's right,' said Louise as they shook hands. 'This is Ellen and I'm Louise. It's very good of you to meet us. In fact it's very good of you to see us at all. We know it must dredge up some painful memories.'

'No, you're wrong. I only have very fond memories of Art, your father, and my sister. Anyway we can discuss all that when we get to my house. Would you like a quick tour on the way of where your father lived and worked?'

'I think most of it has been demolished.' said Ellen. 'A lady in Bexleyheath library, when I tracked down my father's marriage to your sister, told me.'

'She was right. Your dad's road has gone and the school, which I went to, has been rebuilt. But the Common is still the same and I can show you where he used to sit with my sister and plan their future. They didn't know but I used think it a good game to follow them sometimes. The things we did as kids. Stay here for a minute while I go for the car.'

Within five minutes a large four-by-four pulled up and Paul beckoned them to jump in. He took them up through Plumstead and stopped by a muddy and litter-strewn grassy mound.

'This is where your dad's house was in the 60s. The road had completely gone and, of course, so has the pub on the corner. We'll now go up to Plumstead Common.'

He stopped again near a bandstand and they all got out of the car and walked across the grass to stand in it. 'The seats have long gone,' Paul told them. 'But this is where they made all their plans for a long life together. Sadly it wasn't to be.'

They stood in silence for a while and then returned to the car and went up the hill to the large house where Paul lived. Ellen and Louise were surprised at its size and pulled wry faces at each other.

'This is where Jude and I lived as children,' Paul explained. 'I moved back here after my mother died in the late eighties. Dad had died three years earlier with prostate cancer and she never really got over the loss. Her heart gave out one day and that was that. I used to live with my wife Sally in your dad's old house in Welling. My father had kept it after Art moved away and rented it out until I needed a place of my own. All our children were born and brought up there and it holds a lot of happy memories. I can take you to see it if you like.'

'Yes,' Louise nodded. 'It would be nice to see at least one place where he lived before returning home.'

Paul opened the front door and ushered them into the large living room. He called out to his wife and she came from the kitchen drying her hands on a teacloth to meet them. They were introduced to Sally and then Paul motioned for them to down on the settee.

'Can I get you a drink?' she asked. 'Tea, coffee or something stronger if you like.'

'Tea would be fine for me. Milk no sugar,' said Louise.

'Same again,' added Ellen.

'I'll have a coffee please,' Paul requested, 'and some cake if there's any left.'

Sally went out to fetch the drinks and Paul reached down to a side table and picked up an envelope. 'I thought you'd like to see these. When I was about eleven my parents bought me a camera and I took quite a few snaps of the family at home and on holiday in Minehead. I even took a couple at The wedding and that fateful night at the club when Jude was shot. I'd kept all the negatives so I've had some copies made for you to keep.'

He handed them to Louise and Ellen and they looked through them with interest.

'Your sister certainly was beautiful,' Ellen commented. 'And it's weird to see Dad looking so young. The clothes were amazing. I suppose that's you in the suit at the wedding? You did look cute.'

'Not so cute now,' laughed Paul as he ran his hand through his remaining hair. 'I remember the wedding well as I was almost certainly the only one who was sober. They

304

played a Beatles' song to start the dancing. My mother made me dance with her. Jude called it their song. I sometimes wonder what Jude would look like now if she'd lived.'

'I bet that was the one Dad wanted played at his funeral. Was it called "And I Love Her"?'

'Yes, I'm sure it was. It was played at his funeral? He obviously still loved her to the end. Although I'm sure he loved your mother just as much,' he added quickly.

'We know he did but it probably wasn't in the same way.'

Paul looked at the hand Ellen in which was holding the photos. 'I hope you don't mind me asking but where did you get that ring?'

'We found it in our father's bedside cabinet after he died together with a gold wedding band. We thought they must have been our grandmother's. Why do you ask?'

Paul looked wistful. 'Because it's very similar to the one Art gave Jude when they got engaged. I might be wrong. It was a long time ago.'

Ellen looked sad. 'You're probably right. I never bothered to check the hallmark for a date. Would you like to have it to remember your sister by?'

'No. You keep it. It's as much yours as mine and I have many good memories of Jude. Do you have any pictures of your father in later years?'

Ellen rummaged in her bag and gave him a couple of photos. 'These are all I could find. Dad didn't much like being photographed so most of our family photos are of us with Mum.'

Paul looked at the pictures. 'That's a pity. I can see from these that he didn't change a great deal over the years. At least he kept his hair.'

The drinks arrived and the four of them sat and chatted. Paul told them about being in Art's class in school and the trips Art organised. He made them laugh about how Jude had arranged to meet Art in his classroom and how embarrassed he'd been to be roped in as part of it. Then he mentioned their holiday in Minehead when everyone realised Jude and Art were going to marry. A picture of them on Dunkery Beacon and some on the beach showed what a happy time it had been. Paul pointed to a stone sitting by the fireplace.

'That's a fossil I found on the beach during the holiday. It always reminds me of that time and the fun we had.'

The photos taken in the club were not very clear but Ellen could see that the family looked content and at ease with each other. Her father had his arm round Jude holding her close to him and Paul was laughing with Marion. They talked for a little about what life in Liverpool and in London was like as they grew up. Eventually Ellen knew it was time to ask the question that had been bugging her and Louise.

'Why did Dad leave London after Jude's funeral? It doesn't seem to make a lot of sense to us. He always said he returned to Liverpool to look after his mother but she was very ill in a home and didn't live for long anyway.'

'I've often asked myself that,' Paul said. 'Maybe he just wanted to get away from all the bad memories. After the shooting he turned in on himself and we hardly saw him until

306

one day when he came round here with dad. I was at home and could tell something had happened. That was when Art said goodbye. He was quite emotional about it. As I told you my parents refused to discuss it after that. It was almost as if Art had never existed.'

'And why was the club raided?' asked Louise.

'I'm afraid that was part of the more murky side to dad's businesses. It was really organised crime. At that time there were a number of gangs vying to control the area. Dad was mixed up in it a bit and that was probably the main reason for the attack. The police never really got to the bottom of it and no one was ever prosecuted for the murder. When I took over the security firm from dad I heard a few rumours that the man responsible had been killed in a hit and run accident but nothing more ever came to light. The man used to work for dad. I didn't like him. He was violent and disliked Art, especially when Art started working in the business.'

Ellen sat up quickly. 'So that's what he did after leaving the primary school. If he'd carried on teaching we'd never have known any of this. It was those missing years on his pension record that made us want to find out more about his life in London. He never spoke about it.'

Sally took Paul's hand and said, 'I knew very little of this as well. Paul's parents never discussed the past very much except to heap praise on their son. They were kind to me but I was never able to take the place of the daughter they lost. Paul told me that his dad thought of Jude as his own little

307

angel and never really recovered from losing her. It must have been hard.'

'It achieved one thing,' Paul said. 'It made him make the business legitimate. He closed the club and paid off his partners by selling the site. The minicab firm continued for a few years until increased competition made it unprofitable. Only the security company remains and that was the business that Art had built up to be such a success in the short time he was in charge. To this day I owe him a big thank you for what he did. I always wanted to thank him personally but, as you know, had no idea where in the world he was.'

Louise showed Paul and Sally pictures of their own families and in return looked at those showing Paul's three children as youngsters. His children were now grown up and he told them proudly that he now had five grandchildren. 'You must meet all the family one day. After all you are sort of related.'

Louise laughed. 'I liked the idea that we are your nieces-in-law. And you must come up to Liverpool so we can show you where Dad lived and taught.'

'I'd like that,' Paul said wistfully. 'It would put to bed all the worries I had about what had happened to him.'

It was time to go and after they thanked Sally for the refreshments Paul gave them a lift back to the station via Welling where he stopped the car outside the house that Art and Jude had been so happy in as had he when he got married to Sally. Nobody spoke so Paul drove off towards Woolwich.

On the train to central London they sat: still without speaking. They both had a lot of information to digest. Even on the underground to Euston they kept their thoughts to themselves. It was only when they'd settled down in a fairly empty carriage on the train to Liverpool that they felt able to talk about their day.

Ellen spoke first. 'Well Louise that was a day out to remember. I thought Paul and his wife were lovely and welcoming. I'm not sure I'd have been like that if someone had come to me with the news that their father was once my brother-in-law. Paul obviously thought Dad was wonderful. It must have been very confusing for him as a young boy to have to deal with what happened. And to have been there when his sister was killed.'

'You're right. It's impossible to imagine what they all went through. I hope Paul and Sally keep in touch.'

'So do I. But that story Paul told us about the hit and run? Do you think Dad was involved? Was that why he left London and never went back?'

'I doubt it. He wasn't like that. We know he never really lost his temper with anyone. It'll have to remain a mystery as all the people there at the time are now probably dead. Apart from Paul of course and I think he was honest with us. I'm sure he doesn't know any more than what he told us.'

Ellen looked pensive. 'I'm not so sure that Dad would have been able to do nothing. You know he had a hatred of injustices. He always insisted that we owned up to anything we did wrong and made us apologise. We just saw a different side to him than the one he must have shown in London. He certainly wasn't as boring as we and many other people in Liverpool thought he was. Anyway we've really got one hell of a tale to tell our kids when we get back.'

Louise looked again at the copies of the photos Paul had given them. 'Just an ordinary primary school teacher? I don't think so.'

Author's note

Confession time. Yes, the young man on the front cover is me in 1964. And yes, I did live as a penniless student in the tumbledown house in Pattison Road. I also met the sister of one of my pupils at the school swimming gala and we went out together – and on holiday with her family to Somerset. I was a supply teacher in the school whilst waiting to do a teacher training course at Avery Hill College. After that the story goes into the realms of fiction and all the rest is from my imagination although firmly rooted in the many interesting if frightening characters I met at the time.

The houses and the pub (it really was named the Star and Garter) in Pattison Road were demolished in the early 1970s – as was the road itself. I was the last resident to leave.

Acknowledgements

Many thanks to Rob Noble for his technical expertise in producing the book cover. Also to Dharmanātha Porter for his kind work in critically reading my raw manuscript. His efforts were extremely helpful.

Thanks must also go to all the people who lived in Pattison Road in the 1960s. They were the main inspiration for this tale even though some of them were not always on the side of law and order. It was, however, a close-knit community and people would go out of their way to help anyone in trouble or suffering hard times financially. I learned a lot about life from them.

.

37971767R00177

Printed in Poland
by Amazon Fulfillment
Poland Sp. z o.o., Wrocław